"Without rules to know how to act," Luci said.

Mateo stepped farther into the hall. He'd vowed never to fight with Luci in front of the students. Could they call this a spirited discussion of necessity? "I don't get it. Why are you so determined to have a strict set of rules?"

"So the kids will know what's expected of them and how to act."

"They know how to act. They spend eight hours a day together. And if someone has a few socially awkward moments, it's not the end of the world. I'm not buying your 'clarity is kindness' argument. I need a better reason for coming up with a fifty-page code of conduct."

"Not everyone is like you," she said.

"What does that even mean?"

"Not everyone is kind and polite and has impeccable manners. If everyone were like you, sure, we wouldn't need rules."

Mateo furrowed his brow. Her words sounded like a compliment but somehow also an insult. How did she do that?

Dear Reader,

It's hard to believe this is the final book in The Teacher Project!

If you've been following the series, you know that social studies teacher Luci Walker is hiding a big secret, while her coworker Mateo Lander is hiding his feelings for Luci. When Luci and Mateo are put in charge of the new boarding school, it's hard to keep anything on the down-low. Can Luci come to terms with her past and open up to a future with Mateo?

I come from a family of teachers. My grandma, as one of the only college-educated women in a small farming community, was asked to fill in at the high school for a few weeks in 1956 and stayed for twenty years. My mom started out teaching first grade and went on to teach at every level from preschool to college. Life in education means always being ready for the unexpected.

I'd love to hear what you think of Luci and Mateo's story! You can find me on social media and at my website, anna-grace-author.com.

Happy reading!

Anna

HER SECRET HOMECOMING

ANNA GRACE

Harlequin

HEARTWARMING

Harlequin®
HEARTWARMING™

ISBN-13: 978-1-335-05145-5

Her Secret Homecoming

Recycling programs for this product may not exist in your area.

Harlequin Enterprises ULC
22 Adelaide St. West, 41st Floor
Toronto, Ontario M5H 4E3, Canada
www.Harlequin.com

Printed in U.S.A.

Award-winning author **Anna Grace** writes fun, heartfelt romance novels about complex characters finding their way with humor and heart. Anna's Oregon roots and love of family and community shine through in her Harlequin Heartwarming series, Love, Oregon and The Teacher Project.

Whether exploring the West in a remodeled Sprinter van or wandering new city streets in search of an art museum, Anna loves to travel and spend time with friends and family. You can find her on social media, where she's busy stamping likes on images of cappuccino, books and other people's dogs.

X: @AnnaEmilyGrace
Instagram: @AnnaGraceAuthor
Facebook: Anna Grace Author
Website: Anna-Grace-Author.com

Books by Anna Grace

Harlequin Heartwarming

The Teacher Project

Lessons from the Rancher
Winning the Sheriff's Heart
Mistletoe at Jameson Ranch

Love, Oregon

A Rancher Worth Remembering
The Firefighter's Rescue
The Cowboy and the Coach
Her Hometown Christmas
Reunited with the Rancher

Visit the Author Profile page
at Harlequin.com for more titles.

For my mom and grandma, two amazing teachers
who were always up for a game of pinochle

CHAPTER ONE

MATEO LANDER TOOK a sip of espresso, then examined his cup.

A stylized sloth appeared to grip the rim, urging the reader to Hang in There!

Yeah, that wasn't going to be a problem today. The sun was out, the espresso machine at Mac's was working and the school's volunteer principal was out of town at a real-estate conference.

Life was good.

Early spring sunshine warmed his face as he stood on the wide-planked front stoop of Mac's store. The scent of his espresso mingled with the morning dew evaporating off sagebrush. The breeze stirred something in his chest, sparking a feeling of possibility, as though the season had good intentions but wasn't revealing them just yet.

Mateo jogged down the steps, surveying the seven buildings that made up downtown Pronghorn, then stepped into the empty street. Mostly empty, anyway. Connie, a tuxedo cat with only one ear fully intact and a crooked tail, sat sentinel in the middle of the highway. She turned her head, briefly acknowledging Mateo and his good mood.

He and his coworkers had certainly weathered their share of bumps and scrapes over the last several months. The five young teachers had been recruited from the cities of Oregon's I-5 corridor to revive a tiny high school in the state's least-populated county.

At times it felt a little like they were crammed in the back seat of a clown car. A clown car that was on fire, skidding on thin ice, heading for a gaping canyon, driven by a committee of screaming banshees.

But at least his fellow passengers were cool.

Mateo had made a choice the moment he stepped off the bus and onto the streets of this eclectic community. He would be happy, relaxed and look for the positive. It was a choice he'd made over and over in his life, and it served him well. Even if his former classmates at military school had very clearly chosen something else.

Mateo passed the old City Hotel, a beautiful if inaccurately named establishment, where he and his coworkers lived together. It stood directly across the street from the school, a two-story brick building with Pronghorn Public Day School scrawled in bright yellow over the main entrance. If the lettering was a little off-kilter and overly enthusiastic, well, that was an apt metaphor for secondary education. Nothing ran perfectly where teenagers were involved, and he'd choose enthusiasm over order any day of the week. Particularly when he could prepare for that enthusiasm with his favorite espresso drink.

No, it was a great day, and Mateo was excited to start the week. As a math teacher, he helped kids feel comfortable working through the complex, sequential subject matter. His approach was to smile and share a joke when he could. He cultivated an ability to get along with everyone, which wasn't always easy but was essential in his line of work.

And that ability had other, unexpected benefits. Mac, the proprietor of the one store in town and owner of the sole espresso machine, had asked Mateo what his favorite coffee drink was, then he'd perfected it. A cortado—two shots of espresso with an equal amount of steamed milk was just what he needed heading into work this beautiful Monday morning.

He raised the cortado to his lips.

"Where are you going with that?"

Mateo spun around at the voice, then froze.

Luci Walker: brilliant social studies teacher and wily nemesis.

Okay, he could get along with *almost* everyone.

She stood in the arched opening to the hotel's courtyard. The climbing roses framing the entrance were not yet in bloom but thinking about it. Luci wore penny loafers, a knee-length pink wool skirt and an argyle sweater. Her arm was looped through a wicker basket covered with a soft, cream-colored scarf. She couldn't have coordinated better with early spring if she'd tried. She was pretty, with wide, lively eyes and blond hair pulled back in a neat ponytail. The slight ski jump to her nose and intermittent dimple made him think of a fairy. But not like a sweet, wish-granting, smiley fairy. A Shakespearean fairy, stirring up trouble and outsmarting any mortals who got in her way.

She looked like she should be rushing a sorority at Dartmouth but was more likely to be running a centuries-old secret society.

The one thing about Luci's carefully curated look that never quite seemed right to Mateo was the pair of tortoiseshell-framed glasses she wore. If eyes were the window to the soul, Luci didn't want anyone to get a clear view.

"I'm going to school." He gestured with the cup to their place of employment, where both of them were due in minutes.

"With coffee?"

The breeze, warm only minutes ago, was now tinged with a sliver of ice, as though a mountaintop miles away had blown them a warning.

"We all agreed, no food in class," Luci reminded him.

"This is a drink."

"A person could argue that anything is a drink. And I will remind you, one student has taken up that argument on a number of occasions."

"Mav takes up every argument," Mateo said. "Did you hear him arguing with the ref at the spring soccer game last week?"

"Everyone in Pronghorn argues with the ref during soccer games."

"About why free-form poetry is superior to the sonnet?"

She waved away the comment, returning to her previously scheduled concern. "We decided, as a staff, anything that could make a mess counts as food."

"This is four ounces of coffee."

"We never specified the size of the mess."

Mateo widened his stance. Luci narrowed her eyes.

If either of them had holsters, this is where they'd square off across the empty street.

"You need to get rid of your coffee before the students arrive." She glanced over her shoulder, as though all thirty-four students were about to arrive en masse.

"Yet it's okay for you to arrive at school with a family of hedgehogs?"

Luci drew the basket to her chest. "What's wrong with hedgehogs?"

"A basket full of animals has got to be more distracting than one math teacher finishing his coffee."

Luci wrapped a second arm around the basket, pulling it closer. "Look, I didn't ask for these hedgehogs. I never signed on to be their caregiver, but their caregiver I am. I'm not going to leave them home alone all day."

"They're nocturnal," Mateo reminded her. "They sleep all day."

"So they're not a problem at school."

Luci lifted the soft shawl/blanket thing she'd taken from her own wardrobe and used to make her pets more comfortable. Her face relaxed as she gazed at the sleeping creatures. No one had ever gotten the full story about why Luci's room at the hotel had come with four hedgehogs, but knowing their volunteer principal, it could have been anything. What was clear? The animals couldn't have been gifted to a more attentive owner. And Luci wasn't the only one on campus to love these improbable, spiny little peanuts. Kids stopped by her classroom on breaks to spend time with the "hedgies." Occasionally, the basket could be found in the reading nook under the care of a student having a bad day, like very small, sleepy, therapy animals. They really weren't a problem, but neither was a cup of coffee.

"I'm sorry, Luci. We all get through this world the best we can. I don't see any problem with students, or staff, enjoying a beverage in class if that makes the day a little brighter."

Luci threw her head back and puffed out a breath. "Did you learn nothing during our practicum?"

Mateo furrowed his brow in mock seriousness. "No, I think I learned something during the ten-month placement. Gimme a minute."

"Do you remember how kids were about coffee? Students were constantly leaving campus to go to the Dutch Bros, coming to class with sugary, caffeinated drinks, regularly coming in *late*, with coffee." She shuddered, as though *late with coffee* was the worst offense a person could commit.

"With all of the trouble kids get into in this world—" Mateo gestured broadly, attempting to remind her of worse crimes than cappuccino "—I don't think late with coffee is that bad. I'd rather students feel comfortable in my class."

Her eyelid twitched in annoyance. "*Everyone* feels comfortable in your class. With your cozy tables and lamps and rugs. It's like some kind of math spa. Trust me, sipping a latte isn't going to make anyone feel better."

"Was that supposed to be an insult?" he asked. "Because that's exactly what I'm going for. Math is a tough subject. My classroom needs to be calm and comforting."

"I prefer my classes to be exciting." Her eyes lit up.

He nodded. "Makes sense. If I taught something as boring as history I'd try to liven it up, too."

Her lips set in a thin line as she shook her head. "That's cold, Lander, even for you."

"You started the argument," he said.

"You started it. With your coffee."

"That's like saying I started the argument we had last night about grading papers on the reception desk because I was grading papers at the reception desk."

"Exactly."

Mateo turned to the cat. "Can you believe this? It's like that time in ed school—"

"*You* started that debate." She pointed to the center of his chest, as though he might misunderstand and think someone else in this tiny town had ignited the argument that raged between the two of them for eighteen months.

"I expressed my opinion," he reminded her. "And I stand by it. Standardized testing is arbitrary and a waste of student time and taxpayer money."

"Standardized testing is imperfect, but it's *the only* practical way we have of assessing student progress on a large scale."

"So we can produce reports and studies?"

"So we can hold schools accountable for teaching to standards."

He scoffed. "I hardly think schools are just going to skip over math and reading."

"Schools skip over important concepts all the time. A standardized test says to educators, this is the baseline. You can do your cool projects and dive deep into iguanas or ancient Egypt or whatever you're into, but you have to teach the baseline."

"What would you know about the baseline?" he asked. "With your hundred-thousand-dollar, prep-school education? You were miles over the baseline. You probably couldn't even see it from up there."

The color drained from Luci's face. She gritted her teeth. "As I have mentioned, numerous times, I didn't pay for my education. I was on scholarship."

IF LUCI NEEDED any proof that Mateo Lander was set on earth to infuriate her, this was it. He got her back up on a normal day, with his easy smile and loose interpretation of the rules. They couldn't be more different. Intellectually, she understood it was good for their students to be exposed to teachers with different points of view. It prepared them for life.

She was a better debater than he was, which wasn't surprising. Her subject matter lent itself to spirited discussion, his to patterns of thinking. But when he got tripped up in an argument, his go-to, time and again, was to assume she was the product of wealth and privilege, and therefore couldn't speak to the experience of most students.

Considering she'd done everything possible to present that image, it wasn't entirely his fault. But still...

It would all be so much easier if they didn't have to teach across the hall from one another. If they didn't share a home, a friend group, a common cause.

If she could stop ruminating on the day they had met. The same smile currently infuriating her had been exactly what she'd needed in the moment.

Walking into her first class at grad school, she'd been nervous. That wasn't a shocker. She was nervous anytime she went anywhere new. When you're raised with a disdain for societal norms, it's hard to know how to act in a new situation.

Social cues that others intuitively picked up were as complex to Lucy as the Enigma code, and she had to negotiate them without Alan Turing and a team of geniuses at her back. Over time she'd gotten good at figuring out the unspoken web of signals from others, but there were enough pitfalls that she was rightfully spooked about making mistakes. Humans, as a whole, could be so unforgiving.

She'd walked into class the first day, nervous but

determined. At the center of the room stood, objectively, the most attractive man she'd ever seen.

Mateo was her kind of handsome: dark eyes that crinkled around the corners when he laughed, a compact, muscular frame and a bright smile that lit a spark in her heart, no matter how wary she wanted to be. The first day, he stood in the middle of a group of students that would become their cohort, and he was talking to a duck. More specifically, he was talking to Puddles, the University of Oregon mascot. While Luci understood Puddles wasn't really a six-foot, felt-covered mallard, she loved her mascot.

Like, love-*loved* that duck.

So, yes, seeing a gorgeous man and Puddles made for an auspicious beginning to her education career. Luci paused at the threshold, joy bubbling up in her heart at the excitement and possibility. Her habit was to be suspicious in any new setting, to reserve judgment until she had all the facts. But who needed more facts than a gorgeous man and Puddles the duck? Those were two very strong facts.

It was what Mateo did next that she'd never been able to fully forget, or actively stop reliving—

"I can't understand it, Luci." Mateo's voice brought her firmly back to the moment. He held up his hands, as though surrendering. "Why are you so obsessed with rules?"

"Because rules set reasonable boundaries," she snapped, as though she could erase a memory of Mateo with the right vocal inflection. "When firm rules are in place, we know how to act."

"The vast majority of rules are arbitrary. They're created by people with an authority complex."

"There are rules everywhere, Mateo. Humans clearly don't do well without them. I agree we should be thoughtful about rules and reconsider them as society evolves. But you, I and our coworkers created a code of conduct in the fall. We're all in agreement. I think the clearer we can be, especially with teenagers, the better."

"Clear is one thing. I'm all on board with being clear. But not rigid."

"There's nothing rigid about it. We decided, as a staff, no food. When students challenged us, which they did, because they are students, we broadened the category to anything that could make a mess. Kids can have water."

"Wow. How generous of you," he said flatly.

"Although, personally, I'm suspicious of this whole hydration thing."

"You're suspicious of hydration?" He laughed, incredulous.

"I'm suspicious of the *hype* in hydration. Thirty-two-ounce Stanley cups? Massive Hydro Flasks? It seems like overkill. I survived my teens without a constant source of H_2O."

"I don't buy that for a second. You had to be one of those girls with a pumpkin-spice latte in one hand and a sticker-covered Hydro Flask in the other."

The single whoop of a police siren startled them. Mateo and Luci swiveled toward the sound. Sheriff Aida Weston stepped out of her vehicle and held her hand out, palm up, as though asking *What is wrong with you two?*

Right. They were jaywalking in a town of seventy-four people on a road that got less traffic than a socket-wrench-themed YouTube channel.

"Seriously. What have I told you about arguing in the middle of the street?"

"Sorry, Aida," Luci called to her friend.

Mateo smiled at the sheriff. "Sorry. It won't happen again."

Aida tilted her head, debating the statement. Her partner, Greg, flowed from the vehicle, his brown-and-black fur handsome in the morning sunshine. He trotted over to the sidewalk in front of the school and waited for them, eyeing Luci's basket of small friends.

Luci joined the German shepherd, rubbing his ears and burying her face in his fur until her annoyance at Mateo's comment wore off. She'd had a Hydro Flask, alright. Luci had found the perfectly good water receptacle in a recycling bin, removed all the stickers of ski resorts and island eateries, washed it as well as she could five times, dipped it in boiling water, then covered it with the stickers colleges sent her in their relentless pursuit of her application fee.

She still had that Hydro Flask.

"Let's get to work, bud," Aida called to her dog. Greg gave the basket of hedgehogs a polite sniff then trotted toward his handler/best friend. They took a few steps toward the sheriff's office, then

Aida turned back to Luci and asked, "Can I borrow your blue sweater for Thursday?"

"Of course," Luci responded. "Are you coming over tonight?"

Aida grinned. "I've got a dance lesson with the world's loudest PE teacher."

Luci's gaze shifted to Mateo without her permission. His eyes connected with hers for a flicker of a second, just long enough for a spark to threaten.

So she cleared her throat, because that was a sure-fire way to act like you don't remember floating in someone's arms on a ballroom floor, right?

"Sounds good," Luci said. "Stay for dinner, and I'll grab the sweater for you."

"Thank you. Greg is excited to spend more time with the hedgies."

"We'll be in the courtyard." Luci gestured with the basket.

Aida waved, the sunshine lighting up the diamonds on her engagement ring as she retreated into the small building that served as both the sheriff's office and the post office.

"Well, we can't fault her for not being clear on that rule," Mateo muttered.

"True. And this exemplar allows me more understanding of your position. I concede. Some rules can seem a little arbitrary."

Mateo laughed, his eyes crinkling up at the corners and his smile bathing her in its warmth.

So problematic.

"Which cup did you get?" she asked.

Mateo turned the mug so she could see the little sloth clinging to the rim.

Not long after Mac had learned to work the espresso machine, he decided that paper cups created a lot of waste for a little town with no garbage service. He'd brought in cups from home, then other community members had donated mugs as well. Cup roulette was half the fun of buying an espresso in Pronghorn. Community members were expected to wash their cups and return them within a few days, which encouraged everyone to head back into the store for another espresso on a regular basis.

Not that everyone didn't already visit the store every few days, because it was considered antisocial not to.

"I love the sloth," Luci admitted.

"Me, too."

He gazed at her over the rim as he took another sip. Luci readjusted her glasses.

"But just because we agree on one point doesn't mean I'm not right about everything else."

"There is another point we agree on," he reminded her.

She joined in as he stated the one rule they all held sacred: "Never argue in front of the students."

As a team of six teachers, they faced myriad difficulties. In their various practicums they'd seen what happened when the relationships between the adults in a building were unstable. In Pronghorn, the teachers were committed to working through their issues and standing together.

This wasn't a challenge for the most part. Within the first few weeks, her coworkers had become her best friends. Five young, energetic teachers with big ideas in a challenging situation were going to connect pretty quickly.

And then there was eighty-six-year-old Mrs. Moran, the Spanish teacher who'd worked in Pronghorn for decades. Kind, brilliant and dedicated, she could teach circles around any one of them but was the last to ever suggest it was a competition. Mrs. Moran was an extraordinary educator.

But Luci had known that before she took the job.

"I'm glad we can agree never to argue publicly." Mateo grinned at her, launching a spark in her heart. Luci held her breath, depriving the spark of oxygen. She'd squashed that spark before, and she could do it again. "But since the only other soul present at the moment is a cat, let me take the opportunity to say, no, I'm not moving my grading from the reception desk in the hotel lobby."

"It's a mess!"

"It's not a mess—it's exactly how I want it, and the perfect grading spot. Good lighting, I can stand rather than getting all cramped in a desk, and Vander's always playing guitar nearby. I'm not moving."

"Well, I'm putting a philodendron on that desk. I'm going to give it the best plant food available until it's grown so big you can't even find your grading. It's gonna look beautiful."

"You could put that plant from *Little Shop of Horrors* up there, and I'll just grade around it."

The rumble of an engine sounded, signifying the school bus. Or school truck, rather. The grizzled old rancher, Pete Sorel, pulled up in his crew cab. Doors opened and a tumble of kids, backpacks and noise spilled out. Luci took a step away from Mateo as another group of chattering students approached along the sidewalk.

The teachers expertly flipped their scowls around, smiling as kids headed into school. Neveah, a student they all kept a careful eye on, approached them. "Mateo, did you grade my test yet? I think I did better on this one."

Luci shuddered at the student's use of his first name. It was his business, but *still*. She preferred "Ms. Walker," and was confident that most students didn't even know her first name.

Well…no one here actually knew her *real* first name. But that was beside the point.

"I did." Mateo turned to Luci with a fake smile as he spoke to Neveah. "I had a fabulous time grading your test in the warm sunlight in the hotel lobby yesterday morning."

Neveah pressed her lips together and swallowed. The girl had gone out on a limb asking about the test, but everyone's favorite math teacher wasn't giving her a straight answer, just yammering on about sunshine. Neveah came from a complex situation at home. The family was suspicious of public education, as they hadn't been served well by the system in the past. It had taken a lot of effort to get her to class.

Now, she was here, attending regularly and feeling good enough to ask about a grade *before* class. How had Mateo not picked up on that?

"You've been doing excellent work across the board," Luci told her. "I was really impressed by how well you did as a witness in the mock trial we held."

"Thanks." Neveah tucked her hair behind her ear. "I liked the trial."

Mateo finally seemed to get the hint. He slung his messenger bag off his shoulder and began digging for her paper. File folders were not a modern convenience he utilized. Luci sighed and held her hand out so Mateo could pass off the coffee while he searched.

Okay, it really did smell amazing.

Students shuffled past them into the building. It was an eclectic crew, to be sure. The children of local ranching families came in, work gloves still tucked in their back pockets as they'd had a full morning of chores before school. The nine exchange students Pronghorn's volunteer principal recruited had settled in and were making the most of their time here.

And then there were the kids from the Open Hearts Intentional Community.

You weren't supposed to call it a commune, and it definitely wasn't a cult. But it was a different community, one that had only recently found common ground with the ranchers and townsfolk. Members of Open Hearts believed they needed to be wearing something orange all the time, so the students stood out from the beginning. And a collective disdain for society's norms drew attention to the kids in other ways: their willingness to argue against common societal constructs, an inability to interact naturally with other teens, a lack of understanding of basic cultural references, like *The Little Engine That Could*, or *SpongeBob SquarePants*.

It all contributed to the real issue facing these kids; they didn't know how to behave in the world outside of Open Hearts.

They inadvertently frustrated others, and themselves in turn, when they didn't know how to act. Like arguing with a soccer ref about poetry.

Mav jogged up the steps. His frame was still gangly, but he'd gained confidence in the last few months and stood straighter. He touched his thumb and forefinger to his chest, over his heart, and nodded as he passed Luci. Reflexively, she returned the greeting. Then she said the same thing she said to him, to Antithesis, to Spring Rain and all the other students from Open Hearts, every morning.

"I'm glad you're here."

CHAPTER TWO

MATEO COULD FEEL Luci's attention shift when Mav came ambling up the steps. She greeted the kid with extra care, like she was worried he and the other students from Open Hearts wouldn't feel welcome unless she spelled it out for them every single morning.

Not that welcoming kids was a bad habit. She was just so...intentional about it.

Also, she was still holding his coffee.

"I got an A?!" Neveah asked, math quiz trembling in her hands. "You gave me an A!"

Mateo refocused on his student. "You *earned* an A. You did the work, you learned the material. My job is just to check the answers and add up the points."

His job encompassed a lot more than that. He needed to calm her anxiety, spark an interest, explain the relevancy and then, you know, teach math. But he'd found it was better when the students didn't know how hard he was working.

"You got an A?" Taylor, a confident, well-connected student glanced at the paper. "That's awesome! OMG, is there anything you're not good at?"

Neveah reddened at the compliment but kept a tight grip on her test as the girls headed into school.

"Good morning, Mateo." Mrs. Moran stepped

out the front doors and joined them on the steps. "Good morning, Luci."

Mrs. Moran always seemed to be at school when they arrived, and she was still there, working in her little broom-closet office, when they left. Perfectly calm, as though all the chaos of the school and life was nothing.

She smiled at both of them. "I'm afraid we may have a bit of a situation on our hands. Can you accompany me to the gym?"

A frisson of dread slipped down Mateo's spine.

There was only one kind of situation at this school.

Luci voiced his fear. "I thought Loretta was at a real-estate conference in Klamath Falls?"

"She has returned," Mrs. Moran said, as Loretta's bullhorn blasted out the front doors, echoing all the way from the gym.

"Good moooooooooorning Pronghorn Public Day School! All students report to the gym, immediately!"

Luci's gaze met his.

This was one more thing they agreed on. Anytime Loretta called an impromptu, all-school assembly, there was trouble afoot.

They launched themselves toward the entrance. Mateo got there first. Seven years at a military school dedicated to performative chivalry kicked in and he held the door for Luci and Mrs. Moran.

The run morphed into a brisk walk once they hit the foyer, partly because *no running in the school* but mostly because the space was packed with stu-

dents and there wasn't room to run. The entrance
had a high ceiling and big windows overlooking
the town. Old wooden floors reflected the peculiar
shine of decades of teenage sneakers. A reading
nook with chairs and bookshelves had been built
next to one window, and a couple of readers were
already in place this morning, blithely ignoring the
urgent messages echoing out of Loretta's bullhorn.
On the opposite wall was a bay of bright yellow
lockers, the clicks and slams of opening and closing mingling with students' voices.

Perhaps the most notable features of the entrance
hall were the signs. Every available inch of wall
held a cheesy, painted plywood sign. Most of them
Mateo could agree with.

Be the Reason Someone Smiles Today.

You Are Stronger Than You Think.

These Are Your Good Old Days.

Others felt a little off in a school setting; an Easter
bunny, someone's lake cabin rules, a sign informing
passersby that The Dishwasher is Clean!

But that was a problem for another day. Kids were
heading into the gym, ready to hear whatever the
volunteer principal had in store for them this time.

"How bad can it be?" Tate, the tall, preternatu-
rally loud PE teacher asked, joining them in their
speed walk to the gym.

"You have to ask?" Luci said. "It can be horrifi-
cally bad, catastrophically bad." Luci stopped walking and looked around. "Where's Willa? I need more
descriptors for how bad this can be."

Willa, the school's English teacher and their de facto leader, joined them in the hall. "I believe the term you're looking for is dumpster fire."

"That," Luci said, pointing to Willa.

"She's got to run out of big schemes eventually, doesn't she?" Mateo asked.

"No." Vander, their thoughtful, enigmatic science teacher joined the group. "I don't think she can. She's like a cornucopia of bad ideas."

"Remember the time she suggested we could open a big cat sanctuary at the abandoned property off West Fork Road?" Tate asked.

"And that we let the students run it?" Mateo added, "Because she heard on the radio that taking care of animals is good for students' social emotional growth?"

Luci laughed. She had a bubbly, cheerful laugh with a little squeak in it when she thought something was particularly funny. As much as Mateo wished he didn't care, he loved to make her laugh.

"My favorite was her career-education scheme, where she had kids do clerical work for her real-estate business," Luci said.

"You guys know that Mason actually did her taxes," Mateo told the group. "He did all the math, the deductions, the write-offs, everything..." He trailed off, remembering going over Mason's work once the teachers had caught on to Loretta's plan. The boy had done a brilliant job, and while Loretta's actions were wrong, as Mason's math teacher he was kinda proud of the kid.

No, he was really proud.

Kids continued to stream into the gym as Loretta welcomed them through the bullhorn like an aggressive parrot.

Willa held up a hand. "I think we have to give Loretta some credit. Several of her wild ideas have worked out pretty well." They all groaned, but Willa continued, looking meaningfully at Tate. "While recruiting nine international students and telling them we had a premier soccer program was wrong, and not entirely legal, you have to admit, it was an incredible season."

Tate tilted his head in acknowledgement, then glanced over his shoulder in the direction of the sheriff's office, where his fiancée, and co-soccer coach, was hard at work.

"It turned out okay." His huge grin suggested a little more than okay.

"And Vander," she said, pinning him with a gaze, "would you go back in time and undo the holiday pageant?"

"Not a chance," he admitted.

"Her biggest scheme, by far, was convincing the five of us to come out here, and I for one wouldn't exchange this year, and working with you four, for anything. So let's see what she has to say."

Mateo polished off his coffee as they entered the gym. The students had assembled as instructed but weren't listening to Loretta's rambling. It was wild to think that not so many months ago, students had sat in awkward silence in this gym. It had taken weeks to get comfortable returning to in-person school. The three years these kids had spent relatively isolated, attending online school due to budget cuts, had stunted their social growth. When the school reopened last fall, the lunchroom had been particularly bleak, with students eating alone, staring at their phone screens even when the internet wasn't working. The teachers had done all they could to facilitate students connecting with one another, and the kids caught up fast. By this point in the year, the lunchroom atmosphere was more like a Coachella after-party.

Mateo glanced over to see Luci scanning the bleachers, picking up on some kind of trouble only she was able to see.

All the teachers cared about their students, but Luci seemed to care with a vengeance. She was alert to feelings and subtle social cues, as though she'd done graduate courses in reading body language. Where Mateo was likely to assume everything would work out in the end, Luci was always on the lookout for trouble.

Presently, she was picking up something brewing between Oliver, Mason, Antithesis and Cece. She spun on her penny loafers and stalked across the gym, climbed up the bleachers and set herself right in the middle of the group. It was the type of brave, well-timed move to head off problems that the other teachers had come to expect from her. Luci didn't wait for a fight to start—she was vigilant, constantly on the lookout for any situation that might erupt.

After chatting with the students for a moment, she must have felt his eyes on her, because she glanced up and met his gaze. She blinked, as though surprised at his interest in her.

But Mateo had been fascinated with Luci from the beginning, and witnessing her actions in Pronghorn only intensified his curiosity.

What was it she was so intent on doing here?

"HEY," LUCI GREETED the students.

Nothing at all weird about your teacher joining you in the bleachers out of the blue.

Oliver had not figured out how to flirt with Antithesis and more than once had hurt her feelings when he very much wanted to impress her. A well-timed interruption could give the kids more time to process, and protect Antithesis from his unthinking blunder.

"Do any of you know what her announcement is?" she asked. "Heard any rumors?"

"I think it's like a big field trip," Mason said.

"That would be so fun! Like an overnight field trip." Cece's eyes lit up.

Luci shuddered. There were few things less appealing than twenty-four hours of teenagers. Eight hours? Yes, great, wonderful even. But by four o'clock she was ready for a cup of tea and some adult conversation.

Loretta's bullhorn quieted for a moment as she

handed out a few of her business cards to students in the front row, suggesting their parents might consider buying a vacation home while the market was hot. Then she bustled back to her central spot in front of the bleachers.

"Are you ready for the big announcement?!" Loretta asked.

Luci focused hard on not rolling her eyes. She and her coworkers might have their opinions of Loretta, but they did not need to share those thoughts with the kids.

Who was she kidding? The kids could figure it out for themselves.

"I have three words for you…" Loretta paused dramatically. The students leaned in. Her ideas were always so wacky that they didn't want to miss a word. "Pronghorn Public Day School Boarding School!"

The gym was silent as everyone tried to unravel the mass of words.

Loretta waved her bullhorn with excitement, then positioned it in front of her lips again. "That's right! We are opening the extra rooms at The City Hotel to create a boarding school!"

Luci whipped her head around, seeking out her coworkers. If her ponytail hit an unsuspecting student in the face, that was unfortunate, but not her primary concern at this moment.

Vander looked shocked. Tate laughed. Willa was having a fit since Loretta had promised three words, then used six.

But it was Mateo with whom she locked eyes.
Boarding school.

She might not have much in common with the handsome, irascible math teacher, but they both knew exactly how much trouble a kid could get into at boarding school.

"The dorms will be for any student who lives over forty-five minutes away, and for any of the exchange students who want to live there."

A hubbub arose in the crowd as students evaluated their chances of getting a spot.

"Loretta—" Willa raised her hand and spoke loudly "—if I may—"

"Principal Lazarus," Loretta corrected her, batting her long, tangled false eyelashes.

Willa cleared her throat and managed to avoid gritting her teeth this time as she said, "Principal Lazarus, I appreciate your enthusiasm, but we need time to prepare for a boarding school."

"What do you think spring break is for?"

Willa blinked. "Not working?"

"Pish fish. You'll have lots of help. I know all the parents will pitch in to get their teenagers out of the house."

The color drained from Willa's face. "But Loretta, Pronghorn Public Day School Boarding School is a big ask. It's a huge undertaking. It's… It's…*it's an oxymoron.*"

Luci stood in the bleachers. If Willa's biggest issue was a grammatical error, it was time to get involved.

"Respectfully, there are a lot of issues with boarding schools," Luci said. "Students can unwittingly get themselves into some tough interpersonal problems."

Mateo stepped forward. "Students often struggle when situations are radically different from home life. It sounds fun but can have serious ramifications."

Luci nodded, glad they were on the same page. "Mateo and I both attended boarding schools. We can give firsthand accounts of hazing, substance abuse, academic pressure—"

Mateo picked up the concerns. "Late-night kitchen raids for long-standing, interhouse food fights that could erupt at any time."

She looked sharply at Mateo. He shrugged.

"In extreme cases, intense bullying can erupt," Luci continued, "but more often there is subtle negative pressure on students that's hard to recognize but ultimately damaging."

"Rigid cliques can form, impacting education for everyone," Mateo added.

Luci nodded in agreement. "Bad ideas can spiral and students can find themselves in the middle of an elaborate prank that sounded harmless to begin with—"

"Like hiring a band of bagpipers to follow someone around for three days."

What the...? Luci turned to Mateo again, incredulous this time.

"I mean, eventually the cops showed up. But the psychological damage was already done."

Luci tried her Teacher Eye on Mateo but he seemed impervious.

"It wasn't my idea," he supplied.

She shook her head and refocused on the main problem. "Loretta—"

"Principal Lazarus."

"Principal Lazarus, we need time if we're going to do this."

"And for the record, I *don't* think we should do this," Mateo added.

The gym was silent, as they were all possibly contemplating Luci and Mateo's concerns. Or more likely, still trying to wrap their heads around what kind of psychological damage a band of bagpipers wrought.

Then Suleiman, an exchange student from Senegal, stood in the bleachers, a big smile on his face. "*I* think we should do it!"

"It will be fun," his friend Antonio, who had come from Brazil, agreed as several other students chimed in.

"And even if we don't live far enough away to get a spot, we can still come over," Taylor said.

"See?" Loretta gestured to the kids. "They want to all live together at the hotel. It'll be a riot!"

The room erupted in enthusiasm. Because what teenager didn't think a permanent, coed slumber party with no parents was a good idea?

Luci launched herself from the bleachers, heading straight for Loretta. Mateo joined her.

Behind them she could hear students making

plans. Sisters Taylor and Morgan didn't live far enough away to get a spot, but Cece was already promising to invite them for sleepovers. Mav was questioning what Loretta meant by "forty-five minutes," because if he walked from Open Hearts to school, it was well over forty-five minutes.

"Loretta, this is a terrible idea," Luci said.

Mateo stood shoulder-to-shoulder with her. "Worse than your idea for a magnate clown and circus arts school."

Loretta fluffed her hair and cast a glance at the other teachers. They came to stand behind Mateo and Luci, silently backing them up.

"You do bring up some valid concerns," Loretta said.

"Thank you!" Luci breathed out a sigh of relief and started to turn away.

"But there's no way kids could get bagpipers way out here."

"Loretta—"

"No." Loretta stopped her with an outstretched hand. "I've already talked to several families. They're thrilled."

Mateo crossed his arms. "Luci and I have experience with boarding schools, and we are telling you, there is a lot that can go wrong."

"I appreciate your experience and insight on the matter," Loretta said. "Which is why I'm putting you two in charge."

The sentence seemed to wrap itself around them, tethering them to the spot. Mateo turned to Luci.

It was a truly terrible moment to be struck by how gorgeous his eyes were.

"Hold up." Tate stepped forward. "You can't put this on the two of them. We'll all help out."

Loretta pointed to Tate. "You have your hands full with coaching. Track and field is coming up, and since Steve Prefontaine was born to run in small-town Oregon, I expect his doppelganger to be running here this spring."

"We don't have a track," he reminded her.

"Did that stop Steve Prefontaine?"

"No, because Coos Bay, where he came from, has a track."

Loretta continued, unperturbed by minor details like running a track program without a track. "Willa has her duties with the school board, and you know how she helps me out with administrative doodads."

Luci put a firm arm around her friend's shoulder so she couldn't grab Loretta's bullhorn and bop her on the head with it. Willa ran the school and solved every problem that popped up. Loretta took the credit, and created half the problems Willa wound up solving.

"And this one—" she gestured to Vander "—has half a foot in Nashville, chasing after Harlow Jameson."

Vander grinned. "I'm not chasing her, Loretta. We're engaged."

"Don't you wish! Not that I blame you. Harlow is quite the catch."

"I know. We caught each other. We're getting married in August."

Loretta waved away the words, speaking as though Vander wasn't there. "He's always heading off to Tennessee, or hanging out with her musician friends trying to get on her good side. He won't be of any use in a boarding school."

Vander turned to his coworkers, baffled. Mateo laid a hand on his shoulder and gestured to Loretta. "She'll come around at the wedding."

"Do you need an officiant?" Loretta asked. "Because I'm a certified minister. Online, of course."

Everyone groaned.

"Back to the topic at hand," Willa said. "We will take the idea of a student dormitory to the school board, and discuss it further." Loretta started to interrupt her, but Willa continued, "There's a lot to consider. Parent permissions, sleeping arrangements, finances. No one around here is running a dormitory without a significant pay increase."

Loretta waved a hand. "I've got the finances all accounted for." She grinned at Mateo. "I ran the numbers myself."

CHAPTER THREE

LUCI FLOPPED BACK on her bed, the comforter and pillows letting out a whoosh of air to echo her own sigh. *What. A. Day.*

Her concerns, and Mateo's, did nothing to quell student excitement. Just the opposite. Somehow they'd taken their warnings and woven together an imaginary world of fun and light danger. Pronghorn Public Day School Boarding School had become a mashup of Hogwarts and *The Hunger Games*.

Now, she was emotionally exhausted, with a brain working overtime.

Luci scanned her room, one of the large fourth-floor suites overlooking the main street. Her space was beautiful; pale pink walls and polished antiques. A row of windows let the sunshine in, while thin white curtains moved with the afternoon breeze. There was a sitting room set up by the windows, a central space with a desk and old-fashioned dressing table and finally her cozy bed tucked in a back corner. It was the perfect retreat.

Luci's room had come with four hedgehogs, currently asleep in a basket next to her bed. She'd never outright asked Loretta where they came from, but words like *housewarming gift* and *therapy animals* had been thrown around enough times it was clear the volunteer principal had dropped them off in

Luci's closet. It was a gift she was grateful to receive.

Luci ran her hand over the spiny, sleeping creatures. They'd wake up later this evening, forage in the courtyard for a while, then ramble around her room, their paws scrambling on the wood floor a lullaby as she slept. Luci loved her hedgehogs, loved her room. She loved the hotel, and living here with her coworkers.

It was the first time in her life she felt at home.

And now, that home was about to be invaded by teenagers.

A soft knock sounded at her door. "Luci?"

It was Mateo. She sat up. Mateo had literally never knocked on her door.

He tapped again. "You have time to talk? If you're in there…"

"I'm here." She stood and paced to the mirror. Her ponytail was off-kilter. Luci pulled at the strands, trying to right the lopsided hairdo, then she fixed her bangs.

"Okay. Well, I'm outside your door and—"

"Oh, sorry!" Of course, he was still outside. And she was being weird and impolite by not responding. Why couldn't she get it together and behave normally? Luci marched to the door and threw it open. "Hi. What are we going to do?"

He let out a short laugh. "That's what I'm here to ask you."

"Do you want to come in?" She stepped back.

"Should we sneak out to The Restaurant?" He glanced over his shoulder and lowered his voice.

"Willa wants us to meet as a group and I thought it might be a good idea for you and me to speak first since…"

His voice trailed off but Luci understood. The other teachers didn't seem nearly as upset as she and Mateo were. Tate had gone so far as to suggest contacting the rural boarding school in Westlake to get ideas. Willa had brought up how helpful it could be for certain students. Vander thought it might even be fun, which was fine for him to say. He really did have one foot in Nashville and spent at least half his time in Pronghorn out at Harlow's ranch caring for her horses.

"Good call," she said. "How do you want to sneak out? There's a skylight in the kitchen, or we could go with a standard drainpipe escape."

"Hmm." Mateo looked thoughtful, as though he was considering her idea.

"I'm joking. Honestly, the last thing we want is to illuminate all the escape routes for our future boarders."

"*Possible* future boarders," he clarified. "I think we can stop this."

Her gaze connected with his, his confidence settling her. Always a little disheveled, Mateo looked even more casual than usual. Even more handsome than usual.

He cleared his throat.

Right. This was not a helpful thought pattern.

"Come on." Luci grabbed a sweater. "Let's get

out of here before Willa starts seeing Loretta's point of view."

As it turned out, there was no sneaking involved to exit the hotel. Willa was chatting with her fiancé, school board president and local rancher Colter Wayne, about his daughter's upcoming birthday. Vander was playing guitar in the courtyard. Tate was still at school, working with a group of kids on the soccer field.

Mateo nodded in Tate's direction as they walked past. "Maybe instead of a track-and-field team, we could just have a field team."

"Great idea. Since this part of the state is so sparsely populated, we could call it track *or* field, and every meet will be a grab bag of events."

Mateo laughed. "I like that, it brings an element of uncertainty the sport was missing."

They approached a small brick building with The Restaurant written in yellow paint on the side. When they'd arrived in town last August, The Restaurant had offered only two choices each day and was confined to a bare-bones dining room and kitchen. In the last few months the proprietress, Angie, had added a snug outdoor seating area and expanded the menu to *three* choices.

Things were really hopping in Pronghorn these days.

As they approached the door, Mateo stepped forward to open it for her. It was funny how he trash-talked rules, but had the manners of a gentleman ingrained into him. He stood whenever she entered a room, opened doors, used the correct silverware, knew to wait until everyone was seated and served to begin his meal. He'd been taught easy social graces that allowed him to navigate the world, making others feel comfortable and valued.

"What are you doing here?" Angie barked as they entered. "It's not Thursday."

Angie, on the other hand, had no social graces, easy or otherwise.

"We just wanted to grab a Coke and talk for a bit," Mateo said.

"Coke is cheaper at the store," Angie reminded them.

Mateo gave her his most charming smile. "But it doesn't have the atmosphere of The Restaurant."

Angie turned away, grumbling, then stopped. "Hold up. Is this a date?"

"No!" Luci said, loud enough to attract the attention of Pete Sorel and Ed Gonzalez where they were sipping coffee at a central table.

"No," Mateo confirmed. "Not at all. We are the two least likely people to go on a date in Pronghorn."

"I don't know about that—" Angie mumbled.

Luci cut her off. "We need a place to do a little planning. There's no Coke at the school, nowhere to sit at the store and we need to focus."

"Fine. Take a seat by the window."

Mateo glanced at the back corner. "We were hoping for a little privacy."

"You want privacy? Stay home." She jacked a

thumb toward an open table at the front. "Take a seat."

Luci widened her eyes at Mateo. He repressed a smile, then gestured for her to step ahead as he followed her to their appointed table.

The Restaurant held few patrons at four o'clock: the regular tables of older ranchers, and a small group from Open Hearts, including Today's Moment. Her flowing orange robes designated her as the current leader of the community. She nodded as they passed by. Luci dropped her gaze.

"You two realize you're gonna put me out of a job," Pete grumbled as they passed his table.

Luci stopped. "How so?"

A lot of the teachers had been initially intimidated by the old rancher, but she'd caught on to his soft side. He might act grumpy, but he was the first to show up when the community needed anything.

"I've been driving near about five hours a day picking kids up and dropping them off for school. You open the dormitory and I'll just be driving the Holms girls. And that'll only last 'til Taylor gets her license."

Pete's tone was teasing, but Luci picked up on his relief. Five hours a day was a big commitment. She hadn't thought about Pete in all this.

Angie made a fuss about bringing them drinks. Then brought a basket of fries because she didn't believe in serving Coke without something fried and salty to balance the sweetness. After that she disappeared into the kitchen for a few moments, only to return with a small dish of her special sauce she claimed was cluttering up her fridge.

Luci turned her Coke and readjusted the straw. She glanced at her unlikely ally, resigned to sharing a little more truth about her background to put a stop to the boarding-school idea. Not the whole truth, just enough to turn the tide.

"I very much valued my time at boarding school, but it wasn't easy," she confessed.

"Amen," Mateo agreed.

"I understand this is a different situation, and these are vastly different students than the girls I went to school with, but I'm worried that no one is prepared for the realities of living away from home."

Luci dipped a fry in the sauce and popped it into her mouth. While much of Angie's cooking was questionable, her special sauce really was perfect.

He gave her a sly grin. "While I agree with the second half of your sentence, it's hard to imagine you didn't rock the debutante scene."

She returned the grin with a tight smile. "As I've mentioned, I wasn't a debutante, although many of my classmates did have elaborate coming-out parties."

He was determined to put her in a box he understood. And for the time being it was best she pretend to fit that box. Luci continued with as much truth as she felt safe sharing. "Emotionally, I felt lost much of the time. Kids don't realize how much they rely on their community until suddenly, they're two thousand miles away."

"Loretta will argue that they are not two thousand miles away and can see their families whenever they want."

"I know." She pulled a notebook out of her bag. "So let's come up with more arguments. What was your experience?"

Mateo looked thoughtful as he took a sip of his Coke. He was probably the life of the party, the one leading late-night missions to the kitchen and hiring the band of bagpipers. He crossed his arms on the table and leaned toward her.

"I hated it," he admitted.

She looked up sharply. "You?"

"Middle school was unbearable, high school was worse. I tried to make the best of it, but it wasn't my choice, and I would *never* send my own child to boarding school."

Luci attempted to integrate this new information. "It was a military school, right?"

He nodded, keeping his eyes on the table. Luci had been as surprised as anyone when Mateo first admitted to being a product of a military education. He was so relaxed, so easygoing. The type of person you couldn't imagine keeping a straight face during drill.

"One thing that might be helpful…" He paused for a moment, as though unsure how much to share. "It might be helpful for you to understand how much I value honesty and integrity."

He looked into her eyes as if to see how this landed. Luci nodded to show she was listening, but those weren't radical values. Didn't everyone value the truth?

Except, you know, when the truth was a collection of private facts about yourself you preferred to keep hidden.

"At my school, appearance was everything. You were expected to show up as a valiant scholar soldier—or at least appear that way. And if you did that by cheating, lying, or throwing your classmates under the bus, the authorities turned a blind eye. They preached integrity but subtly encouraged us to practice getting ahead by any means possible." He swallowed hard. "I hated it."

"I'm so sorry," Luci said. "My time wasn't great, but no one encouraged lying."

"It sucked."

"Is that why you became a teacher?" she asked.

"I became a teacher because it's a great job, and service is valued and expected in my family. But, yeah, I do find myself atoning for some of the bad decisions I made at St. Xavier's." He leaned back in his chair and smiled at her. "So before we start scheming together, I have one request. Can you and I be completely honest with each other? I know we haven't always gotten along, but I can handle anything except lies."

Luci kept her gaze steady, knowing full well the gross omission of her past was considered dishonesty. But what he, and everyone else, didn't know couldn't hurt them, right?

MATEO DIDN'T EXPECT to be laughing with Luci over a stack of sticky notes and gel pens when he woke up that morning. It reminded him of their days at the U of O, trying to figure out a professor's baffling grading scheme.

He didn't even mind when she asked him to color-coordinate their different tactics for stopping the boarding school. She was organized. That was what they needed to put a stop to this.

"Let's go over our outline again." Luci flipped her planner around so he could see the neat rows of multicolored squares of paper. "Reason one is the condition of the hotel."

"Right. The rooms on the second and third floors are in bad shape."

"We'd need new mattresses, bedding, furnishings—it will get expensive fast."

"We don't know if the elevator works, so the building isn't up to code."

"Good point." She wrote *Elevator!* in her even, energetic script, then glanced up at him over the sticky note. "What if the elevator does work? We've never actually tried it."

Mateo rubbed his brow. The reason none of them had ever tried the elevator was because it was creepy, and no one wanted to get stuck inside. Did he admit this to Luci, or was it understood?

He glanced up to see her shudder theatrically. It was understood.

"We're going to assume it doesn't," he said. "And even if it does, there's no way it's safe."

She nodded, her ponytail emphasizing the action, and pressed the square of yellow paper into her planner. Mateo grabbed another French fry, then gestured with it as an idea came to him. "Hey, do you think there might be asbestos?"

"Oh, my god, that would be amazing!" Luci said, scribbling on another note. Then she stopped. He tried to contain his smile but couldn't when she rolled her eyes at her own words. "I totally heard myself there. Sorry."

He held up his hands. "I brought it up."

Luci's gaze connected with his. Her eyes were a deep, periwinkle blue, like the sky before sunset.

She grabbed another fry and dipped it in the special sauce. "Okay, I'm going to read back what we have. Our areas of concern are legal issues, building condition, social emotional well-being of the students, social emotional well-being of the *teachers*, finances—"

"Sorry to interrupt!"

Mateo had been so focused on Luci that he hadn't noticed anyone approaching. They both looked up in surprise.

"Ms. Walker, Mateo, hi. I'm Cece's mom."

"Of course." Mateo stood, gesturing to a spare chair. "Nice to see you, Ms. Hayes. Would you like to join us?"

Luci's brow furrowed as she shot him a look. Sure, it was bad timing. He didn't want Melissa Hayes to join them any more than Luci did, but what was he supposed to do, be impolite?

"Oh, no thank you." She waved both her hands, as though to erase her interruption. "I can see you're busy. I just wanted to thank you both in advance."

Luci straightened. "Why?"

"For the boarding school. I heard how Loretta sprung it on you, and I know how she gets. But it's going to make such a difference for us, for Cece."

Mateo didn't know how to respond, so he smiled. It was his go-to, but maybe not the best for this situation?

"You wouldn't know this, but I work from home," Melissa said. "I process medical records. We're an hour out of town, so when I take Cece to and from school every day, that's four hours of driving. With the price of gas, a lot of days I just stay in town."

Mateo glanced at Luci to gauge her reaction. She kept her expression neutral.

"I try to get some work done, but you know how the internet is out here. Unless you have a satellite, you're out of luck. So I wind up bringing her to school, then either drive home and have to turn around and come back a few hours later, or I stay in town and have to work at night."

Luci's expression began to falter. "Can she take the school bus?"

"Pete offered, of course, he did. But we're out past Hart Mountain. His route is on the other side of the valley. If Pete were to pick up Cece, he'd have to get to our house at five a.m. I don't want that for my daughter, you know?"

"We had no idea," Mateo said. "Thank you for making such a sacrifice to get her to school."

She waved her hand. "I'm happy to do it, thrilled even. I wouldn't ever have Cece return to online school. Those days were…bleak." Tears welled up in her eyes. "This year has been incredible for my daughter. She's playing sports and has made so many friends. The dormitory will make such a difference. We've already decided I'll come into town on Wednesday afternoons, so we can spend time together and go out to dinner. Then she'll come home on weekends, of course. But during the week, this is going to make our lives manageable. *Thank you*."

Luci didn't seem to know how to respond any more than he did. Do you say "you're welcome," when you're actively trying to get out of the thing someone is thanking you for?

"I won't disturb you any longer." Melissa's friendly smile returned. "But thank you again, for *all* you do."

Melissa squeezed Mateo's hand, then Luci's, and hurried off.

Mateo flopped back into his chair. Luci stared at the neat lists in her planner.

"Okay, I feel kind of bad right now," she admitted.

"I know…" Mateo trailed off and gestured in the direction of Cece's mom, who was now standing next to her car as Cece finished up Ultimate Frisbee practice.

"Maybe we can come up with another solution?"

Luci said, brightening. "Maybe Cece could stay with friends during the week?"

"Great idea." He pointed to her forehead. "I like the way you think."

"Do you?"

"Most days." He grinned at her.

Luci rolled her eyes, then refocused on her planner. "Where were we? Hotel safety? Or are we ready to move on to legal issues?"

A tap at the window caught their attention. Neveah was standing on the other side of the glass, her elbow pinned to her side as she waved at them. They both waved back. Neveah didn't leave, rather gave them a hopeful look. Mateo gestured for her to join them.

"She is such an incredible kid," Luci said.

"And she's come so far," Mateo noted.

"I loved watching her face as she saw her math quiz this morning. Those are the moments, right? When a kid tries hard and finally gets it."

"Yeah," Mateo agreed. This was another thing he and Luci had in common. They were both dedicated to this tough, demanding work.

She kept her eyes on a French fry she was dipping in the sauce as she said, "I don't think I've ever met anyone who approaches math like you. It's cool. The kids love it."

Mateo warmed at her words. Luci's classes were carefully planned, dramatic events that all the students looked forward to. His were low-key and laid-back, an environment where he could quietly urge his students to excel.

She glanced up at him, her Shakespearean fairy grin offsetting the compliment. "And given that less than one percent of the earth's population actually likes math, that's really saying something."

Mateo leaned forward to respond but Luci glanced dramatically at Neveah as she approached the table. Still grinning, she whispered, "Don't argue in front of the students."

"Hi!" Neveah waved again. Mateo stood and gestured to a chair for her, but the girl was too excited to sit down. "Um. I can't *wait* for the dormitory to open. It's gonna be… *the best*."

Luci's expression fell. Her voice was gentle but firm as she said, "Neveah, boarding school isn't the fun everyone keeps saying it is."

"It doesn't matter if it's fun." Neveah shook her head, like she didn't want to be misunderstood. "I mean, it *will* be fun. But you know getting to school has been…hard. With my family."

Her words dropped off. She didn't need to explain.

Neveah pulled in a breath. "But with the boarding school, everyone will be going to the school, every day. Even you guys! And everyone will have homework, and I can go to the games or maybe play rehearsals and I won't have to negotiate. You know?"

Neveah seemed to lose her words. She swallowed and stared at the floor. Then she nodded firmly. "Thank you. I'm really glad you're here."

Mateo said the only thing he could. "We're glad you're here, too."

Neveah soaked in the compliment. Then she waved again, dropped her gaze and headed for the door.

They stared out the window as Neveah retreated down the street. After Ultimate Frisbee practice she would hop in the school truck. Pete would take her home to a barren patch of ground that was not, technically, forty-five minutes away. But even Loretta, in all her self-promotion and bad ideas, had to intend for Neveah to have a spot in the school dorms.

"How awful are we?" Luci asked.

"When we were hoping for asbestos or crushing dreams?"

"We were hoping to crush dreams with asbestos, so it's really all one and the same."

Mateo let out a breath, then asked the question he didn't want to contemplate the answer to. "What would be good about a boarding school?"

Luci didn't move for a moment. Then she dug in her bag and produced another set of sticky notes, these ones bright green, echoing the colors in her sweater. She pulled off the top slip and wrote *Neveah* in her neat handwriting.

Together they started a new list.

CHAPTER FOUR

"I'VE GOT THE board's decision here," Willa said, waving a piece of yellow paper torn from a legal pad.

Luci didn't bother to look at Mateo. He sat next to her at the wrought-iron table, hunched over, face in his palms. She could feel his dread as powerfully as her own.

It was Saturday. The teachers had gathered in the courtyard of the hotel to wait while Willa attended the emergency board meeting at Colter's house. But insofar as Luci and Mateo had agreed to the dormitory, she wasn't expecting any last-minute opt-out of the impending doom. They were resigned to the inevitable.

Mateo leaned back in his chair and ran his hands through his hair. "Let's hear it."

"The dormitory rooms in the hotel will open the Monday after spring break," Willa said.

Okay. Luci had expected that.

"Mateo and Luci are in charge, and the rest of us will help."

Luci shook her head. "Mateo and I can handle this. You've all already taken on extra duties. Tate, you coach everything. Vander, I know the kids are excited about a spring play, plus you're taking care of Jameson Ranch. And Willa is basically running the school."

"I am effectively running the school," Willa corrected.

"Exactly. Plus you're all—" Mateo waved his hands "—in love and planning a bunch of weddings. Luci and I can take this."

"We'll help," Willa said again. "And you two will be paid a substantial stipend for your work."

Luci straightened. That was good news. Mateo mugged an impressed expression. "Nice." He glanced at Luci. "Maybe we could pool our resources and buy something extravagant for the hotel?"

"Like a toaster?"

"I was thinking a vehicle with actual doors."

"I don't know," she mused, "the ATV we were issued is growing on me."

Mateo winked at her. "Every time you drive that thing, you have a dramatic effect on the proportion of people wearing penny loafers while driving camouflage off-road vehicles."

She grinned back. "I'd like to see that Venn diagram."

Voices from the street floated into the courtyard, along with the sunshine and warm breeze.

Willa continued, "You'll have eleven students living here. Of the nine exchange students, four are opting to stay with their host families, and then there are six students coming from outlying areas."

"Any kids from Open Hearts?" Luci asked.

"It's not far enough away," Willa noted. "With the exception of Neveah, we're being strict about the distance."

Luci crossed her arms tightly over her chest.

Willa consulted her list again. "The dormitory will be open Sunday through Thursday nights. Parents are expected to pick their kids up Friday after school and you'll have the weekends off."

"Yes!" Mateo launched out of his chair and punched his fist into the air. He landed with a sheepish grin. "Sorry. I'm excited. This might be less horrible than anticipated."

"Excellent news," Luci concurred. As she spoke, the voices from the street seemed to quiet a touch, almost like people were listening in. Which led her to question why there *were* people out in front of the hotel. She shook her head and refocused on her friends. "Thank you, Willa. That's going to make a big difference."

Willa held up the sheet of paper. "Honestly, it all looks pretty good. The only thing we didn't cover was finances, but Loretta seems to think she's got it all worked out. The state can kick in some funds. She's already spoken to families and gotten commitments. Payments are on a sliding scale, so families that can pay more will and help cover the fees of students who don't have the resources."

Mateo placed a hand on her shoulder, as though thinking the same thing she was. The community of Pronghorn, no matter how contentious and frustrating it could be, rallied for their kids. The two of them could rally for the next three months, too.

Willa studied the list, then looked hard at Mateo

and Luci. "I hate that you two are stuck doing something you don't want to."

"It is what it is," Luci replied. "The whole thing is hard enough without having to rehash it. Mateo and I are mature enough to understand that our sacrifice can have a positive impact for students this spring. Or at least I am."

Mateo gave her something in between a scowl and a smile. It probably wasn't supposed to make her heart give a little shimmy, but it did.

"*This* spring," Mateo confirmed. "Luci and I are on board to run the dormitory until the end of the year. We will reassess in June. We make no promises about next year. Except for Luci. She promises to keep color-coordinating her socks with every outfit and ironing her sweaters."

"I steam my sweaters," Luci corrected, then addressed the group. "We need an immediate solution for our students who live farther out, but we're not committing to anything past the end of the school year."

"Understood," Willa said.

"We appreciate what you're doing." Tate ran both hands through his thick black hair. "I don't think I could do this."

"I know I couldn't," Vander admitted.

Luci caught Mateo's eye.

Can we do this?

They both had a lot of baggage from their own time at boarding school, and working together had never been their strong suit.

The voices outside the courtyard seemed to intensify. Tate looked over his shoulder and finally asked the question that had been gnawing at her. "What's going on out there?"

"Um, yeah." Willa glanced at the opening to the street, where Luci now noticed Colter blocking the entrance. "People want to help."

"Help?" Luci asked.

"With setting up the dormitories."

Vander looked stricken. "How many people?"

Willa waffled her hand back and forth. "Most of the people?"

Their coworkers hopped up and headed to the opening into the street to have a look, leaving Mateo and Luci at the table.

"Are we really gonna do this?" he asked her.

She nodded. "We are. We're gonna do it and we're going to make it look easy."

He held her gaze. "It can't be like my experience. We can't have long lists of random and arbitrary rules everyone is just trying to work around."

It couldn't be like hers, either. With myriad unspoken rules that everyone knew except the weird girl on scholarship.

"Honesty and integrity," she said, reminding him, and herself, of his core values. "Let's start there."

He held out a hand to shake on it. Luci slipped her fingers into his, feeling the warmth of his grasp spread through her chest. Her hand always felt so at home in his, like it could comfortably rest there.

But that was just what Mateo's good manners

did. They made everyone feel comfortable and at ease. No surprise that her hand got the same signal as the rest of the world.

He smiled, his eyes crinkling at the corners. "Honesty and integrity."

A loud voice sounded on repeat, like a late-night car alarm that no one responds to.

"I guess Loretta's here," Luci said, not breaking eye contact with Mateo.

His grin widened. "Help strikes again."

Luci laughed.

Willa gave Colter the all-clear signal and in seconds the courtyard was overrun. Angie arrived with cleaning supplies, barking directions to a group of students she had in tow. Raquel Holms, Pronghorn's most opinionated mom, bustled in with an industrial vacuum. She took a significant amount of time and space in the courtyard explaining why this machine could clean the carpets better than any other, as though she had serious vacuuming competition and was *not* gonna miss out on her shot at cleaning rugs. The older generation, like Mac and Ed, made a quieter entrance. Those two had toolboxes at the ready as they headed up the stairs to begin tackling the dilapidation that had overtaken most of the hotel.

After the first flood of help, Luci found herself dealing with attempted donations. Old furniture. Old tablecloths. Old towels. Old everything. People wanted to contribute. They also wanted to get rid of their old stuff.

There had been similar donations at the school. The library was packed with back copies of *Field & Stream* magazine and the complete canon of Barbara Cartland romance novels. People offered Tate old basketballs no longer capable of holding air. Vander was the recipient of half-finished, 3D models of dinosaurs.

And the gift that people couldn't stop giving Luci? Old *National Geographic* maps. Stacks and stacks of them. Maps of the Holy Land. Maps of Dutch settlements in Indonesia. Maps of countries that hadn't existed since the fall of the Berlin Wall. Some maps were useful in a social studies classroom, of course. But all the maps? It was a bit much.

In her years as a scholarship student at an expensive school, Luci had learned to how to act grateful when someone gave her something she neither wanted nor needed. But she'd never learned to like it.

This was a different situation, though. The hotel might need to house eleven students, but she had no intention of storing other people's junk. As she was trying to politely decline a set of no-longer-nonstick pots and pans that originated in the Reagan years, Pete Sorel came strolling into the courtyard with a huge box.

"Where do you want the new sheets?" he asked.

Luci glanced at Pete. "*New* sheets?"

New sheets were something she was willing to discuss.

"New sheets," he confirmed. "I got 'em off this site called Amazon."

"Oh. Okay. That's great. Thank you, Pete."

"You been to that site?" he asked.

A flash of yellow caught Luci's attention. Someone in a polyester pantsuit was heading into the hotel lobby.

"To Amazon?"

"They've got everything there."

"Um—"

"Sheets. Breakfast cereal. It's where I got all the flag stickers for my truck." Pete, like many people in this area, drove a white truck with an American flag sticker on the back. When nine exchange students had arrived in town, he'd added international flag stickers to support the kids, along with a Senegalese flag he flew in honor of Pronghorn's star soccer player.

"Sounds amazing, Pete, it really does—"

"And you just put what you're looking for into the search bar. Like with sheets, you type in thread count, color, whether or not you want the sheets to have lions on them—"

A box crashed in the next room, followed by the sound of a nail being pounded into a wall. With Loretta, that could only mean one thing.

"I'm going to catch the rest of this later," Luci promised. Although was she really going to listen as Pete gave her a tutorial on Amazon? She sprinted out of the courtyard, into the lobby.

There, balanced precariously on the early 20th century art nouveau reception desk, high heels leaving prints on Mateo's grading, was a woman in bright yellow, hanging up a sign that read Good Vibes Only.

"No!" Luci shouted.

Loretta wobbled in her heels.

"Whatever are you yelling about?" Loretta asked.

Luci pointed a finger and said the only word she could think of. "You."

Loretta looked baffled. Luci managed to find her voice. "You may not hang up that sign. Any signs. Or anything."

"Don't be such a spoilsport, Luci. A few words to inspire the kids won't hurt anything."

"I'm not having signs in here telling kids what kind of vibes they are, and are not, allowed to have."

Loretta turned back to pounding a nail into the fragile 1920s lath-and-plaster walls. "Everyone could use a few good vibes. Especially you."

"No." Luci widened her stance and crossed her arms. "This is where I draw the line."

"Oh, for heaven's sake, it's just a sign."

"It's not *just* a sign." Luci scanned the room for the evidence she knew she would find. "There are two full boxes of cheesy sayings painted on plywood. Where do you even get all of these?"

Loretta turned her attention back to the hammer and nail. "Don't think you can steal my shopping secrets, Miss Luci Walker."

"I don't want your shopping secrets. I don't want this sign, or any of these signs. Ever. Anywhere."

"You don't want good vibes?"

"I don't want good vibes. I don't want—" Luci pulled a sign out of a box. "Man cave rules? In what way is this possibly appropriate for a boarding school?"

"Well, you don't know what they'll be getting up to on the boys' side."

Luci studied the conglomeration of demands regarding a space set aside for beer and football. "I don't know what's more disturbing, the fact that you bought this sign, or that there's now a cave of men somewhere with no guidance on who the remote belongs to."

Loretta braced a hand against the wall and tried to pry the sign away from Luci. Raquel chose that moment to bustle in with the world's most effective vacuum cleaner.

"You two mind if I do this room next?"

"Wait until I'm finished. Who knows how these cookie-cutter walls are gonna crumble."

"You're putting nails in these walls?" Raquel asked. "The plaster is original."

"And so are these signs," Loretta chirped, pointing to an ultimatum about living, loving and dancing like no one was watching. It was wedged in next to some very strict instructions about what kind of vehicle could be parked in Mark's garage.

"No." Luci climbed up on the reception desk next to Loretta, making sure to avoid a stack of geometry quizzes. "We're not doing this."

"Oh, fiddle faddle, everyone loves an inspirational sign. And a few good vibes never hurt anyone."

Luci grabbed the sign, pretty sure she could hurt someone with these vibes right here and now.

"What's going on?" Mateo appeared in the doorway, looking disheveled and happy, a tool belt slung across his hips.

Like Luci didn't already have enough problems on hand? Attractive men should not be allowed to walk around wearing tool belts. It was one thing to be gorgeous, but throw in useful? Unfair.

"Is everything okay?" he asked.

"Nope."

"This one is impeding my progress," Loretta snapped as she climbed off the desk, scattering several statistics worksheets. "I'm here, trying to serve my community, and *Miss Walker* keeps butting in." She grabbed another piece of plywood. This one explained to the reader that in the Maxwell family, they keep their promises, laugh often, make mistakes, apologize, say thank you, get rowdy and know they are loved.

Not like all those *other* families.

"Isn't this the cutest?" Loretta clucked, scanning the walls for a good place to let the Maxwells wax on about their harmonious family dynamics.

Mateo stepped farther into the room. "Loretta, let's hold off a bit on the decorating. We need to get the hotel in order first."

"No!" Luci snapped. "We're not holding off. We're stopping. There will be no signs in this room, not now, not ever." Luci waved the sign threateningly. "No man-cave rules, no Maxwell family bragging, no requirements for dancing, no parking and no good vibes, or any vibes of any kind. This is a *vibe-free zone!*"

She intended to turn a cold look on Loretta, only to see many, many pairs of eyes on her.

Great. She had an audience.

At some point during the argument, students, community members and coworkers had drifted into the room, like wasps to a family barbecue. And now, Luci was standing on the reception desk, Mateo's grading at her feet, attacking the existence of vibes. Everyone was staring.

Real normal behavior.

Raquel Holms cleared her throat, then stepped forward. "That's a nice sign."

Tears of frustration blurred Luci's vision. Raquel had mellowed out considerably over the year. But, *of course*, she was here to catch Luci at her worst, arguing with the volunteer principal over a piece of plywood with a relatively reasonable message on it. Raquel's daughters, Taylor and Morgan, exchanged a glance. Luci lowered the sign, then sat on the reception desk. She'd made a spectacle of herself, again. And now every time she walked through this room it would not only be plastered with signs, but would also be a reminder of her humiliation. How many places in her life were now tainted with the shame of her not being able to act like a normal person?

Raquel walked over to Luci and examined the sign, then said to Loretta, "May I buy this sign from you? I'd like it for my workshop."

She liked the sign? That was ridiculous. Raquel

had excellent aesthetic sense. She created gorgeous jewelry and was responsible for the tasteful holiday decorations the town displayed. She might be a little opinionated and judgy, but the woman was an artist. There was no way she liked this sign. Unless…

Raquel continued, "In fact, I'd like to buy all these signs from you, Loretta." She gazed around the lobby and sniffed. "This room can't quite pull off a fun, modern decor. I'll take these boxes with me and load them into my car."

Colter's jaw dropped as Raquel came to the rescue. Mateo gave her an appreciative nod.

Raquel glanced at Luci, with the smallest spark of mischief in her eye.

Luci really, really wanted to hug Raquel, but she still had a tight grip on Good Vibes.

"Well. If you insist." Loretta scanned the room. "I was just trying to liven the space up for the students."

"I think the students will make it plenty lively," Raquel said. "I know my girls would love to stay here, but I thought ahead when purchasing our home and we're close enough that it's not a burden to get to school. Plus, Taylor will be driving in another month. She passed the permit test on her first try and I'm sure she'll do the same with the driver's exam."

Raquel flipped from saving the day to quiet bragging so fast Luci's head spun. Mateo glanced at her and she had to look away before his attempt to repress a laugh made *her* laugh.

Nevertheless, Raquel was the hero of the hour.

Luci gave her a smile of gratitude as she handed over the sign. *"Thank you."*

"I can carry these boxes out to your car for you," Mateo offered.

Raquel blinked, uncomfortable with the direct gratitude and offer of help. Then she glanced around the room. "Why is there math homework all over the floor? When *I* was a teacher, I kept my student papers organized."

MATEO COULD STILL hear the cheerful hubbub of the hotel renovation, but he was fairly certain no "volunteers" would make it as far as the second-floor atrium. For the most part, Mateo didn't crave solitude. The middle of a busy group of friends was his happy place. It was part of the reason he loved living with his coworkers at the hotel. There was always something happening. He'd set up his grading on the reception desk so he was at the center of things, always able to join in a conversation, or take a break with a coworker if the opportunity arose.

He glanced down at the penny-loafer-shaped smudge on Ilsa's Algebra 2 assignment. The reception desk wouldn't be an option with students living here.

The atrium, on the other hand, had possibility. It was small, maybe a hundred and fifty square feet, with a sloped glass ceiling. The walls were at least half windows, and the view of the backs of other brick buildings and a narrow alleyway reminded him of small, family-run hotels he'd stay in on his travels. The atrium must have held plants and maybe citrus trees back during the hotel's heyday. Now, it was a little dusty but largely untouched by age. Old boxes were stacked in the corner, two café tables sat in the center of the room, and what must have been a service counter at one point was perfect for grading.

As he set the space up for himself, he worked through the confusion building in his chest. How on earth were he and Luci going to handle this? They needed to step up, that was clear. But what would it be like when they did?

This year of living with his coworkers had been fun. More than fun, it was fantastic. Their very first night in Pronghorn they'd nearly gotten kicked out of The Restaurant, sealing the friendships that hadn't wavered. But Willa was moving in with Colter and his daughter as soon as they were married in June. Tate would live with Aida. And Vander was already splitting his time between the hotel and the Jameson Ranch. Plus, with his frequent trips to Nashville, it felt like he was gone more than he was here.

Mateo had been worried about himself and Luci rattling around the hotel together, with no one to interrupt their arguments. No one to distract him when she came downstairs looking adorable in her argyle sweaters. No one to act casual around when he offered to grab her a cup of tea once she was snuggled into her favorite chair in the lobby, reading one of the many Barbra Cartland novels before she went to bed at night. No one to stop him from falling even harder for her, day by day.

Luci was an enigma. For the most part she was so confident, completely in control of herself and any situation she found herself in. But occasionally glimpses of vulnerability shone through.

From the first day he met her, he was fascinated. Mateo had been chatting with Puddles the duck, as much as one chats with a guy in a duck suit who communicates in a rudimentary form of mime. But Puddles was there to welcome their cohort, and Mateo could talk to anyone, so he happily chatted with the big bird.

Until Luci walked in.

She seemed to shimmer in her eagerness to start the education program. This beautiful woman who could have found a welcome anywhere looked straight at him. He smiled, because, *obviously*, and she seemed to relax.

He was surprised by the feeling she sparked in him. Meeting her felt like coming home. She walked right up to him and the duck. Puddles's miming became more animated, because there was, after all, a guy in that suit somewhere. Luci laughed as Puddles tried to kiss her hand with his duckbill. But then Luci glanced at Mateo again, and he caught that flash of vulnerability. She was nervous.

And while Mateo could be better at a lot of things in this world, he did know how to put people at ease. He introduced himself to Luci and everyone else in the room seemed to vanish as they chatted.

He was annoyed when their cohort leader had them circle up for introductions. Mateo already had the intro he was interested in. The leader asked everyone to say their name, where they'd done their undergraduate studies and which Pixar or Disney character they most related to. Since Mateo hadn't been able to take his eyes off Luci, he witnessed her reaction. She seemed to turn in on herself, like she was afraid of answering the question incorrectly, even though that wasn't possible.

Of course, the instructor called on her first.

Luci planted her penny loafers on the tile flooring. She pulled in a breath, voice quavering a touch as she said, "Um. Let me think. Disney or Pixel character."

"*Pixar* character," someone had corrected her with a chuckle.

Luci blinked. It was almost like she didn't know any Pixar or Disney characters.

That's when Mateo had jumped in. "Who's the girl in *Brave*?"

Luci locked eyes with him, her Shakespearean fairy grin breaking out as she realized what he was doing. "Oh, right, that one girl. The brave one?"

"Yeah." He'd grinned back. "What's her name?"

"Merida!" another girl in the program said. "That's what I was going to say, but I'll pick Elsa instead."

"Thank you," Luci said to the woman, then glanced at Mateo in gratitude. "My name is Luci Walker, I relate to Merida, from *Brave*, and I graduated from Dartmouth."

His head swam with questions. What kind of woman graduates from Dartmouth and can't readily compare herself to a Pixar or Disney character? And how was he going to focus on his studies with such a cutie in the program?

He'd attempted to ask her out after the meeting, but inadvertently wound up inviting the whole cohort.

Then they started arguing.

Mateo shook himself out of the memory. Yeah, he'd been worried about getting a second crush on Luci, or a relapse of the first, once all their co-workers had moved out and couldn't distract him anymore. But there was nothing like opening your home to eleven teenagers to put a damper on a romantic mood.

Mateo flipped over Ilsa's paper to grade the back. As usual, she'd made a few comments in the margin about the superiority of the Dutch national soccer team and drawn soccer balls to accompany her thoughts. Mateo responded to her comments, adding his own opinions on the undeniable glory of Real Madrid. But her math was excellent, and her devotion to her home country was understandable.

After brushing off the loafer smudge to the best of his ability, he picked up Mason's paper. Mason was in a class of his own, already working on calculus. His paper included margin notes about how cool continuous differentiability was, and questions about alternate applications for formulas. Mateo took his time, responding to each question and enthusiastic comment.

There was a shuffling noise in the hall. Mateo

looked over his shoulder. There weren't supposed to be kids on the second or third floors, but it was probably just someone exploring the hotel while they had the chance. No one ever noticed this door.

A draft scooted Mason's paper several inches to the left.

Correction, no one ever noticed this door except for the person currently opening it.

Mateo glanced up to see a woman in a striped sweater sneaking into the room.

"What do you think?" Luci spoke directly into her basket. "Should we hole up in the atrium? Because the courtyard is looking a little busy right now." She readjusted a file folder under her arm and laid her hand over the spiny, probably sleeping creatures in the basket. "I think we should hang here."

"Welcome."

Luci jumped back, so startled she almost lost her hedgehogs. "Mateo! Ugh, you scared me."

"I'm just grading. Which I agree can be a little frightening when your papers are covered in footprints."

She closed her eyes, a dark flush running up her neck. "I'm so sorry about your papers. About standing on them. This day! Seriously." Luci spun back toward the door. "I'll get out of your hair."

"No!" The word shot out of his mouth. "No, stay."

She paused, then tilted her head to one side. "How do you even know about this room?"

"How do *you* know about it?"

"Fair point. I'm nosy, I like to explore. You?"

"Something like that." Mateo smiled. "I like the windows, and the light."

"Me, too."

"Then stay." He pulled out a chair at one of the café tables for her. She hesitated, then approached the table and sat. Mateo resumed his spot at the counter.

They worked in silence for a few minutes. Luci straightened her file folder, laid out a row of gel pens and picked one up.

Then she set the pen down.

"You have the best manners. I don't get it. You're sloppy, and you don't like rules, but you're so polite it's astounding sometimes."

He chuckled. "Is that a compliment?"

"It's a question," she retorted.

Mateo shrugged. Good manners were a reflex. His parents had taught him to be polite, but at St. Xavier's, urbane gallantry was honed like a weapon. Students would smile and greet the custodian even as they planned to egg his car. Stand and offer a chair to the mother of the kid they bullied during class. Lie to the school's staff, plagiarize their papers, cheat on their exams, so long as they held the door open for their instructors and thanked them for the lesson.

And since it was difficult to catch and punish individuals for their pranks, staff would reprimand students on technicalities. You could be punished for wearing a uniform incorrectly, forgetting to make your bed. He'd been accused of insubordination for asking reasonable questions during class.

Rules at St. Xavier's did nothing to shape positive behavior. They were simply an added challenge for inappropriate actions. A means by which adults exercised power over their students.

It made him sick to think about it. He wanted to inspire his students to be good people, to act in the best interest of their community.

A crash was heard from somewhere above them. Luci's gaze connected with his, and she smiled but didn't say anything.

"If it *was* a compliment, I'd give you one in return," Mateo said. "I'd thank you for saving the lobby from Loretta's signage."

She reddened. "That was all Raquel."

"No, it was definitely you, standing on a pile of math quizzes, threatening Loretta with her own cheesy decorations."

Her face warmed further as she shook her head. "I kinda lost it there for a minute."

"Thank God. The lobby is beautiful. You did good."

"See? There you go again, being polite."

"I'm being honest. You were a rock star."

She ignored the compliment, studying the table as she opened her file folder and drew out a stack of essays. "I've got a compare-and-contrast of post-classical civilizations."

"Nice."

"How about you?"

"Umm, a little of everything."

She nodded, then uncapped her spring green

grading pen, burying herself in the rough handwriting of a sophomore. Mateo refocused on his own papers.

A breeze came in through the open window, pushing Luci's bangs against her forehead. She brushed back her hair and readjusted her headband without pausing. A smile glimmered as she read, then she aimed her pen at the paper, scribbling notes on the margin.

Mateo picked up Oliver's Algebra 2 assignment, which had been done quickly and with little thought to detail. Ever since performing in the holiday pageant, he was planning on being an actor, or a comedian, or a famous YouTuber, and was already assuming he'd have people to do his taxes, manage his wealth and attend to any home repairs. Mateo sighed as he marked up the paper. Oliver was a good kid, but he would glance at the grade then throw the paper in the recycle bin.

"Did you really hire bagpipers to prank an administrator?"

Mateo looked up to see Luci gazing at him.

"You're pausing," she noted, "which means yes, because you're too honest to say no."

He didn't like to relive the experience. Their attempt to embarrass an administrator had gone on long after it stopped being funny. "It wasn't my idea."

"It wasn't? Because it seems like the creative kind of trouble you'd get into."

It wasn't his idea, but he *had* been the point man

on coordination. The main difference between Mateo and his peers was an ability to realize when they'd gone too far, when to call off a prank.

"And I'm supercurious about those...what did you call them, 'late-night kitchen raids for long-standing, interhouse food fights that could erupt at any time'?"

"Those were actually fun. Fun, but wasteful, looking back." Like so much of his experience, it had been fun in the moment, but decidedly not fun as the ramifications of their actions set in. The food fights *were* wasteful and created hours of work for the housekeeping staff at St. Xavier's.

"How about you?" he asked. "I'm guessing you didn't spend your entire high-school experience without stirring up something."

"Believe me, I did my best to keep from stirring anything. I was grateful to get a good education."

"You must have taken part in a prank or two."

"I didn't."

"Not one?"

She shook her head, ponytail emphasizing the movement.

"I don't buy it. You are a mastermind of strategy when it comes to snowball fights, pinochle tournaments, dealing with Loretta."

She glanced at him, her dimple peeking out. "Is that another compliment?"

He chuckled. "It's a compliment and a question. You're a bit of a mystery, Luci Walker."

She held his gaze for a moment, then pulled another essay out of her folder.

Mateo glanced back at his own work. It took him a moment to refocus on the task at hand, or even remember what his task was. Then he chuckled.

"What?"

"Just Mav, wondering why we have to use established formulas for math." He held up a paper for Luci to see the long paragraph written next to an equation. "He feels like it would be better if they all got to make up their own formulas and wonders why mathematicians are trying to squelch his creativity."

Luci grinned. "That kid is something else. I wonder—"

She looked down and placed a hand on a hedgehog.

"You wonder?" he prompted.

"I mean, it's gotta be hard for the kids at Open Hearts, right?"

"It's hard for any kid at this age. It's an awkward time, and throw in this—" Mateo gestured out the window, trying to come up with a word for the increasingly complex world they were living in.

"Right. But I sometimes get the sense Mav might like to move away from his community, go to college. That's not supported or encouraged at Open Hearts. In fact, there's a pretty strong bias against the outside world. And I get it, I do. They all live together, they grow organic hothouse flowers and have a whole system."

"Do you distrust their system?" Mateo asked.

Luci got very quiet, staring hard at an essay. Finally, she looked up and seemed to choose her words carefully. "Our work as teachers, as I see it, is to set kids up for a life of their choosing. Kids should graduate from high school with the skills and knowledge to shape and direct their own lives. Mav has developed so many interests this year. I'd like to see him have the chance to explore those interests. But moving away from Open Hearts…" She shook her head. "That won't be easy, if it's what he wants."

"Why is it—" Mateo started to ask why she took such care of the kids from Open Hearts. From day one, Luci had had more patience with, more understanding of, those students than anyone else had. She managed to defuse arguments, explain processes and help kids find their way. These were the students most likely to challenge rules, even reasonable ones, so why was Luci the first to jump in when anything came up with a student in orange?

"Why is it I'm looking out for those kids?" Luci gazed at him, the set of her chin telling him in no uncertain terms that she wasn't going to discuss this any more than she had in the past. "I'm looking out for all our students."

"I know you are."

He smiled. She gave him a brief nod of acknowledgment, then turned back to her papers. The sun shone through the windows, and a light breeze crept in through the warped casings. Beyond their sanctuary, he could hear excited voices, hammering, Raquel's industrial vacuum cleaner. Mateo pulled

Cece's quiz out of his stack, eyes scanning for the first line of a joke that she always wrote at the top of her papers. If he couldn't guess the answer she'd tell him the next day in class.

Why do bees have sticky hair?

He thought for a moment then made a guess.

Because they use honeycombs?

He graded her paper, then the rest of the stack. Luci's pen darted over her own papers in bursts of energy.

After a while, she set down her pen and glanced at him. Mateo's heart picked up pace. She had that look, like she was about to share something with him. And while logically he knew she wasn't going to say something awesome, like *Let's take the ATV for a drive and I'll tell you all about my past,* he couldn't help hoping.

Instead, she sighed. "We should probably start talking about rules for the dormitory."

Mateo stiffened. Not what he'd been hoping for.

"I was thinking we could sit down with the students and come up with group norms."

"Group norms?" One of her eyelids twitched.

"Yes."

"Mateo, these are teenagers, all under one roof together. This isn't the time for wishy-squishy, feel-good conversations. We need rules."

"We need student buy-in, so they behave without threats."

"How about 'follow the rules or you get kicked out?' How's that for buy-in?"

Mateo drew in a sharp breath. He didn't want their time together to end in another argument.

"Let's table this for now," he said. "I'm sure we can come to a compromise."

Her blue eyes connected with his, her lips quirking up. "Or if we can't compromise, I'm sure I can convince you of my way of thinking."

He braced his arms on the counter and leaned toward her. "Or the inherent superiority of my way of thinking will become clear to you all on its own."

She raised an eyebrow. "Keep dreaming, Mr. Bagpipes."

"Sure thing, Ms. Vibe Police."

Luci laughed, then bent her head to her grading again.

Mateo gazed at her a moment longer. What was it in her background that made her such a champion of strict behavior systems? She was impossible to understand and harder to work with when she wouldn't explain the reasoning behind her thinking.

But these kids were not going to be given a list of arbitrary rules to try to break. Not on his watch. He planned to help the kids develop strong moral codes. The guidelines for student behavior needed to be flexible, not so brittle the rules were easy to break. It didn't matter how much he wanted to get along with Luci, this was one issue he couldn't compromise on.

CHAPTER FIVE

THE WEEK BEFORE spring break was officially worse than the one prior to the winter holidays. Way worse, in Mateo's estimation.

Across the country young people flocked to the beaches of Florida or California to party during their one week off in the spring. The kids in Pronghorn didn't seem inclined to wait for the break, or a beach. His students, already amped up with longer, sunnier days and the promise of a week off, could barely contain themselves as they anticipated the opening of the school dormitory.

"Mateo?"

He turned from where he was helping Neveah with an equation. Cece had a hand up.

"We good here?" he asked Neveah. She nodded and Mateo rose from the seat at her table and headed over to Cece. The moment he walked away, Neveah abandoned the equation and started talking to Taylor about whom she hoped she'd be rooming with at the hotel.

"What's up?" Mateo asked Cece.

"What time is our curfew going to be?"

Mateo rubbed his forehead. "Did you have a question about math?"

"We just want to know," Mav chimed in.

"You're not even staying at the hotel," Mateo reminded him.

Mav crossed his arms defensively. "I know."

"But all his friends are," Oliver said. "If there's something going on in town Mav shouldn't have to miss it."

"Ms. Walker and I haven't decided on the curfew."

Ms. Walker and Mateo hadn't been able to agree on anything yet. She wanted a rigid, clearly outlined code of conduct and a promise from him that every rule would be enforced in letter, spirit and all varying interpretations. He championed flexibility, addressing individual situations as they arose. Kids knew how to behave. He and Luci needed to foster an environment where students were intrinsically motivated to do the right thing.

"Mateo, I have a question." Sylvie raised a hand.

Mateo moved around the tables and sat next to Sylvie. He looked at her paper. It was blank.

Next to her, Sofi, an exchange student from Armenia, asked, "When can we start having sleepovers at the hotel?"

Enough was enough. Mateo stood abruptly.

"Can I get everyone's attention?"

"Is this about the curfew?" Oliver asked.

"No," Mateo snapped. He drew in a breath to settle himself. "Quick reminder—this is math class. Math is not only practical, and required for sixty percent of college majors, but it also strengthens your patterns of thinking and problem-solving abilities. We are in *math class*. Not on spring break. Not in the hotel dormitory. You all have the freedom to move at your own pace as you progress in my classes, but that implies you're actually making *progress. Claro?*"

The students mumbled apologies and got back to work.

Ninety seconds later they were placing bets on what time curfew would be.

Mateo paced out the open door of his classroom so he could breathe in deeply before he lost it. He didn't want to bark at his students the way he'd been yelled at in high school. But dang, today was tough. He took a step into the hall, just as Luci came charging to the doorway of her own classroom.

They stared at each other for a moment. Then she gestured over her shoulder and widened her eyes in frustration. Mateo nodded, confirming he was in a similar situation.

She glanced around to ensure the hall was empty.

"This is ridiculous!" she whispered. "No one is getting any work done."

"No one in my class is acknowledging the existence of work. All anyone wants to talk about is the dormitory."

"It's a nightmare. I have a full room of students who will never be able to understand the major players in pre-Columbian North American trade patterns. They're too busy trying to figure out what time we're going to wake them up in the morning."

"We have to wake the kids up? Don't they have alarms?"

"You've never slept through an alarm?" she asked.

"Whatever. Point being I can't get anyone to focus this week."

Luci glanced over her shoulder to where kids weren't even looking at the large maps spread out on their desks. "I'm *not* going to let this week go by without a single one of these kids being able to pinpoint Cahokia on a map. We should just decide on the rules now and be done with it. We can post them and the kids will stop asking questions."

"I have made several suggestions," he reminded her.

"'Wait and see what happens' isn't a suggestion."

"I don't have a problem with general guide-lines—"

"Guidelines are for a creative-writing assignment, not a living situation with eleven teenagers all under one roof."

"If we hand them a list of rules, they're just going to spend their time figuring out how to break them," Mateo whispered back loudly.

"Without rules, the kids aren't going to know how to act," she said, for what had to be the six billionth time.

Mateo stepped farther into the hall. He'd vowed never to fight with Luci in front of the students. Could they call this a spirited discussion of necessity? "I don't get it, Luci. Why are you so determined to have a strict set of rules?"

"So the kids will know what's expected of them and how to act."

"They know how to act, Luci. They already spend eight hours a day together. And if someone has a few socially awkward moments, it's not the end of the world. We all have cringe moments we look back on. I'm not buying your clarity-is-kindness argument. I need a better reason for coming up with a fifty-page code of conduct."

"Not everyone is like you," she said.

"What does that even mean?"

"Not everyone is kind and polite and has impeccable manners. If everyone were like you, sure, we wouldn't need rules."

Mateo furrowed his brow. Her words sounded like a compliment but somehow also an insult. How did she do that?

Luci continued, "Look, I'm not suggesting we use the Code of Hammurabi."

"I don't even know what that is."

"You don't know what the Code of Hammurabi is? First known code of law in human civilization?"

"Musta missed that day."

"You know what? I feel sorry for you. Like there is sadness in my heart because you don't know the pleasure of riffling through Hammurabi's Code. It's a fascinating insight to ancient culture and human behavior. I also feel sorry for you because while you claim to love flexibility, you're not being very flexible in this discussion."

"Agreeing to being inflexible with rules isn't a sign of flexibility."

A burst of laughter erupted from behind him. Luci looked over his shoulder into his classroom. "Oliver is dancing," she told him.

Mateo's jaw twitched. All year long his easygoing, connected approach to teaching had meant that he didn't need to set strict rules in the classroom. *No dancing* wasn't something he'd come right out and said, but up until now he really hadn't needed to.

Mateo exhaled. "Is he any good?"

"On a proficiency scale, I'd say he's emerging."

"I'd better get back in there," he said. "Let's sit down tonight and—"

What? Discuss this further? They'd been having the same argument since graduate school. And while they could ask for help and advice from their coworkers, or look to other rural boarding schools for guidance, he and Luci would ultimately be in charge of this crew. They had to establish a system that worked for both of them, and their boarders.

A paper airplane sailed out of Luci's classroom, and it appeared to be made out of a map. Luci snatched it up and spun around instantly.

"Hey. What did I say about paper airplanes? Only during simulations, and only with paper out of the recycle box." She spread the map out on Antonio's desk. "We're having a quiz in twenty minutes." The class groaned. Luci spoke over them. "You will be expected to accurately locate major trading centers of pre-Columbian North America, along with the items they traded. I'm talking Cahokia, Choonkian and Pueblo sites. Everybody involved and everything on the trade network."

Her students complained but Luci stood firm in her loafers and spoke sharply.

"Gripe all you want. This quiz is worth twenty points, and anyone who gets less than fifteen questions right will have to come in after school tomorrow to retake it because I am *not* letting my students loose in the world without this basic information. You got it?"

Students grumbled, but got busy with their maps.

Mateo turned back to his own classroom. Pop quizzes and using points to shape student behavior weren't his favorite strategies. But as Luci's class bent their heads to the work, he had to admit her method had some merit.

IT *WAS FINALLY* 3:00 P.M.

Luci was pretty sure the school days before spring break were lengthening. Like, there was something about the earth's rotation that made them take longer. She'd have to ask Vander. She didn't understand much about the space-time continuum, but as far as she was concerned, the theory of relativity had solid proof in these school days.

Her strategy was to keep the kids busy, which meant she was *extra* busy. And even the most carefully planned lessons could hit the skids. Right now, it seemed like the only thing her students wanted to know about social studies was where the next party was happening.

Luci glanced into the hallway. Mateo was surrounded by a cheerful group of students. He always managed to keep his cool. You'd have to know him really well to see the strain in his smile, the exhaustion in his brow.

Eventually, the kids headed down the hall, some to the library for rehearsal, others outside for Ultimate Frisbee practice. Mateo slung his messenger bag over his shoulder, his exhalation of relief audible. As always, he'd held it together, been encouraging and cheerful, up to the last minute of student contact.

Unlike her. She really hadn't wanted to snap at her students. There was nothing worse than losing her cool. And yet, these kids needed to know history. She wasn't going to sit back and let them cruise through the class period without learning.

It was a balance. For her, anyway. She knew she was "the strict teacher." The others managed to get the kids to learn without even breaking a sweat. Tate was fun, Vander was cool, Willa was inspiring, Mateo was warm and friendly, and eighty-year-old Mrs. Moran was simply magical.

Luci didn't have their natural gifts. She worked hard and held her students accountable for doing hard things, too. While *she* knew it was good for the kids, it might be years, or never, before *they* knew it. But she couldn't pretend like history didn't matter. If a pop quiz got her students focused on learning, then a pop quiz it was.

She glanced down at her pile and allowed herself a moment of satisfaction. The average score was an A minus.

"'Bye, Ms. Walker!" Antonio called, like she hadn't totally yelled at him in class.

"'Bye, Antonio." She scrambled around for something nice. "Have fun at practice."

"Are you coming to the tournament?" he asked.

Luci hadn't heard about an Ultimate Frisbee tournament, and had no idea when or where it was. But this was a small town and there was only one answer. "Of course!"

He waved and headed off down the hall. Luci shook her head. Then she rose from her desk, gathered up her bag and the basket of hedgehogs and headed for the door.

But she wasn't quite ready to go home.

Luci wandered into the main hall. The door to an old janitorial closet was propped open.

"Mrs. Moran?" Luci called.

"Well, hello." Mrs. Moran dropped a shawl over a panel with a blinking light on it. "Would you like a cup of tea? You're just in time."

Luci was always *just in time* for tea with Mrs. Moran. She suspected teatime was on the same unpredictable schedule as the school's sporadically working internet.

"Yes, please." Luci sat down on the upturned bucket that served as an extra chair. Mrs. Moran claimed a china teacup with dainty yellow flowers off a shelf and set it next to her hot pot.

"Earl Grey?"

"Thank you," Luci said. "My favorite for afternoon."

"Mine, too."

Luci sighed, exhaling the tension of the day. She'd never had Mrs. Moran as a teacher but had known the caring, clever woman by sight. More than once Mrs. Moran had a smile or kind word for the lost girl in orange, wandering around town.

Of course, Mrs. Moran showed no sign of recognizing her. No one did. And while that was for the best, it was also depressing. Luci had been disconnected from her childhood since she left Pronghorn, but somehow every day she was back and unrecognized made her wonder if she'd really been that lost little girl.

Mrs. Moran set the tea on a stack of old textbooks. "How were your classes today?"

"Wild."

Mrs. Moran chuckled. "The week before spring break is always a bit of a kerfuffle."

"In two of my classes I was running a simulation of the stock market leading up to the crash of 1929, so at least it was on theme."

"You're always so good at getting your students involved." Mrs. Moran set a plate of cookies next to Luci's tea. Where had the cookies even come from? "I love teaching, but I cannot tell you how I look forward to this moment, with a cup of tea after a long day."

Luci took a sip of Earl Grey. She loved the snacks but what she really looked forward to was soaking up the calm wisdom of the older teacher.

"How are plans for the dormitory coming along?" Mrs. Moran asked.

"Not well," Luci admitted.

Mrs. Moran gave her a gentle look. "And how are things with Mateo?"

"Worse well?"

"You two can pull this off as well as anyone. Better, even."

"We're not finding a lot of common ground," Luci admitted. *Or any common ground.*

"That takes work."

Yeah. Work that Luci didn't know how to do and Mateo didn't want to do.

Luci scanned the broom closet. Her coworkers marveled that Mrs. Moran was comfortable in this little space. Willa had tried to convince her to take one of the bright, airy rooms in the main office. But Luci understood Mrs. Moran's attachment to this particular nook. It was warm and cozy, with stacks of books and bins of teaching supplies. The walls were a mosaic of pictures, starting in black-and-white, then faded color, then Polaroids and finally bright new images, of students, friends and townspeople. There was a snapshot of Today's Moment and Pete Sorel cheering together at a soccer game. Another of Raquel Holms laughing with Harlow after the holiday pageant. A black-and-white photo of two women in bell-bottoms had to be Mrs. Moran and Flora Weston, Aida's grandma. The whole history of Pronghorn High School was laid out across the walls in candid shots. Luci could only dream of having touched this many lives.

An image caught her eye.

"Who is that?" she asked, pointing to a man posing next to a Shinto shrine.

"My husband."

"You had a—" She meant to say *husband*, but what she actually stopped herself from uttering was *life*.

"Yes," Mrs. Moran said, answering both questions with a gentle smile. "You wouldn't have known him. He passed away many years ago."

"I'm sorry."

Mrs. Moran kept her eyes on the picture. "So am I."

Luci studied the image, then scanned the walls to see the same man appearing again and again, ranging in age from late twenties to early seventies. There was something immediately appealing about him.

"He was a social studies teacher, like you."

That was what it was. He had an air of curiosity.

"It looks like you two went all over the world."

"Come upstairs someday, and I'll show you the photo albums."

Luci pointed to the ceiling. "You keep your photo albums in the abandoned upstairs of the school?"

Mrs. Moran ignored the question. "When you

live in a small town, you can't wait for the world to come to you. You have to get out and see it."

Joy bubbled up in Luci at the thought of Mrs. Moran traveling the world. Of Mrs. Moran having a husband and travel buddy. What other secrets did she have up the sleeve of her hand-crocheted sweater?

She glanced over to see Mrs. Moran gazing at her. An unexpected urge to spill her secret welled up in her chest. She'd just learned something major about Mrs. Moran, and she wanted to respond in kind.

You're a world traveler! That's amazing. I grew up at Open Hearts and have been lying to everyone about who I am for the last eight months. We're basically the same.

Because a huge mess definitely wouldn't ensue once that news got out, right?

Instead, Luci said, "I'd love to travel someday."

"Haven't you already done a fair amount of travel?" Mrs. Moran kept her gaze steady.

Luci had indeed traveled—two study-abroad programs in Europe, a school-sponsored trip to Belize and a solo trip to the Yucatán Peninsula between undergrad and her education program. But nowhere had seemed as far or foreign as leaving Open Hearts for boarding school. Was there something about Mrs. Moran's gaze that suggested she already knew it?

No, she didn't. And she didn't need to.

Day by day, Luci's childhood self seemed to drift further away. Maybe one day the little girl known as Evening Light would no longer exist at all. She'd just fade into the past, like all the other unstudied and forgotten histories.

"Some," Luci admitted. "But not nearly enough. I'm excited to see the world."

Mrs. Moran nodded. "I've learned that the best way to get comfortable traveling is to first set your bags down in a place you call home."

The hotel was Luci's home, the first place she'd ever felt comfortable unpacking her bags. But it was on the verge of being overrun, and she was damaging her relationship with the one person who would remain in that home with her.

"It must have been nice to have a travel partner." She studied a picture of Mrs. Moran and her husband by the Colosseum in Rome.

"Yes. We had some wonderful times."

Unbidden, an image floated into Luci's mind. Finding her way through the cobbled streets of an ancient city, laughing with Mateo as they got more and more lost. Luci shook it off.

She had plenty of friends she could travel with now. Aida, or Harlow, or Willa. Maybe all three? *That* could be a fun trip.

Luci's imagination unfurled, bringing all her friends together at a villa in the south of France. Okay, this might need to be a real plan. Being with her favorite people exploring little villages, cooking together.

Without warning, her wily imagination invited the guys along and reminded her that Mateo was the best cook among their crew. And suddenly, the two of them were lost on cobblestone streets again.

Luci rubbed her forehead.

There was no world in which she and Mateo would be part of a couples, or any, vacation. They couldn't agree on basic rules. They couldn't agree on what counted as a breakfast food.

That's not the person you book airline tickets with.

Luci lifted her cup and swallowed the last of her tea.

"Thank you. I should get back to the hotel. It's Thursday and Angie always expects us for dinner on Thursday nights."

"Hmm. Careful there. Rumor is she has chicken-baked steak on the menu today."

Luci groaned. Mrs. Moran nodded in confirmation.

"I know Angie has a champion in Harlow, but I would still avoid that particular menu item. Along with her vegetable soup."

"Noted," Luci said with a grin. "Besides, it's been such a long day, I may not be able to stay awake long enough to order."

Mrs. Moran patted her arm. "The days before spring break are always long. Then spring break itself will pass in a flash."

Luci smiled, but inside her stomach dropped. Spring break would pass in a flash, and she would wake up at the end of it to move-in day.

CHAPTER SIX

"It's move-in day!"

Luci's tea sloshed over the edge of her cup at the sudden appearance of Loretta in the courtyard. It was *not* move-in day, and even if it was, why would move-in start at 8:00 a.m.?

"It's Saturday," Luci reminded her. Then checked her watch as though the analog timepiece would confirm the day of the week.

Loretta bustled into the courtyard, casting a shadow over Luci's homemade scone. "Families want to get their kids settled in."

"Families want to get their teenagers out of the house," Luci noted dryly.

As promised, spring break had passed in what felt like thirty minutes for the teachers. But for families grown used to the luxury of having their kids in school all day, the last week would have been long. Many of the host families took their exchange students to see American sights like Disneyland or the Grand Canyon. As much as Luci loved her students, she didn't envy anyone on those road trips.

"Well, somebody woke up on the cynical side of the bed."

"I haven't fully woken up at all." Luci gestured to her tea. And after a fitful night of anxiety dreams, it was going to take more than one cup of English

Breakfast to get her there. "Mateo and I still have a few things to iron out before we're ready."

"Well, you need to strike the iron while the sun shines, because kids are arriving today."

Luci shuddered at the mixed metaphor, glad Willa wasn't around to hear it. Then she shuddered again, because try as they might to strike while the iron was hot or even tepid, Mateo and Luci hadn't made any progress. They were gridlocked in a battle over dormitory rules.

They had tried, and failed, to agree on anything concerning the dormitory. As of this moment, they had almost nothing to go on. Even the Maxwell family and man-cave rules would have provided more structure than their current lack of plan.

Luci took a deliberate sip of her tea. "We agreed the dorm would host kids Sunday through Friday nights. We're not prepared."

The sound of a car parking out on the street came floating into the courtyard, then doors slamming.

"Well, then I guess it's time to get this show off the road." Loretta hopped up as another car arrived.

"What's going on?" Mateo ran into the courtyard, still in the sweats and T-shirt he slept in, hair sticking up in the back.

Antonio appeared at the arched opening into the street, Stetson on his head, two large duffel bags at his feet. "Welcome!" he cried to himself.

Suleiman came in juggling a soccer ball that Ilsa quickly stole from him, launching a scrimmage across the brick courtyard.

Mateo turned to Luci, panicked. She wasn't awake enough to panic and instead took a bite of her scone and wondered if this was another anxiety dream. But those always took place in the cafeteria of the Breasely-Wentmore school for girls.

No, it was time for Luci to admit she was good and fully awake.

She made eye contact with Mateo, trying to communicate something along the lines of *What are we going to do now?*

He widened his eyes, clearly stating *How would I know?* then he looked over his shoulder in the universal gesture for *Where's Willa?*

But Willa hadn't yet returned from spring break in her hometown in western Oregon. Vander would be flying in from Nashville late tonight, and Tate, who could sleep through a land invasion, seemed to be doing just that.

It was only her and Mateo. And Loretta, who was currently pulling out her bullhorn as the courtyard was overrun with students and families. This called for immediate action.

Luci grabbed Mateo's hand to steady herself and climbed up on her wrought-iron chair. She clapped her hands together. "Listen up!"

Families and students settled, staring at her expectantly.

"You are all a day early."

The crowd groaned. If rotten fruit had been available, they'd have hurled it in her direction.

"You are a day early, but we're going to let you go

ahead and get settled. Here is the schedule…" Luci paused, scrambling to come up with a schedule.

Mateo took over. "We've created two dormitory rooms upstairs and assigned the bunks. Girls are at the east end of the hall, boys are on the west and the teachers' rooms are in the middle. Move-in is from now until noon." Mateo glanced at Luci to make sure this was okay.

Fine by her.

"We're not providing lunch, so you'll need to feed your kids at The Restaurant."

"But what if we already ate there this week?" Raquel asked.

"Do it again," Luci said. "Directly after lunch we'll hold a parent meeting, after which families are free to leave. Then we'll go over the rules with the students."

Mav raised his hand. "When's dinner?"

Luci hadn't even thought about dinner. They'd gotten a huge load of groceries from Lakeview, but turning those groceries into meals? Still a mystery. "Um… Yeah, dinner…"

Mateo chuckled. "Mav, you're not moving in. Open Hearts is twenty minutes away at best."

Mav crossed his arms, hurt and defensive. "I'm just curious."

"Dinner is at six thirty." Luci chose the time randomly. "Mateo and I are not assuming responsibility for students until one o'clock today. We have some important work we still need to do."

This bought them four hours to agree on the issues they hadn't been able to come to terms with for the last two weeks.

"Any questions?" Mateo asked.

He fielded a number of queries as Luci gazed at the crowd. The kids were excited. Neveah stood next to her aunt nearly trembling in anticipation. Melissa Hayes blinked back tears but was clearly happy to see her daughter connecting with friends. Ilsa's host family looked exhausted.

"Okay. Let's do it," Mateo said. He probably hadn't had breakfast, or coffee, or a shower, but he motioned to the students to follow him. "Head on upstairs, everyone."

Families and students rushed into the hotel. Mateo headed up to help people get settled. And, hopefully, put on something other than sleepwear.

The courtyard was empty, except for a tall, lone student in orange.

"Mav, it's nice to see you," Luci said.

Mav glanced around, looking a little lost. She could relate.

"Are you here to—" she fumbled to explain his presence "—help?"

"I guess. Not like I can move in since I don't live far enough away."

Luci didn't say anything, but let the silence settle.

"Not that I want to," Mav clarified.

"But it would have been nice to have been given the option," she said.

Mav shrugged. She remembered the feeling. You understood there was a world outside of Open Hearts, were desperate to explore it, but felt guilty for that impulse. You grew up surrounded by people telling you the outside world was chaotic and unstable, but you suspected it might also be exciting and vibrant.

"What are you up to right now? I could use some help." If he accepted her offer, she'd have a tall, slouchy, grumpy shadow as she negotiated the chaos of move-in. But she could deal with it for Mav's sake.

"I might go help Mac with the espresso machine," he said.

"That's thoughtful. With everyone in town, he'll probably get a lot of business today."

Mav gazed in the direction of the lobby, where all his friends were getting set up to live together. Then his head drooped and he turned and headed into the street.

Luci watched him retreat, then pulled in a sharp breath.

Mav could take care of Mav for now. She had a job to do.

If there was one thing Luci disliked on the same level as unclear rules, it was not being appropriately prepared for a situation. And it would have been hard to prepare for this situation no matter what. Right now, she had several hours until the parent meeting and was determined to have something to say before it started. Then she'd catch Mateo and they could hammer out some basic rules for the kids beyond "Thou shalt not steal."

Luci opened up her planner and started a list.

No stealing was as good a place to start as any. Even if stealing in a small community like this was pretty pointless. If you took someone's coat, everyone else would recognize it when you showed up wearing it the next day.

But still, it was going on the list.

No stealing.

No roaming the second and third floors.

No parties upstairs; social gatherings are only allowed in the hotel's common rooms.

No food upstair—

"Ms. Walker, can we keep these snacks in our room?"

Luci looked up from her list to see Antonio and Suleiman with grocery sacks of crackers, energy bars, chips and electrolyte drinks. Instinctively, she pointed to the rule she was in the process of writing, opening her mouth to say *Absolutely not!*

And yet.

Both boys were athletes, and probably burned through calories like Tate did. Cece and Ilsa were also athletes, and who knew what types of fast metabolisms other students had? Luci didn't want to have to drop whatever she was doing and fix snacks every time one of these kids got hungry. They were going to need to feed themselves.

On the other hand, Suleiman and Antonio were seventeen-year-olds, not an age group generally associated with cleanliness. The hotel was already infested with teenagers—she did *not* want it infested with mice.

"I'll tell you what—I'll label a cabinet for you in the kitchen, where you can keep your snacks. Food needs to stay downstairs, but you can grab it anytime you need it."

Too bad Mateo wasn't nearby to see her dealing with a situation as it came up like a boss.

Suleiman nodded. "Cool! Where's the kitchen?"

Parents and students continued to drift in and out of the courtyard, hauling bags into the lobby, realizing last-minute needs. If she stayed here, she was a sitting duck for questions. Luci scanned the courtyard.

Neveah's aunt, Amber Danes, stood with her arms crossed, baseball cap obscuring her face. She glanced over her shoulder, like she was ready to get out of here but had business to attend to first.

And Luci was pretty sure that business included her.

"Ms. Walker?" Sofi appeared at her side. "We don't have enough closet space in our room. Can we keep some of our clothes in the room next door?"

"Um… Let me…"

A flash of rumpled T-shirt caught her attention. "Mateo!" she called.

He stopped abruptly, in the middle of a swarm of kids following him around asking questions.

"Sofi and Ilsa are wondering if they can keep some of their clothes in the room next to theirs, as there isn't enough closet space. Can you help them?"

Mateo scowled at her, then smiled at the girls. "Sure! Let's check it out."

Luci strode across the courtyard. Amber gave her a brief nod.

"Is Neveah getting settled in?"

Amber shrugged. "I guess so. I don't know if this is a good idea, but no one asked me."

Luci contained the very real and strong urge to say *Me neither!*

Instead she said, "The parent meeting is right after lunch, and I hope you'll bring up any concerns or questions there."

Amber scoffed. "I'm not stayin' in town for lunch."

Oh. Right. The Danes family had very little money. She hadn't even thought of Amber when she ordered everyone to feed their kids at The Restaurant. She'd made a blanket statement assuming everyone had the means and inclination to eat there.

"Is there something I can help you with?" she asked.

Amber looked over Luci's shoulder. "Can I talk to the other guy?"

"Mateo?"

"No, the one with the guitar. The guy that did the pageant. Mr. V."

"Vander's not here right now," Luci said. "Is it a question about the dormitory? Because Mateo and I—"

"No, it's not about the dormitory. You got eleven kids under one roof. I know exactly how that's gonna go."

Luci didn't like the implication that this was going to be a complete debacle, but it was hard to deny.

"Is there something else *I* can help with?" Luci asked. "Neveah's doing great in school, and we'll keep an eye on her here at the hotel."

"I know she's doing great." Amber looked uncomfortable, then scanned the courtyard again. "I'll come back and talk to Mr. V later this week."

Her eyes landed on her niece. Neveah was talking

excitedly with Cece, not even noticing the aunt who took such ferocious care of her. Sadness clouded Amber's face, quickly replaced by studied disinterest. Then Amber sauntered out of the courtyard without looking back.

MATEO PLACED HIS hands on the steel countertop, leaning against the island at the center of the industrial kitchen. He wasn't a big fan of arbitrary rules and strict schedules, but even he could see they might have come in handy today. The hotel, his home and sanctuary, felt like it had been overrun by...whoever those folks were that overran the Roman Empire. Luci would know.

But Luci didn't seem very interested in speaking to him today. And rightfully so. Why had he been so stubborn about refusing to come up with a few reasonable rules?

Because "respect yourself, others and the environment" really *did* cover it all, no matter what Luci argued to the contrary. Loretta could just hang up a piece of plywood stating something to that effect and they'd be good to go.

The parent meeting had been alarmingly brief. Over the course of the school year, the teachers had worked hard to gain the trust of the community. Apparently, they'd done a great job because the families were completely willing to drop their kids off and hightail it out of town.

"Okay, I'm getting serious Visigoth vibes." Luci strode into the kitchen. "You?"

"Visigoths!" Mateo hit his palm against the island. "That's the word I was looking for."

Luci took a few steps toward him. Instinctively, he gestured to the countertop.

What, was he offering her a space to lean in frustration?

Luci planted her palms next to his and sighed.

"I'm really nervous," she admitted.

"Me, too."

Tate's voice came floating in from the courtyard. He and Mrs. Moran had jumped in to entertain the kids, giving Mateo and Luci a few minutes to plan their next steps. But Tate needed to leave for a spring soccer meeting in Adaline. This evening Mateo and Luci would be on their own with eleven inmates. They could handle it. Hopefully.

"Let's think it through," Mateo said. "What are we afraid of? What's the worst that could happen?"

They both fell silent. Luci gazed at the ceiling.

The intermittent dripping from the sink started up again.

Yeah, there were *a lot* of answers to that question.

Luci finally broke the silence. "Beyond huge catastrophes, which I am absolutely worried about, I'm concerned about subtle bullying, the sneaky kind we never see."

Mateo nodded. These were good kids, but as he well knew, good kids could do bad things, and situations could compound themselves pretty quickly.

"I'm worried about drugs and alcohol," he admitted.

"That was my first concern, but I talked to Aida about it, and she doesn't think it's going to be an issue."

"Oh, yeah? What's the sheriff have to say?"

"Apparently, the area is so remote, most teens who get involved with drugs have access through a family member. While there are families in the area with substance-abuse issues, I don't get the sense that any of the kids staying with us come from homes with access."

Mateo thought it through. "You're right. And Mac doesn't sell alcohol at the store, so they can't get it there. Angie only stocks PBR, and she keeps a close eye on everything."

"So being in the middle of nowhere is in our favor."

Mateo nodded. "That takes a load off my mind. Drugs and alcohol lead to bad decisions, and in turn can be used to dull the shame of those bad decisions, leading to even more."

"I agree," Luci said.

They were both quiet for another moment. Cheerful student voices rose in the courtyard, followed by a burst of laughter.

"I'm worried about these kids developing a pack mentality and leaving the ones who don't live here out," he said.

"I'm worried about the kids staying here not getting along with each other and creating competing cliques."

"I'm worried about cooking for them."

"I'm stressed out about the messes they'll make."

A blast of music startled them. Student voices

rose to compete with the loud bass beat, then someone readjusted the volume. Now, they were just loud, rather than public-nuisance-level decibels.

Luci pointed her thumb toward the courtyard. "They're having an awful lot of fun. Should we be concerned?"

"Tate's with them," he reminded her, then checked the clock. Tate needed to get going soon. He glanced around the beautiful old kitchen. "I'm seriously concerned about this building falling apart."

"I'm worried they're going to tear it apart."

"I'm worried about Neveah," Mateo admitted. "Did you see her aunt this morning? It's like she knows we think it's better for Neveah to be here. And then she didn't stay for the parent meeting."

"Amber was real cagey about wanting to talk to Vander this morning—he's the only one of us she trusts. And then there's Mav—"

"Mav doesn't live here," he reminded her. "Let's just focus on our concerns about the dormitory." He flashed what he hoped was a comforting smile.

She was shaking her head before he even finished the sentence. "But that's my point. It's hard enough for Mav already."

"It's hard for all kids," he reminded her. "Luci, you don't need to worry about every little thing with the kids from Open Hearts."

"Don't tell me who I can and cannot worry about," she snapped.

Mateo turned away, frustrated. The drip of the faucet kept steady in their silence.

Luci drummed her fingers on the steel counter-top. Noise from the courtyard rose again.

He felt a soft pressure against his arm, followed by warmth spreading through his body. Luci had briefly touched her shoulder to his, and now was pulling back, a wry smile on her face.

"I'm worried about us," she admitted, waving a hand between them.

Mateo's breath caught. His body turned toward her more fully. Did she feel this, too? Did she sometimes wonder what might have happened in grad school if they hadn't been so intent on arguing all the time?

She gazed into his eyes. "I know I'm not the easiest person to live with, or get along with."

He blinked. That wasn't what he was expecting.

"You probably wish you were running this dormitory with anyone else on earth."

"Luci, that's not true."

Sure, she could be confusing, and sometimes he upset her when he didn't mean to. But he loved sharing this hotel with her. Way too much. *That* was the issue.

"Okay, fine, I'm a better choice than Loretta."

Mateo sputtered out a laugh. Luci started to speak again but he placed a hand on her arm. "You're a better choice than anyone."

She gave him a frank look, then rolled her eyes. Mateo combed through his upbringing to find a polite, kind and honest way of telling her that even when she drove him crazy, he still wanted to be around her.

"Look, I'm not going to tell you what you can and cannot worry about again. But, Luci, you're not hard to live with. If anything our difference in style sets us up for success."

She searched his face, her expression suspicious. He wished he knew more about her upbringing, her years at boarding school. What happened in her life to make her erect this wall, and how could he find a way past it?

He could start by trying harder. Luci could be a puzzle, but he was good at figuring things out. There was every possibility that they could run this dormitory, work together and come through it with a better understanding of one another.

Maybe this was what they needed to work out their issues and finally, maybe—

"Hey! No way," an angry voice cried from the courtyard.

"You can't do that!" another responded, panic lacing the words.

Mateo and Luci locked eyes. A low, smug response came from another voice. The bullying had already begun. They sprinted out of the kitchen.

She was already yelling as they burst through the door into the courtyard. "What's going on—"

Luci skidded in her penny loafers, grabbing Mateo's arm to steady herself as they stared at the scene before them.

And while the situation absolutely did not call for it, he couldn't help flexing his triceps.

Mateo scanned the scene, trying to place the angry outburst, to find evidence of bullying.

But all he could see were students sitting in groups of four at the wrought-iron tables, juggling oversize fans of playing cards. Tate amicably laid a card on the table, then chuckled as someone picked it up. Making up the fourth in another group was Mrs. Moran, wearing a pair of Ray-Ban Wayfarer sunglasses and a devious smile on her face.

Next to her, Suleiman slapped his hand of cards against the table and bellowed, "Clubs? You can't call clubs as trump."

"Oh, I think it's still legal in most states." Mrs. Moran, who'd taught the students to play pinochle during their first days of in-person school, calmly nodded to her partner across the table. "Shall we play?"

Luci exhaled, pressing her forehead against Mateo's shoulder as she tried to repress a laugh. Relief ran through him. This wasn't an illicit party. It was a pinochle tournament.

And Luci was using his shoulder to keep from laughing.

"Okay, this could be worse," Mateo said.

"That should our boarding school motto—'it could be worse.'"

"What is that in Latin?" Mateo thought back to the seven years he'd spent learning the dead language.

"Posset esse peius," Luci said. "But I think in this situation a translation into pig Latin would be more appropriate."

Mateo laughed, the first real laugh he'd had in a while. It felt good. They could do this. He and

Luci had their differences, but together they could pull this off.

Tate saw them and sprung up from his chair, checking his smartwatch and grabbing his bag as he headed for the door.

"There they are!" he announced. "I'm off, but Ms. Walker and Mateo are here. I'm sure they have the rules ready to share with you." He waved and slipped out of the courtyard.

Did they? Mateo looked at Luci. She gave a slight shake of her head, but opened up her planner and pointed to a list.

Of course, she had rules ready to go.

Mateo glanced at the list, then back at Luci, an idea forming. He might not totally agree with whatever she had on that list, but it was a start. They could present Luci's ideas to the students and invite feedback, then as a group decide on norms. He and Luci would model compromise.

Her brow furrowed as she mimed something related to the list. He glanced at her planner again. The list looked good enough, short and to the point.

"Listen up!" Mateo called. "We need to have a conversation about expectations."

Everyone turned to look at them.

"We need to talk about these rules," she whispered.

"Right. We'll all discuss them as a group." This was actually a great compromise. Luci's list would set basic expectations, and then the students could discuss her ideas and agree upon a framework for behavior. Perfect.

Mateo cleared his throat and addressed the students. "You are all good people, and we expect you to treat yourselves, each other and your environment with respect and kindness."

"Vague much?" Luci muttered so only he could hear.

"Ms. Walker and I have some ideas we'd like to share with you to start." He took her planner and read from it. "No stealing. No roaming the second and third floors. No parties upstairs, social gatherings are allowed in the hotel's common rooms." He looked up and grinned. "So you're all doing the right thing. No food upstair—" He furrowed his brow at Luci. "Did you mean upstairs? I think that's something we'll all want to discuss. It would fall under respect for our environment but—"

She snatched the planner and turned so the students couldn't see her speaking. "I'm nowhere near finished with this list, and I'm not particularly interested in feedback. We need to be specific and clear."

Mateo held eye contact. She wanted specific? He could be more specific. "Do you all understand what I mean by respecting our environment?" The kids stared at him blankly. "Okay, another example might be, no water guns, super soakers or water balloons allowed in the hotel."

There, that was a solid rule. It made sense. This felt good. He looked at Luci to confirm he'd done a good job of making up a rule to illuminate the point he assumed she was making with no food upstairs. Her expression of horror was a bit of a surprise.

Mateo continued, clarifying his meaning for the students. "I realize it might sound fun, but water can cause a lot of damage. Every spring when the water battles would break out at the boarding school I went to, they inevitably spilled into the classroom."

"Um… Mateo—" Luci began.

"I mean, sure, if we're all having a friendly water fight on the soccer field that's one thing. But at St. Xavier's, kids were packing concealed water guns, spraying people from under their desks during tests. Water balloons were a favorite, because if you're stealthy enough when you throw it right in the middle of class, no one can figure out where it came from. So no water fights. Inside, anyway."

The students murmured to one another.

Luci's expression was now frozen in furious disbelief, so he tried again. "We want you to be honest with us. Like if you need to leave the building after curfew, come talk to us. Don't try to sneak out. Besides, Ms. Walker and I already know how to sneak out of this hotel using the skylight in the kitchen, the downspout in the southeastern corner and the slider off the dining room, so don't even think about it."

Luci gripped his arm, hard.

"What?" he asked.

"If they weren't thinking about it before, they sure are now."

"I'm trying to be clear." He *was* trying, but he could admit this wasn't going as well as it had when they'd come up with group norms in his classroom.

"What else should we *not* do?" Ilsa asked.

"Just be smart about things," Mateo said.

"Could you give more examples?" Antonio gestured in a circular motion, suggesting Mateo continue. "What would be 'not smart'?"

"You know, the normal things. Don't put your friends down the laundry chute. Because that's only fun until someone gets stuck. Don't launch bottle rockets out your windows. And I don't want to hear even the suggestion of a food fight. It's hard enough to get groceries out here, and if you waste food hurling it at one another, I'm not taking an extra trip to Lakeview to go shopping. And, while it really doesn't need to be said, no bagpipes. No bagpipes, no mariachi bands, no wandering minstrels—"

Luci gripped his arm harder. The kids murmuring intensified.

"What?" he asked Luci. "You wanted rules."

"You're not giving them rules," she whispered. "You're giving them ideas."

"You were the one who asked for clarity. I'm being honest."

"Being honest doesn't mean sharing every last bit of information."

"That's exactly what honesty means."

Her face, which had been steadily deepening in color, was full brick-red now. "I think we should table this discussion."

Frustration piled up in his chest. "You're the one who had to have rules. You started it."

"Well, you complicated it. And we're not going to get anywhere at this point."

Mateo was baffled. He'd done exactly what she wanted, and now she was mad. It felt unfair, reminiscent of his school years, of being called out on a technicality.

The kids spoke among themselves, words like *laundry chute*, *bottle rockets* and *water balloons* rising above the low rumble of conversation.

Luci clapped her hands. "Okay! It's four o'clock. Dinner will be served at six thirty. Mateo and I will post the rest of the rules first thing in the morning."

He turned to Luci and spoke in a low voice. "I thought we just went over the rules."

"We're going to need rules to keep them from acting on the 'rules' you put in their heads." Luci turned on her heel. "I'm going in to start dinner."

"What's for dinner?" Mateo asked.

"I have no idea." She strode back into the hotel.

Mateo closed his eyes, frustrated. He wanted to work with Luci. He was trying. But if she was dismissive of his ideas there wasn't much he could do about it.

He had to untangle his emotions from their working relationship, to get over her once and for all. They had to work together, but he was not going to let his heart get thrown around anymore. She wasn't interested. He could accept it and move on. There was no romantic future for him and Luci.

There were, however, eleven students now living under his roof. That was a challenge enough.

CHAPTER SEVEN

IT WAS TUESDAY NIGHT, they'd finished dinner and Mateo desperately wanted to get to his grading.

And Luci was making a face.

"What?"

"We're just gonna let everyone off the hook with cleanup?"

"Willa is giving a test in all of her classes tomorrow. They need to study."

She looked over his shoulder to where the kids were sprawled out in the hotel lobby. "I don't see a lot of studying going on."

Mateo didn't glance back, choosing not to confirm or deny.

"Without a cleanup schedule, what happens on nights like tonight?" she asked. "Who does the dishes?"

"I'll do them."

"There's a literal mountain of dishes in there."

"You're lucky Willa's not in the room to hear you misuse the word *literal*."

She huffed.

He puffed out a sigh.

But the breathwork didn't blow down the hundred-year-old structure. The City Hotel stood firm, and they were still in charge of eleven kids.

Three days in, and he and Luci had not found a way to magically work together.

He could now admit they were not adequately prepared for the behavior issues. Strategies that worked for the classroom didn't directly translate to the boarding school. She'd been right—they *should* have sat down and created a list of guidelines for the kids. But admitting Luci was right was not his strong suit.

Nor was creating rules.

Nor, for that matter, was running a boarding school.

He tried again. "Look, I'm sorry. I don't know how to do this right out of the gate. Can we give ourselves some grace to make a few mistakes the first week in?"

"Not if those mistakes are due to our lack of basic forethought," she snapped. "Not if our mistakes wind up allowing these students to harm themselves and others."

"No one is harming anyone."

"Something is up tonight." Luci scanned the room. "I can feel it."

"What do you suggest?" Mock serious, Mateo gazed at the ceiling. "I set up an interrogation room? You call in the sheriff and we grill each student individually to see if anyone is plotting to sneak a granola bar past the second floor?"

"Allowing them to take food upstairs is asking for an infestation of mice and ants."

"But hedgehogs are fine?"

Her expression grew serious. "You leave the small friends out of this. I am barely hanging on by a thread this week, and the hedgies are the only thing holding me together."

Mateo bit down on the urge to laugh, because heaven knew that wouldn't help the situation.

"Look, we're not getting anywhere tonight. Why don't I take over with the kids for now? I can get them upstairs and give the speech about staying in their rooms after curfew."

One of her eyelids twitched. Because what was more annoying than offering her an out for the evening?

"Why, because you're the *nice* teacher?"

"Because you're being unreasonable, and I want to give you some space away from people right now."

The color drained from her face. Mateo understood instantly that he'd said the wrong thing. He'd snapped that last thread she'd been so clear about clinging to.

"Luci, I'm sor—" he began, but she held a hand up to stop him.

"Yeah. Great idea. You get the kids settled and I'll wash all the dishes."

"That's not what I was suggesting."

"Someone has to clean up. And since I'm not fit to be around people right now, it may as well be me."

"I'll clean up in the morning."

"You have to go to work in the morning."

"Luci—"

She shook her head, lips pinched together, as though trying to hold in her emotions. When she finally spoke, her voice was low, almost a whisper. "Please don't talk to me right now."

She brushed past and headed for the kitchen, leaving him, the students and her hedgehogs without a word.

How had he messed that up so quickly? It was like Luci was expecting him to hurt her, and she was watching for it. And then he'd gone and done exactly as she expected.

Awesome.

In the name of the impending English exams, Mateo coaxed the students into their dorm rooms earlier than normal. The occasional bursts of laughter and murmurs of conversation suggested no one was getting to sleep early, but they were in their rooms.

He rubbed at his stubble and headed back to the kitchen. The lights were on and seemed overly bright as he walked into the large industrial space.

And at the center of the chaos of dishes and leftovers was Luci. She still wore the white jeans and pink sweater she'd dressed in that morning, not a smudge or speck of dust on her outfit. Even dirt was afraid of Luci.

She checked the temperature of the water in the sink, then glanced at the mound of dishes. With a sigh, she picked up a plate.

"Hey."

She didn't look up at his voice.

"You still not speaking to me?" he asked.

"I was never not speaking to you," she countered. "I have a great deal to say to you."

Mateo joined her at the sink. He grabbed a plate and scraped it into the garbage can. Luci took it from his hands, rinsed it, then set it in the dishwasher. They worked in silence, the only sound was scraping, rinsing and stacking plates.

"Please don't be mad at me," Mateo said.

She set down a plate and pressed both palms at the edge of the sink. After a beat, she said, "I'm sorry. My emotions are running high right now. It's probably not the best time to talk it out."

Mateo chuckled at her reference to Open Hearts. When any of the kids from that community got upset, they'd say their emotions were running high, or accuse others of needing to do some breathing exercises. "Yeah, we should wait until we can go into the sun."

She turned a hard look on him, then swallowed.

"Look, we haven't handled the first few days very well," he said.

"We have not."

She picked up a load of silverware and dumped it in the sink. Mateo grabbed the soup pot and ladled the leftovers into a container. They worked in silence again.

Then Luci surprised him by saying, "Do you remember that one professor we had in grad school? The guy with the baffling grading schemes?"

"Oh, yeah."

"There was so much work to do, and we couldn't figure out what to prioritize. Some assignments he would give us full credit without even glancing at our work, and others he would nitpick to pieces, remember that?"

Mateo did remember. But not so much because the class was frustrating. His memories were of sitting with Luci and laughing as they discussed the *Alice in Wonderland* experience of trying to get a good grade in this guy's class.

"That's what this feels like to me. I want to do the right thing, but I don't know what the right thing is."

Mateo set the soup pot on the counter by the sink.

"I hear what you're saying," he finally replied. "And I'd like to ask that you aim your frustration at the situation, rather than me."

She looked up at him for the first time. He continued, "This is as hard for me as it is for you. I know I come off as easygoing and positive, but that's because I work hard to be easygoing and positive."

She set down her sponge and faced him fully, listening. Mateo had never really explained his philosophy to anyone, not because he was hiding anything but because no one seemed very interested in *why* he was happy. They just assumed he was born that way.

"I make a choice to be happy. I started when I was in school, my peers were frustrated, my teachers had anger issues. I didn't want that."

"It seems like the whole world is angry sometimes," she murmured.

"Because we glorify feelings of indignation and anger, as though there is moral superiority in being outraged. It's easier to be angry than it is to do the work to make the world a better place. But in reality those emotions just make us feel powerful in the moment, and we need more than a well-worded rant to make the world a better place."

She gave him the glimmer of a smile. "That is an astute observation of society."

"It's based on my experience. I'm not saying there aren't times for anger, and there's certainly plenty to be angry about. But I function better, and contribute more to society, when I'm happy. So I do what it takes to stay positive."

"How..." Luci's words trailed off as she focused on the dishes. Then she looked him fully in the eye. "How?"

Mateo gestured for her to finish the question.

"That's it. How? How do you keep positive?"

She held eye contact with him. Was he really going to admit this?

He was, because honesty mattered.

"I googled it."

Luci's laugh rang out in the kitchen, accompanied by the little squeak.

Such a pretty sound.

He stepped closer to her. "I found a lot of good stuff. It sounds simple, but I count my blessings.

When I get mad or frustrated, I make a list about what is good about the current circumstances."

"I should do that," she admitted.

"I also watch what I say. I try not to complain about something I'm not willing to work to change. I've agreed to run this dorm. I'm going to see it through until June, so I'm not going to spin my wheels talking about what a raw deal it is."

Luci gazed at him. "That's really wise."

"Thank you. It also frees up a lot of spare time."

A little smile curled her lips. He took another step to stand next to her at the sink.

"What's good about this situation?" Mateo asked.

Luci picked up the soup pot and turned on the water.

Mateo lifted the pot from her hands and took over with the washing, then repeated, "What's good about this situation?"

She stared at the sudsy water. He waited.

"I have a home."

"We have a great home," he concurred. "I love living here."

"I have a job," Luci continued.

"We have engaging, important work."

Luci glanced down at her top. "I love this sweater."

"It's very pretty."

She turned her Shakespearean fairy smile on him. "What about you?"

"What about me what?"

"What's good about your situation? Do you love your old Seattle Seahawks sweatshirt?"

He smiled, and she seemed to relax.

"I'm healthy," he said.

She nodded.

A thought came unbidden to his mind and he pushed it away, instead saying, "I have a college education and a master's degree, and no one can ever take that from me."

"Same."

"I have good friends."

She held eye contact, inspiring him to continue. "And if we have to run this dormitory, I'm glad I'm doing it with someone I trust."

She blinked, then grabbed a sponge and turned away to wipe down the island. They worked in silence, the persistent, unnerving thought bumping through his head.

I'm grateful to be here with you.

It didn't make sense. They hadn't exactly knocked it out of the park as partners in this endeavor. But somehow, he was still glad she was the one he was in this mess with.

LUCI LAY IN BED, unable to sleep.

Something was up.

It wasn't just thoughts of Mateo keeping sleep at bay. Heaven knew this wasn't the first night she'd lain awake analyzing his actions. Charming, gorgeous, easygoing, unworried; he was a perfect foil to her every flaw. It was hard to be crushed out on someone who's good at everything you struggled with.

But it literally—and she was using the word correctly this time—wasn't Mateo keeping her up.

There was a whiff of trouble in the air. Somewhere, someone was up to something.

And that someone was probably right down the hall in one of the dorm rooms.

A hedgehog skittered across the floor. On a normal evening the soft patter of their feet served as a lullaby. Tonight it was like a dramatic motif in a suspense film.

Luci flipped over her pillow and tried to get comfortable. Mateo had been very solicitous, coming down to the kitchen to clean up. Helping her focus on the positive. Apologizing.

And while that was sweet, it left her stewing in her own reactions. It was so frustrating when she snapped like that. She didn't want to get mad. She wanted to be cool and rational, and not take every little thing so personally.

She flipped onto her back, twisting her pajamas until she had to kick her legs to readjust them.

Were those voices she heard? Or just the wind?

Luci opened her eyes and stared into the darkness. A soft clicking sound, almost imperceptible, wafted down the hall. She propped herself up in her elbows.

Then the creak of an old floorboard, followed by total silence.

There it was.

Luci flung back the covers and launched out of bed. After flipping on her light, she took a long, decisive step into the hallway.

Her arms were already crossed, face set, as she turned on five, fully dressed boys.

"Good evening."

The boys froze in midsneak. The only movement was their eyes as they glanced at one another. Luci bit down on the inside of her cheek to remind herself this *wasn't* funny.

"Um." One meaningless syllable from Oliver was all any of them was able to muster.

Expression intentionally bland, Luci glanced down at her watch. The seconds ticking by filled the hall.

"Hello, Ms. Walker," Antonio finally said.

"Good evening, Antonio." She kept her voice steady. "It's after midnight. You must be aware that your curfew is eleven o'clock. And I hear you have a test in your English class tomorrow."

"I know, but—"

Luci gazed at the boys. She and Mateo hadn't been superclear about the rules in general, but they all knew their curfew. Not sneaking out past eleven would fall under the common sense Mateo kept insisting the kids had.

"We were just…" Oliver's voice trailed off as he looked at his friends.

The door to her right flung open and Mateo ran into the hall. Luci kept her eyes on the kids, as

Mateo managed to look extra adorable when he'd just woken up.

"Is there something I can help you with?" she asked the students.

"No," Suleiman blurted. "We were only—"

"You were only—?"

Mateo moved more fully into the hallway. She risked a glance at him to make sure he had her back here. His concerned gaze connected with hers and a spark of humor caught. Her lips twitched and she looked away from her coworker. She could *not* smile.

There was the briefest pause before all the boys started talking at once, a loud burst of excuses.

"I was thirsty and thought—" Antonio said.

Oliver gestured broadly. "There was a noise, and we were going to check—"

"I just remembered I left my homework on the—" Suleiman began.

Each boy continued with his unique reason for being up, fully dressed and in the hall with friends at midnight. The contradiction in the stories only made each boy speak more loudly, as though confidence while lying would make them more believable. Mateo was barely keeping a straight face as the boys spoke, getting further into their excuses, and sounding more absurd as the seconds ticked past. The garbled spray slowly trickled off as the boys realized how weak it all sounded.

Antonio was the last to give it up, his voice barely more than a mumble as he finished with, "—getting some water from the kitchen, because it tastes better."

"Huh." Luci nodded, as though all their nonsense was perfectly reasonable. "Do you think you could wait until the morning to grab your homework, help me put the dishes away, look for your socks in the ballroom, get a drink of water and check to see if any pronghorn have gotten into the courtyard?"

Out of the corner of her eye, she saw Mateo turn away, shoulders shaking and face flushed but not actually laughing. Luci chomped on the inside of her cheek.

There was a long silence until finally Oliver said, "Yes, Ms. Walker."

She smiled at him. Bad idea. A smile was way too close to a laugh. She kept a straight face by thinking about European disasters of the fourteenth century: war, plague, famine.

"Why don't you head back to your dorm room?" Mateo suggested. "We'll talk further in the morning."

The boys hung their heads, shuffling as one unit back to the room.

"Good night." Luci waved them in, then shut the door behind them.

When she spun around, she caught Mateo's eye and the need to laugh made her head swim. She could feel the heat rising through her face as she retreated down the hall.

The hotel was silent. Luci managed to pull in a breath.

Then a string of cursing in French, Portuguese and English erupted from the boys' room.

A giggle escaped her throat. Mateo shook with silent laughter, and the more they tried to repress it, the funnier the whole situation seemed. Tears streamed down her face as she tried to laugh quietly. Finally, Luci let out a little squeak and that made Mateo laugh even harder. She gave up, and laughed out loud until her sides hurt.

"Well done," Mateo finally said, still laughing.

Luci wiped a tear from her eye and leaned her head against the wall behind her, gasping. "That was the worst attempt at sneaking out I've ever seen."

"To give the guys credit, they haven't had much practice."

A snuffling sounded at her feet. Luci looked down to see her hedgehogs were also making a break for it. She sat down and scooped Chai into her lap. The hedgie waddled across Luci's pajamas and nibbled at the sleeve.

Mateo sat on the floor across the hall from her, tapping his finger to get the attention of Rooibos, who hesitated in the doorway.

"That was awesome. You were so calm. How were you so calm?" Mateo leaned his head back and wiped at a tear. Then he started laughing again. "Oliver's face."

"Right?"

Mateo snickered. "Nicely done, Ms. Walker. You called it. Something *was* up tonight."

Rooibos waddled farther into the hallway. Mateo reached over to pet her, and she instantly folded in on herself, hiding her sensitive face and belly with her coat of prickles.

"I don't think she likes me." His face fell, like he was seriously disappointed there was a creature on earth who didn't respond to his charming smile and perfect manners.

"She doesn't know you. You have to go slow."

Luci reached across the floor and tapped the carpet next to Rooibos. The hedgehog, who in Luci's estimation was the bravest in the bunch, peeked out. When she saw it was Luci, she unfurled herself and waddled over.

"Lean down, so she can see your face."

Mateo lowered his head and smiled at Rooibos. The hedgehog stopped walking but didn't disappear into herself.

"It takes time," Luci said.

"Have I ever mentioned how cute these guys are?" Mateo asked.

Luci warmed, as though she was personally responsible for their cuteness. Rooibos sniffed his hand, then poked her nose at the sleeve of his sweatshirt.

"They are adorable." Earl Grey braved the hallway, shuffling toward her. "They are widdle waddlers." She leaned down so she was nose-to-nose with the hedgehog. "Are you a widdle waddler?"

Mateo laughed.

"I love these guys," she said. "Other small creatures, not so much. Like, guinea pigs kind of stress me out. And don't get me started on rabbits."

"You find bunnies stressful?" he asked.

"A little bit," she admitted. "But hedgehogs are roly-poly friends." She kept her eyes on Earl Grey, then pulled in a deep breath and admitted, "You may have noticed that sometimes I get really stressed out and lose my cool."

"It's happened a few times."

"It would have been way worse this year without the hedgehogs." She ran a finger along the spiny fur of her small companion. She felt Mateo gazing at her. "What?"

"I have an idea."

"That's…great?"

He rolled his eyes. "About making sure the kids stay in their rooms."

"I'm listening."

"Okay, I didn't love this when I was a student. But sometimes, if we'd been on a tear of bad behavior, the instructors would randomly put tape under the doorknobs, taping the door to the jamb."

"They taped you in? Doesn't sound supereffective."

"The point wasn't to keep us in, it was to catch whoever was sneaking out. If someone left their room, it would break the tape, so all our instructors had to do was walk down the hall and look for broken tape."

"Ooooh. That's good."

"If we told the students in advance about the tape, they'd know not to even try to sneak out."

"I love that idea." She leaned her head back against the wall. The release of the laughter and the relief brought about by Mateo's plan washed the adrenaline out of her body. She suddenly felt very tired.

"You should get to bed." He stood and offered her his free hand, pulling her to her feet. "We can share this plan with the kids in the morning."

He passed Rooibos to her, then herded Earl Grey back into Luci's room.

"Thank you," she said.

"Thank *you*. That was epic." He gazed at her for another moment. "Good night, Ms. Walker."

She had to clear her throat before she was able to respond. "Good night."

Luci stepped into her room and closed the door behind her. Her bed felt particularly soft and welcoming. She pulled the covers up to her ears, listening to the scratching little paws of her hedgies. Across the hall, Mateo would be spilling back into bed as well.

Then she closed her eyes, drifting off to sleep as she made a list of all the good things about her situation.

CHAPTER EIGHT

"IT'S LIKE MATEO and I are parents to eleven teenagers, and we can't even decide on a brand of peanut butter."

Willa and Aida laughed out loud. Harlow hurried back from the kitchen, and asked, "What? What did I miss?"

"Just more of the same," Luci said, rolling her eyes at herself. Her one moment of common ground with Mateo had not miraculously morphed into a hundred more. They literally agreed on only one thing: tape.

Harlow set an artfully arranged tray of snacks on the coffee table and sat down next to Luci on the sofa. "Tell me, anyway. I'm loving the dormitory drama."

"Good to know someone is."

They were one week in, and while none of the kids had had a meltdown, exhibited major behavior problems, or set the building on fire, Luci's patience was stretched so thin she was on the verge of doing all three.

But today was Sunday. Harlow, their big-time Nashville lawyer friend, was in town for the weekend, and she'd invited Luci, Aida and Willa out to her luxurious ranch for the afternoon. Luci's plan had been to eat fancy snacks and simply listen and enjoy as her friends discussed wedding plans and honeymoon options.

Instead, they wanted all the latest on the boarding house, the kids and Mateo.

Luci grabbed a plate and loaded it with cheeses, salamis and spreads. Harlow had the most well-curated fridge imaginable. No, scratch that, she had the most well-curated *life*. Everything Harlow surrounded herself with was chosen with care. Even the sunshine streaming through the massive windows seemed made to order. Hanging out at Harlow's ranch felt like stepping into a Pinterest board. It was the perfect house for a friend to have. Luci could come over and enjoy it, but it wasn't something she had to create or maintain. In fact, she preferred the quirkiness and the old-world glamor of the hotel. But it was fun to visit Harlow's beautiful home and enjoy her impeccable taste, before returning to her patchwork life.

Luci snuggled deeper into her corner of the sofa.

"So what was the thing about Mateo and the mac and cheese?" Harlow asked. "Vander started to tell me about it, but I don't think I got the whole story."

"Yeah, what was that?" Willa asked.

Luci sighed. "Okay, you know how Suleiman gets, like, really homesick every once in a while. But he doesn't want anyone to know?"

The women nodded. All the exchange students had bouts of missing their families. Suleiman's habit of acting like he was fine intensified the feelings and made it hard to help him.

"I try to be there for him," Aida said. "But sometimes even soccer doesn't help."

Because in Aida's world, if something couldn't be cured by soccer, could it really be cured at all? Willa patted her arm, her smile acknowledging what everyone else was thinking.

"So Wednesday evening, Suleiman gets home from practice and goes straight upstairs and we can tell he's homesick. I offered to drive him out to Pete Sorel's house to use the internet there to call his family, but by that time it's two a.m. in Senegal."

"His mom would totally get out of bed for a video call," Willa said.

"Oh, I know. But calling his mom at two a.m. her time makes it look like he's homesick."

"Which he is," Harlow added.

"Right. So Mateo's all, I'll make mac and cheese with barbecue beef on top. Which he normally reserves for when someone is heartbroken, but he decided homesick counts."

"Is that what I missed on Wednesday night?" Willa asked. "I'm so bummed! That meal is amazing."

"Oh, I'm not saying it isn't." Luci's mouth watered at the memory. "There are days I've almost wished someone would get their heart broken, just so Mateo would make it again."

"Same," Aida concurred. "Remember the one time when Vander was all upset and playing sad Beatles songs nonstop and then…" She trailed off, just now remembering that was the time Harlow and Vander had nearly sabotaged their relationship.

Harlow raised an eyebrow. "Do tell. What was so wonderful about that time?"

"Not a thing. It was the worst." Aida gave a firm nod. "And we really should have brought you out some leftovers because mac and cheese with barbecue is incredible."

"While the meal *is* incredible, it takes hours to make," Luci reminded them. "Hours on a normal day, but Mateo was making it for fifteen people."

Everyone groaned.

"So now, Suleiman is homesick and hungry. The rest of the kids are hungry, too, and they don't understand why dinner's taking so long. I ran across the street and asked Mrs. Moran to come over and help, since everyone else was gone that night."

"Mrs. Moran was still at school?" Harlow asked.

Luci bit her lip. "Yeah. She was just doing some… I don't actually know what she was doing. Whatever. Anyway, we get back and I can't find Suleiman."

"Oh, no," Aida groaned.

"I probably don't have to remind you that Suleiman has a track record of taking off on ATVs without permission. So then I'm really freaked out. Miraculously, we had an internet signal that night, so Mrs. Moran hung out in the lobby and asked the kids to explain TikTok to her. I head into the kitchen to tell Mateo we have a situation and what do I find?"

"What?" Harlow asked. "What happened? Was Mateo gone, too?"

"Nope. He's in the kitchen, with Suleiman, and the two of them are listening to a podcast on theoretical calculus while they make dinner."

Luci's friends responded with blank stares. The severity of the situation seemed entirely lost on them.

"What?"

"That's pretty sweet of Mateo," Willa said.

"I mean, sure, it was a nice gesture..." Luci grabbed another one of the perfect wheat crackers Harlow knew how to find.

"Did it work?" Aida asked. "Did Suleiman feel better?"

"It always works," Luci reminded them. Suleiman had eaten a big helping, then asked Luci if they could drive out to Pete's the next morning before school. They did, and she'd had tea in the kitchen as Suleiman chatted with his parents and little brother. She and Pete got to meet the family and were issued a standing invitation to come visit Dakar.

"Okay, I hate to say this," Willa said, "and I know it's not what you want to hear, but in my opinion..."

"Oh, my god, just say it!" Luci grumbled.

"In my opinion, you two are doing a pretty good job at running the boarding house."

"The fact that the building is still standing after one week and there have been no major injuries doesn't make us good at this."

Willa shook her head. "The kids are happy. They're getting their homework done. They're not exhausted from driving all over the county. I no longer have to grade essays that were finished in the back of Pete's truck on the way to school."

Luci shrugged one shoulder. Willa wasn't wrong.

There had been a few adjustments, but for the most part it was good for the students.

"How does it all…work?" Aida asked. "Like, where do they sleep? Where do they shower? Because even though I've been upstairs in the hotel, all I can picture is the dorm room Little Orphan Annie and Pepper slept in."

Luci laughed. "It's not so grim as that."

"It's not at all grim," Willa said. "The kids love it. Sylvie is begging Colter to let her move in."

"We created shared rooms with the two big suites on the top floor. So all five boys are in one room, and all six girls are in the other. We thought it would mitigate some of the fear of missing out and also help hold kids accountable. One person can sneak past us and swear their roommate to secrecy. It's a lot harder with half a dozen people."

"Yeah, we all heard about that one," Harlow said, pointing a finger at Luci.

Luci grinned. It really had been an epic save.

"And Mateo agreed to all the night checks, right?" Willa turned to the others. "He sets an alarm and gets up to check every night at a different random time."

"That's nice of him," Aida said.

Willa looked pointedly at Luci. "He offered because he was worried about the stress of this whole thing on Luci and wanted to make sure she wasn't losing sleep on top of everything else."

The room reacted: palms covering hearts, big doe eyes widening, the word *Aww!* sighed out across the sofas.

The guy did *a chore,* it wasn't like he was saving puppies or anything.

"What are you all thinking for your weddings?" Luci asked, flipping the subject. "We really need to start planning because I have to get my guest wardrobe together."

"Please stop trying to redirect the conversation," Willa said.

"Please stop assuming you're going to be a guest," Aida added. "You're on serious bridesmaid duty this summer."

Harlow nodded. "She's right. I've already ordered your dresses, BTW. But we were discussing Mateo."

"Did I tell you all about the laundry?" Luci asked. "The hotel has an amazing laundry room and I took everyone down for a tutorial on Thursday."

"You are the only person I know who gets excited about a laundry room," Aida said.

"And the only person who is able to redirect conversation away from a fascinating topic, like Mateo being a total sweetheart, and on to laundry," Willa noted.

"Ugh!" Luci threw up her hands. "Why can't we talk about something important? Like shoes."

"How about this for a deal." Harlow leaned forward in full negotiation mode. "You let us bug you for five more minutes about the dormitory and Mateo, then we can pull up Pinterest boards on the big screen in my game room and start making wedding decisions."

"Thank you!" Luci said, emphasizing the words

with her hands. "Yes, that's fair. What do you want to know?"

"Is it true Mateo made cocoa for all the kids on Thursday night, then made you a special cup of Sleepytime tea because he knows it's your favorite evening drink?" Aida asked.

Luci groaned and covered her face with her hands. Her friends were relentless.

What they didn't get was that Mateo was just polite. His behavior was ingrained. Sure, he brought her tea, but he also made warm beverages for eleven other people. He held doors, stood when others entered a room and had a smile for everyone, even Loretta. The tea meant nothing specific to her. It *was* delicious, with the perfect amount of honey and a little half-and-half in it, but it wasn't any kind of a gesture of friendship. If he really cared about Luci, he'd have sat down with her weeks ago and come up with a plan for managing the dormitory.

"It's just a lot," Luci said into her palms. "Sometimes, I question what I'm even doing."

Willa settled an arm around her shoulder. "Here's my question. Are *you* doing okay? With all of this."

Luci dropped her hands from her face. "I'm fine."

"Are you?" Willa asked. "Because you don't have to do this."

Luci looked up sharply. "I do have to do this. I mean, technically I could have said no to supervising the dormitory, but I'm not heartless."

"No, I mean teach in Pronghorn," Willa said. "I would hate for you to leave. That's the last thing

I want. But with your skills and background you could teach anywhere."

"But I want to teach here," she said. Her friends wore expressions somewhere between concern and confusion. Since she'd spent the last hour complaining about this job, it was no wonder.

Harlow's gaze connected with Luci's. She was the only person in town who knew about Luci's past because she'd been a key part in that past.

Luci had been a curious little girl in orange the day she met Harlow. The now-glamorous lawyer was an argumentative ninth grader, who tipped off Luci about the outside world and introduced her to the concept of public school. One conversation had changed the course of Luci's life. It had been an unexpected gift to get to know Harlow as an adult. Harlow was shocked when she finally put the pieces together and recognized Luci, but had promised to respect her privacy. It was just another in the long string of reasons why Luci adored Harlow.

The others didn't get why teaching here was so important to Luci. They couldn't get it.

And honestly, Luci was tired of hearing herself complain.

"I'm happy." And if she wasn't always happy, at least she was satisfied. "Mateo and I aren't arguing about everything. And the good thing about the whole mac-and-cheese situation—"

"—is that you got to eat the best meal ever," Aida mused.

"Yes, that. And we've finally agreed on one

thing—whoever is prepping dinner needs to start by four thirty. If we've got the ingredients out and a game plan, it's pretty easy to rope a few kids into helping cook. Mateo and I have been taking turns, and now we're in agreement about the start time."

Luci slipped out from under Willa's arm to load dried figs and the most amazing soft cheese onto her plate. It was Mateo's night to prep, and he was far and away the stronger cook of the two of them. She didn't *want* to spoil her dinner with Harlow's snacks, but she was well on her way.

"Is it Pinterest time yet? I have so many opinions on centerpieces."

Harlow checked her watch. "It's time. And just so you all know, I'm going way over the top with this wedding."

"I fully approve." Luci stood and stretched. "Someone needs to compensate for Tate and Aida, who are basically just hosting a soccer game at which they'll get married."

"Soccer is part of the reception," Aida clarified.

"Did you hire the ref to officiate yet?" Luci quipped as they headed into Harlow's perfectly organized game room.

"Also, dancing." Aida spun around and walked backward as she spoke to Luci. "You'll remember my fiancé taught us all to ballroom dance?"

Luci laughed. Tate had learned to ballroom dance as part of his bachelor's degree in physical education and had used that skill in his enthusiastic wooing of Aida. Aida had forgotten that Luci and Mateo already knew a slew of ballroom dances from their private-school years.

He was an excellent dancer.

"When is Tate going to teach a dance unit in his PE class?" Luci asked. "Dancing is a useful life skill. These kids need to be prepared for all the world is going to throw at them. Including the Lindy Hop."

"Speaking of, who's going to be there to greet the kids this afternoon if they arrive early?" Willa asked.

"Mateo and the guys are there," Luci said. "Surely they can handle things for a couple of hours, right?"

MATEO LAUNCHED THE Frisbee into the air. Tate and Vander sprinted to the other end of the field, attempting to cut each other off. Tate jumped up and knocked his fingers against the edge but didn't manage to get a grip. The disc waffled in the air and Vander caught it.

Mateo laughed as Vander claimed a victory for STEM teachers. The sunshine, warm and welcome, fell on his back, even if he could see dark storm clouds gathering on Hart Mountain. He had time before the students returned to the hotel, and a good half hour before it started to rain. Life was good.

Vander threw the Frisbee and Tate took off. Mateo raced him to the point of contact. Tate, who was a good foot taller than pretty much anyone, leaped up. Mateo couldn't compete with Tate's height, but he'd been a solid wrestler in high school. He drove his shoulder into Tate's side and scrambled after the Frisbee. Tate responded by trying to push Mateo out of the way and they both tripped over their own feet. Aida's German shepherd seized the opportunity, springing into the air and snatching the Frisbee in his teeth.

"Greg for the win!" Vander called, laughing.

Greg dropped the Frisbee at Tate's feet and sat, waiting for a victor's ear rub.

"Who's a good dog?" Tate asked. "Who's the Frisbee champion? Is it Greg?"

Mateo flopped down in the grass beside them to catch his breath.

Good friends, sunshine and a Frisbee. If rain was on the way, it was on the way. Worrying about the storm clouds gathering wouldn't change anything.

"Hey, how's it—" Vander gestured toward the hotel. "How is it?"

"Uh. I don't know." Mateo sat up. "Kids are fine. Luci's stressed out. It's like school, only at home."

"Are you doing okay?" Tate asked.

"We're fine."

Tate and Vander exchanged a look.

"And the kids, are they getting into trouble at all?" Vander asked. "I heard some of the boys tried to sneak out Tuesday night."

Mateo chuckled. "Well, they tried. But Luci's got a sixth sense, or knowing Luci, it's more like a seventh or eighth sense."

Mateo revisited the memory: Luci in her soft pink pajamas, hair in braids, staring down the boys as they tried to explain away their behavior.

"Why are you smiling?"

Mateo blinked. "Was I smiling?"

"Yeah," Tate said.

"I don't know. I guess it was funny. By the time I got out there she had it taken care of."

"I'm glad you and Luci are getting along."

"I didn't say we were getting along."

"You don't have to," Vander noted. "The smile is pretty clear."

"I'm not smiling about Luci. It was funny to watch those guys try to make excuses."

"Okay." Vander glanced at Tate.

"What?"

Tate shrugged. "For two people who don't get along very well, you sure talk about each other a lot."

What did Tate even mean by that? It wasn't like he talked about Luci half as often as he thought about her.

Or wait. Maybe... Did Luci talk about him?

No, she didn't. And he was in the process of getting over her, moving on.

"I don't talk about Luci."

"You were just talking about her," Vander said. "Thirty seconds ago."

"Because he asked." Mateo gestured to Tate.

"I asked about the dormitory," Tate said.

"The dorm I'm running with Luci."

Tate rolled his eyes. "And there's her name again."

Mateo punched Tate in the arm. Greg let out a warning growl.

"I'm only joking," he reminded the dog. Greg maneuvered himself next to Mateo, indicating that he'd accept this defense on the condition of an ear rub.

Mateo petted the dog, then glanced at the sky. He had about twenty minutes before the rain came, before the students returned and he needed to get inside and start dinner. He should make the most of it.

Mateo grabbed the Frisbee and sprang to his feet. Greg, having clearly forgiven him, dropped into a play bow, ready to go. Tate and Vander scrambled up and started running. Mateo spun the disc in their direction.

"Can I play?"

Mateo startled to see Mav standing right next to him. *That kid.* He had a singular ability to appear out of nowhere.

"What are you doing in town?" Mateo asked.

Mav shrugged.

"Mav, go long!" Tate called.

Mav backed up, then started running. He made a decent catch, then had a little difficulty with a throw. A drop of rain landed on Mateo's arm. The heavy rain clouds were rolling in. It was probably time to get back to the hotel and start dinner prep, but they could play for a few more minutes.

The sound of car doors slamming altered him to the arrival of students.

"One more catch!" Mateo called.

Tate threw the Frisbee and Mateo and Mav raced to catch it. But before either of them could get there, Suleiman launched himself onto the field and sped past them, hovering in the air as he jumped to catch the Frisbee.

"Cece!" Suleiman called, gesturing to another new arrival. Cece gave her mom a quick hug, then ran out to join them on the field. Rain spattered on the dry ground, releasing a scent of sagebrush and steam.

"Three on three!" Tate called. "We'll use the soccer goals for the end zone."

"Four on three!" Antonio announced, sprinting over as his host family waved goodbye.

Mateo ran, loving the feeling of blood pumping through his system. The students laughed as they jostled one another, gunning for the Frisbee.

The game, and the rain, intensified.

Mateo absolutely intended to stop playing and head back inside and start dinner. But the friendly game quickly grew competitive. As other students returned to the hotel, they couldn't resist joining in or cheering the teams on. Mateo relaxed and found himself having fun, fully engaged in the moment. Rain drenched them, and the muddy field gurgled up at their feet, soaking their shoes.

"Mateo!" Neveah called, waving her arms. Her hair was plastered to her forehead, getting in her eyes. That was going to make the Frisbee hard to catch, so Mateo launched a gentle throw. Mav intercepted, but then slipped in the mud, taking two kids down with him.

"Everyone okay?" Mateo asked.

The kids jumped back up, muddier and laughing harder than before. The rain beat down steadily, but everyone was warmed by the activity, by the fun and camaraderie of the impromptu game.

He had time for one more catch. Just one more.

"Whoa! I gotta get cleaned up," Vander said out of nowhere, checking Tate's watch. "Harlow's gonna be here in ten minutes."

Mateo froze. If Harlow was going to be here in ten minutes, so was Luci. How late was it?

"Okay kids, we gotta get back to the hotel. Get ourselves cleaned up before—" He was on the verge of saying *before Luci gets back*, but managed to stop himself. They hadn't done anything wrong, and so long as kids toweled off and left their shoes outside, it would be fine.

And even if they did track mud through the building, Raquel had that industrial-strength vacuum she was always boasting about.

He corralled the kids off the field and into the courtyard, then instructed them to take off their shoes and wait until he could return with towels.

Mateo ran into the hotel, wet hair still dripping water into his eyes. He sprinted to the linen closet, where he was reminded that all they had were white towels. *Oh, well.* A few stained towels were well worth the price of the fun they'd had. He grabbed a stack and headed back to the courtyard.

He got there right as Aida, Willa, Harlow and Luci entered.

Luci stared, horror-struck at the mass of muddy, dripping kids.

"I'm definitely getting Little Orphan Annie vibes," Harlow remarked.

Greg gave himself a good shake, then trotted over to Aida. "Looks like you and Tate had fun," she said, then flexed up on her toes to kiss Tate's cheek.

Luci made eye contact with Mateo and shook her head, as though he'd personally covered each kid in mud.

They were back to square one. Again.

"Towel off, kids," Mateo called, ignoring Luci. "You've got plenty of time to shower. Dinner's going to be a little late today."

"You don't have dinner started?" Luci asked.

"Nope," he answered, not looking at her. The afternoon had been fun, a great bonding experience, and he was not sorry.

He saw Harlow greet Vander, placing her hands on both sides of his muddy, wet face to kiss him. That was what Mateo was looking for in a relationship—someone who could love him even in a mess.

Not a woman who turned up her nose at anyone who didn't steam their sweaters.

"Students, please get showered up," Luci called, frustration barely concealed in her voice. "I need help getting dinner started so as soon as you're finished, head down to the kitchen."

"I'm going in to start dinner now," Mateo said.

"You need to shower first," she said crisply. "I'll do it."

"No, it's my turn."

Luci ignored him, following the students into the hotel.

Mateo reached out to grab her arm but stopped before he could get mud on her sweater.

She crossed her arms and faced him.

"I don't know what I did wrong here, Luci. I can tell you're mad, but I can't come up with any moral issue with playing Frisbee."

"You were supposed to have dinner started."

"Well, I don't. We were having fun."

"Yeah. I see that. Glad *you* had fun. Now, I'm going to do your job and then clean up a muddy hotel."

"*I* will start dinner, and the kids can clean up after themselves."

Color rose to her face, like her emotions were so intense she couldn't even speak to him. One minute everything was fine, and the next he'd committed some crime he didn't even know about. It was a lot like St Xavier's, where there was always someone waiting to catch you out for a rule you weren't following correctly.

"It's just mud, Luci." Mateo held eye contact with her. "It's not alcohol, or drugs. It's not a social-media addiction. It's not a mental-health crisis. In fact, it may well be the antidote to those things. I'm not going to apologize for having fun playing Frisbee with our students. Dinner's gonna be a little late, but if I had this afternoon to do over, I wouldn't change a thing."

Luci swallowed and dropped her gaze. Then she walked around him, calling after the kids. Mateo glanced up at the sky as the rain began to fall again.

CHAPTER NINE

"Ms. WALKER, why do I have to chop the onions?" Ilsa asked.

Luci pressed her lips together. It was the fifth why-do-I-have-to question in the last five minutes, and the urge to yell *Because I said so!* was strong.

"Because we're making minestrone for dinner, and it won't taste right without sautéed onions."

"I hate chopping onions," she complained.

"Well, we've got fifteen other people living here, so the next fifteen times we need onions, you get a pass."

Ilsa grumbled, but she kept chopping.

Luci could empathize. She was mad. Steaming mad. Sizzling-onion mad. Logically, she understood she needed to regulate these feelings. Mateo had chosen to play Frisbee with the kids, which had resulted in them making a mess. It wasn't a crisis. So he hadn't gotten the meal started like he was supposed to. It wasn't like he'd skipped town.

But she was furious, anyway. Mad at him for making her unreasonably mad. Disappointed in herself for caring that he made her mad.

To the girls at Breasely-Wentmore, emotional regulation was an art form. Her classmates had been raised to be cool and in control. Growing up at Open Hearts, Luci had been encouraged to feel deeply, and share every passing emotion. A middle ground had to exist, but for the life of her, Luci couldn't find it.

And her go-to in these situations was to hold it together, not show or feel anything, until the emotions stacked up precariously, one overlaying the next until one wrong word could send them scattering. An unstable, teetering tower of hurt, frustration and insecurity.

Her feelings swayed precariously as Mateo came jogging into the room, showered, gorgeous, with a bright smile, as he asked, "How can I help?"

Help?

Here she was, doing his prep work, on his day, and he wanted to know how he could help her do his work?

"I've got it," she said.

His expression fell, as though he was disappointed to find that one smile wasn't enough to turn everything around.

"Ms. Walker, is this enough?" Ilsa asked.

"Not quite. I put out four onions. Please chop all four."

Mateo stepped close to her and spoke quietly. That wasn't helpful, because for whatever reason the inexpensive soap they got at Mac's smelled really good on him.

"Luci, I'm sorry. I know it was my day to prep, and it still is. You go take a break."

"I've *got* it."

She met his gaze, conveying a frank reminder

that they didn't argue in front of students, and if he kept this up, that's where they were headed. Around them, the students continued to complain about having to help out.

"Kids, stop griping," Mateo said.

"They wouldn't be griping if we had a set schedule and they'd known in advance they'd be prepping dinner," Luci said quietly.

"I agree, it would be easier if we had a schedule regarding who is helping when. But they still wouldn't be prepping because that's my job."

"But you didn't do it, because you were busy being the fun teacher. Now, I'm mean ol' Ms. Walker, making everyone work."

"Again, I could be doing this on my own."

"If we wanted to eat at eleven o'clock at night, sure."

"What's my job?" Mav seemed to appear right in between them, his head drooping next to theirs. *That kid.*

"How'd you get cleaned up?" Luci asked.

Mav looked down at himself, as though surprised to find he was clean.

"I showered."

He had showered like everyone else, but unlike everyone else he didn't have an extra set of clothes. He wore a pair of Antonio's sweatpants that were both too large and too short, and Ilsa's Dutch national team soccer jersey, for some orange.

Mateo turned to him with his bright, easy smile.

"Dude, you don't live here. You don't have to help, or even be here right now."

Mav's shoulders slumped, his lanky form folding like a blade of grass protecting a seed head in a rainstorm. Luci did not want to snap at Mateo, not again. She knew she was being unreasonable about the Frisbee game.

But how did he not see the effect his words had on Mav?

Sure, the kid didn't live there. And yeah, they had their hands full. They didn't need another kid around. But Mav needed *them*.

"Your job is to help me reach the upper cabinets," she said, walking past Mateo and pointing to a cabinet she'd never been able to reach and had no idea what was inside. "I'm not sure where they keep the soup plates."

"What's a soup plate?" Mav asked. "And what's wrong with a regular bowl?"

"I want to use soup plates. Please check for me."

Luci had Mav opening and closing cabinets, which added to the turmoil of teens attempting to cook a dinner Mateo should have gotten started this afternoon.

Luci kept her chin high as she directed the mayhem. Mateo didn't leave the room.

"Ms. Walker, what do you want with the carrots?" Antonio asked.

"Leave them over here and I'll—"

"What are these?" Mav picked up a dainty champagne coupe by its stem.

"Those are—"

"We could eat soup out of those," Oliver suggested.

"No, I think we'll—" Luci began.

"Can I dump the carrots in this pot?" Antonio asked.

"In a moment, but first we need to—"

"No way!" Ilsa cried. "You can't eat soup out of a champagne glass."

"Technically you can," Mav countered.

Luci turned back to Antonio, who was now receiving a lesson in sautéing carrots from Mateo. She glared at her coworker. He held her gaze.

The scent of sautéed vegetables filled the room. Kids chattered away, and Luci kept herself as far from Mateo as she could while still making soup. The tension slowly dissipated.

She ducked into the pantry, searching for shell pasta. He followed.

"What was that about?"

Luci kept her eyes on the dry goods, attempting to sound nonchalant. "What was what about?"

"With Mav. We have too many students as it is, the afternoon is already chaotic and you suggest Mav stick around and get in everyone's way?"

"The afternoon didn't have to be chaotic," she reminded him.

"Well, it was. And I don't regret it. And for the tenth time, you don't have to be here cooking right now. It's my night."

She grabbed a box of pasta off the shelf, gripping it tightly enough that the cardboard crumpled.

"You can be mad if you want. I won't stop you and goodness knows I wouldn't be successful if I tried. But what is your deal with Mav?"

"There is no deal. He's a kid who needs a place to be right now."

Behind them Luci could hear Mav practicing Dutch words with Ilsa. It was fun to watch their friendship grow and see Ilsa expand his understanding of the world.

"It's not just Mav. It's all the kids from the commune."

"It's not a commune, it's an intentional community."

"See, like that," Mateo said. "Why are you so good with those kids?"

"They're not *those kids*. They're kids." Luci looked sharply at Mateo. "I hope I'm good with all my students."

Luci walked past him and set the pasta on the counter next to the soup pot. Her tower of emotions wobbled, the pain of tears pricked the back of her eyes. Another minute in this room and she was going to embarrass herself as her emotions would spill all over the floor, flooding the unsuspecting people around her with her frustration.

She couldn't continue like this. They had three months of running a dormitory together, and she had to find a better way to deal with her frustration than focusing it on the man she was supposed to be working with.

Luci closed her eyes briefly, then managed to lift her chin and walk out of the room, leaving the meal and the teenagers to Mateo.

MATEO GLANCED INTO the lobby again, where all eleven kids were sprawled out watching a movie. Aida was there, too, along with Greg, who was sound asleep across the laps of Cece, Ilsa and Suleiman.

No one was getting into any trouble tonight. Except for him.

Mateo shook his head.

What was good about today?

A rowdy game of Ultimate Frisbee in the mud.

He had fun.

The kids felt more connected with each other, and their teachers, after the game.

It wore everyone out.

Mateo sighed, stepping over Antonio as he headed into the courtyard. Luci would be there, watching her hedgehogs have a ramble. Hopefully, she'd be in a mood to talk and they could work this out.

But her getting mad when he didn't meet all her expectations, all the time, couldn't continue. Her anger tonight had been hurtful, and it was made worse because she wouldn't talk about it.

From the courtyard, he could hear Vander strumming his guitar. The notes would float from the hotel, throughout Pronghorn, as a signal to every-one that they could relax and unwind now.

The music relaxed Mateo, too. He stepped confidently into the courtyard, ready to talk whatever this was out with Luci.

There he found Vander, four hedgehogs and no social studies teacher.

"Where's Luci?"

Vander kept playing as he nodded to the arched entrance into the courtyard. "She's outside. I think she wants to talk to you."

Mateo buried his face in his palms. She should be sipping tea, watching her spiny little creatures forage for the food she intentionally planted for them. Instead, she was outside, probably getting madder by the minute at him for something he didn't know he was supposed to be doing in the first place.

"I've got an eye on the hedgehogs," Vander said, as though unsupervised hedgehogs were the issue.

"Thanks, great. I'm gonna go find Luci."

Mateo headed out to the street. Luci sat on the steps, framed by the roses blooming around the archway, watching the sun as it slipped toward the horizon. The rain had dried up as quickly as it had appeared, leaving its fresh scent mingling with the sagebrush.

"Hi, Luci."

She looked up. Unreadable emotions flickered through her eyes, then she patted the step next to her and returned her gaze to the horizon. Vander's music drifted out, a soundtrack to the fiery sunset over the Coyote Hills.

She kept her eyes on the riot of color in the sky. The rain clouds had passed over and brightened as they emptied, intensifying the outrageous beauty of the evening.

Finally, Luci spoke. "You like honesty, right?"

"Yep. I like honesty. I like people telling me what I've done to make them mad."

Her eyes flickered in his direction. "I have trouble relaxing."

Mateo leaned forward, elbows resting on his knees. That wasn't a major revelation.

"I can't relax when there's clutter, or a mess, or if I have grading left. I prefer to get everything finished, then I can relax."

Mateo opened his mouth to question her, to tell her to just let things be.

"I'm sorry I lost it about the mud today," she continued. "I really regret it. I was wrong, and I'm sorry I snapped at you."

Mateo blinked, surprised by the wash of relief he felt.

"I'm sorry I didn't get dinner started," he said.

She nodded, hearing him, but still not looking at him. "Thanks. Although it sounds like you all had a lot of fun. And you're right. It's not drugs or social-media addiction. It makes sense that you chose to continue the game."

"Thank you for...getting that."

They sat in silence for a moment, eyes on the horizon. A herd of pronghorn antelope picked their way across the open land beyond the school.

"They're back," she said. "I love it when they come home."

Mateo turned a questioning look on her. This was their first spring in Pronghorn, the first time the antelope had come back on her watch.

"Can you see the babies?" She pointed.

Mateo scanned the herd, dark outlines of animals against the glowing sunset. Little ones teetered on thin legs next to their mammas.

"This is gorgeous," he said.

She gestured to the sun. "Sometimes I can't even believe how beautiful it is, you know? Like how is a sunset so beautiful?"

He nodded, watching the pink and gold light play across her face.

"I love the evening light," he said.

She turned to him, shocked. Then quickly mastered her expression and said, "Yeah. Me, too."

After another moment, she pulled in a deep breath. "You appreciate honesty. I thrive with order. I like to know what's expected, I like having a plan. I had expectations of you, and a plan for my afternoon when I returned here. I didn't react well when things didn't unfold the way I thought they would." She finally looked at him. "It felt like I didn't get to do what I wanted, because you had gone ahead and done what you wanted."

Whoa. That hadn't even occurred to him.

"Luci, I'm so sorry. I didn't think about it that

way." He paused, then tried to articulate his concerns. "But you didn't have to start dinner. You could have gone ahead and done whatever you were going to do."

She nodded. "I know. But the kids would have been hungry if they'd had to wait. I don't like chaos and there are few things more chaotic than hungry teenagers."

"Okay. I hear you, and this won't happen again."

She looked up, her pretty blue eyes connecting with his. "Thanks. And when it does, I'll try to react differently."

He laughed. She smiled. The connection they'd felt their first day of graduate school glimmered between them.

"I can be a little like a hedgehog," she admitted.

What, cute and funny? Up at night being busy when everyone else was asleep?

His face must have shown his confusion because Luci continued, "I throw up my defenses, fold in on myself when I feel threatened. That's not a great communication style and I know it."

Mateo resettled his elbows on his knees. "You wouldn't need to worry about your communication style if I wasn't always making a mess of things."

"I don't get off the hook that easily," she said. "We'll just keep…getting better. How does that sound?"

"It sounds great." He gazed at her, the rush of relief giving way to the attraction and respect that always rumbled so close to the surface when he was with her. "What, uh…what was it you had planned for the afternoon?"

"I was going to hang up my outfits for the week and make sure everything was steamed and ready to go."

"Steaming sweaters was your Sunday, fun-day plan?"

She nodded, a spark of mischief in her eyes. "I love getting my outfits in order."

"Is that why you always look so—" Mateo stopped himself before he could say *beautiful*, scrambling for a more appropriate word "—put-together?"

"I guess so. I also appreciate having the right clothes. I like my clothes. It's fun."

"Where do you shop?" he asked. "You have this endless stream of preppy clothing, but Mac's selection consists of work gloves and ball caps."

"It's a secret," she said.

"What, you're afraid I'm going to steal your source and run them out of argyle before you get there?"

She laughed, then gazed at him for a moment. "You want to know?"

"Yes. This is the first and only time I've ever been curious about where a person gets her clothing."

She scanned the empty street, as though there were informants lying in wait to hear her secrets. Her eyes landed on Connie.

"It's a service. When I first got to boarding school, I didn't have the right clothes. One of the other scholarship girls told me about this woman in Boston who puts together boxes of preworn clothing. It's all the right brands, high-end but not too flashy. She has my size, knows the things I like and I've been buying a few boxes a year ever since." She grinned at him. "Now, you know my secret."

"It's a cool secret. I like it."

She pulled off her glasses and retrieved a chamois cloth from her pocket, then began earnestly wiping at an imperceptible smudge.

Mateo let the facts about Luci marinate. She was a scholarship kid, which she'd mentioned before but he'd never really bought it. She ordered and wore secondhand clothing.

She was brilliant. Far and away, the star of their education program at U of O. She was creative.

She'd come here, to this tiny town where she taught, as though her life depended on it. Or someone else's life.

Going for casual, he asked, "So what's your boarding-school story? Did your parents send you away or did you want to go?"

Her gaze connected with his, eyes momentarily exposed. Then she slipped her glasses back on.

"What's *your* boarding-school story?" she asked.

"I asked you first."

"I just told you my deep dark secret."

"No one's deep dark secret includes blue striped sweaters."

"Those are called Breton stripes, and since you

are literally the only person who knows, it totally counts."

Mateo furrowed his brow. "I'm the only person who knows?"

"Well, you and the woman who fulfills my orders."

"You didn't even tell Aida?"

"The only conversations Aida and I have about clothing are interventions."

Mateo nodded. He suspected Luci had a great many secrets, but he liked being in on this one. Maybe the way to get her to open up was to open up himself.

"I don't have a deep dark secret, because I don't like secrets. My boarding-school experience was terrible."

"Did your parents send you?"

"They did. I come from a military family, going way back. It was expected." Mateo ran his hands through his hair. "At first, I was excited to get out of the house. My parents are amazing. They're both military officers—tough, smart people who believe in service to community and country. But they didn't have time for a lot of nonsense."

"And your feelings on nonsense as a kid?"

"I was a big fan."

Luci's Shakespearean fairy smile snuck out. "I can imagine."

"I thought boarding school was going to be a blast," Mateo admitted.

"I have to be honest, those water fights sounded superfun."

He chuckled. "They could be. I had a few good times. But St. Xavier's was a terrible environment to grow up in. The thing I'm still upset about is how easily I fell into the same patterns as everyone else. I was there, I had a pack of friends and I just went along. Everything about the system indicated it was okay to lie, steal, cheat and blame others. And if you didn't, you got a reputation as a chump. Underage drinking was normalized, which compounded the problems. It's easy to be stupid when you're under the influence. It's easy to pretend what you did was okay when you can drink and not think about it."

"What did you do?"

"Sorry?"

"What was it you did, that you still feel so bad about?"

He chuckled uncomfortably. "Wow. You zeroed in on that one pretty quick."

She gazed at him. "It fits. You're a good guy, patient, kind. You would be far more upset about hurting someone else than you would be about someone hurting you."

Her observation rubbed at the sharp edges of the uncomfortable memory. It was true, he was ashamed of how easily he let himself join in the roving packs of bullies.

"I just went along with it all. I laughed at the kids we targeted. While I am ashamed of specifics, it's the whole picture that makes my stomach turn."

He shook off the memory. When he glanced up, Luci was leaning toward him, her blue eyes full of sympathy. It struck him that her eyes were the same color as the Pronghorn sky just before sunset.

"It's amazing how we are shaped by our surroundings, isn't it?" she asked. "We don't even realize the subtle pressure until we walk away."

He nodded.

"I hope we can provide our students with an environment where the culture is uplifting and encouraging. I'm not saying we won't have our problems. These are teenagers."

"Amen." He nodded.

"But we've done a pretty good job so far this year. All evidence points to us continuing on this trajectory."

"Okay, let's start with us." Mateo leaned toward her. "The adults in the room need to be on the same page."

"We do," she acknowledged.

"You thrive with order, I thrive with flexibility, honesty and information."

Luci leaned back, propped her elbows on the step behind her and crossed her legs. Casually, she flagged a hand between them. "So when I get mad and refuse to speak to you, that's *not* working?"

He laughed. "It's about as effective as me being unwilling to sit down with you and come up with some basic rules before the dormitory opened."

She smiled in acknowledgement. "Then let's

come up with a strategy. For the next time this happens."

Mateo's first instinct was to say it wasn't going to happen again. His second instinct was to say they could solve issues in the moment, as they arrived.

So it took a minute, but finally his third, and correct, instinct was to listen to Luci. She wanted a plan. The only problem was he had no idea what that would look like.

She waited for him to speak, then shook her head. "Maybe we should google ideas? Or ask ChatGPT how to get along?"

Her smile was so pretty, Mateo couldn't help flipping back to his previous page. "But, it *won't* happen in this way again, because we're gonna come up with some rules for this barrel of monkeys."

Delight lit up her face. "You want to figure it out right now?"

He did want to talk now. He wanted to talk all night long. But this was what always happened with Luci. Their relationship seesawed back and forth, and that wasn't good for him. She needed a strategy to deal with him, and he needed one to keep from falling for her.

They could set up a time to talk the next day, when they weren't bathed in the glow of the setting sun, stars beginning to appear overhead. When he wasn't feeling his crush return like a tidal wave over his heart.

"Right now, I was hoping to spell you on dormitory duties so you can go get your clothes ready for the week."

A glimmer of mixed emotions flickered across her face. Then she grinned. "But when will you plan *your* outfits? Because those sweatshirts aren't going to wrinkle themselves."

"Actually they are going to wrinkle themselves. That's the one thing a sweatshirt is capable of."

Her laugh rang out, warming Mateo, drawing him closer to her. "I'll fly uncharted for the week to come. But what about us?"

She pulled her head back at the inclusive pronoun. Mateo explained himself quickly. "What about us, as in, when are we going to plan out some rules for this crew?"

"Um. How about Wednesday after school? That will give us a couple of days to think about it."

"Sounds good. I'll bring the spreadsheet."

"Really?"

He'd been joking, but didn't want to let her down now. "Sure."

He held out a hand to shake on it. She slipped her fingers into his. The crush washed through his chest, tossing his heart in a wave of warmth and unwarranted hope. Notes from Vander's guitar, romantic and timeless, floated on the breeze, like the rose petals loosened by the afternoon's rain.

Mateo reacted on instinct, turning her hand in his, raising it to his lips like he was some kind of knight from her history books, ready to slay the dragon of unstructured dorm life for her.

She blinked, surprised. Then smiled, her face alight and happy in the setting sun. "Are you trying to charm me into a meeting to establish norms?"

He grinned back, keeping hold of her hand. "I wouldn't dream of it."

A flicker of vulnerability crossed Luci's face. Then she dropped her hand and stood abruptly.

"Thanks. I'm gonna grab the hedgies and—"

Mateo stood as well, shoving his hands in his pockets. "Yeah, I'll go see about the kids—" He gestured with his thumb in the wrong direction. "You take off, with the sweaters." He gave an awkward wave and finally managed to say, "Have fun steaming!"

"You know it. I'll be back at nine forty-five to help get the kids upstairs."

Luci remained in place, the evening breeze ruffling her ponytail for an instant. Mateo didn't move, either. A fresh wash of rose petals floated around them onto the cracked sidewalk.

"Okay." She spun and headed into the courtyard as Mateo said, "Right. See you later," while walking into the courtyard next to her.

He made a point of talking to Vander, who simply gave him a sly grin as he continued to play the guitar. Hedgehogs in tow, Luci slipped from the courtyard, leaving Mateo with the beginning of a plan.

CHAPTER TEN

"GOODBYE, MATEO! See you in two hours." Neveah waved as she headed out of his classroom on her way to rehearsal.

"Nice work today!" he called back from the doorway. Neveah joined her friends and together they flowed into the library.

He glanced across the hall at Luci's classroom. Through her open door, he could hear her talking with a student.

Mateo switched off the lamps he'd set up at each student worktable, until the room was only illuminated by the afternoon sunlight streaming through the windows. That unidentifiable spark of anticipation stirred within him. Or maybe he *could* identify it, but he was choosing not to at this moment. Across the hall, Luci continued to work with her student. Mateo shuffled a few papers on his desk. He'd managed to wait until after school to present his spreadsheet to Luci, but it hadn't been easy.

Not that an Excel sheet with three columns was something to write home about. But he'd thought long and hard over the last few days about a strategy to ensure he and Luci got along. It was a simple start to a complex problem, but it might just work.

He didn't even need to resort to AI for the answers. A glance at the clock told him school had been over for a full twenty minutes. Most kids had already headed out to other activities. Vander was directing a student-written play. Somehow, Tate managed to run spring soccer and Ultimate Frisbee simultaneously. He could probably even fit track *or* field in there if he had a mind to.

Voices continued to emanate from Luci's classroom. Mateo was not impatient by nature, but he'd been waiting to show her this since eleven thirty last night. He grabbed his computer and strode across the hallway to the open door.

"But I get so nervous," Sylvie said. "Why can't I give the presentation to you after school?"

"It's okay to be nervous," Luci said. "In fact, it can be good to be nervous. Challenging ourselves with new things is part of life."

"But what if I mess up?"

"Then you mess up. I mess up all the time in front of class."

Sylvie scoffed. Mateo wasn't sure he'd buy that from Luci, either.

"I do," Luci said. "I make mistakes, I forget the word I'm looking for, sometimes I mix numbers up, I forget where I put papers."

"But you're a teacher. You're used to being in front of people."

"I'm used to it, but it still makes me nervous. I'm nervous every morning before school and before class starts. I'm worried I'm not prepared enough, or someone won't like my lesson, or Pronghorn antelope will get into the school and Vander won't be on hand to help me get rid of them."

Sylvie managed to smile, but it faded as she said, "What if I get a bad grade because I freeze up and can't talk?"

Luci handed her a piece of paper with one of her intricate grading rubrics on it. "If you look at the score sheet, you'll see you've already earned nearly full credit before you've even gotten to the presentation of knowledge. Your research was impeccable, that's ten points. Your slideshow is clear and easy to follow, eight points there. You've done your revisions. You could get the lowest possible score on the actual presentation and still get an A."

It was *such* a Luci assignment, challenging for the kids, but with enough scaffolding so everyone could succeed. Then, of course, Luci checked and rechecked their preparation to make sure they were *going* to succeed before they stood in front of their peers.

Mateo leaned against the doorframe. Luci glanced up and smiled at him, then refocused on Sylvie. "Learning to get comfortable being nervous is one of the most important skills you can develop. And your social studies class, with eight people who all like you, is the perfect place to practice. Plus, everyone is stoked about your topic. Social movements and fashion? That's awesome."

Sylvie let out a breath. "Okay."

"Okay?"

"But can I go first tomorrow? To get it over with?"

"Absolutely. Now, you'd better get to rehearsal."

"Thank you." Sylvie turned away from Luci and headed to the door. Mateo stepped aside to let her pass but Sylvie spun back around. "No, wait, can I go second?"

"Sure," Luci said.

"Thanks, Ms. Walker. I'll see you tonight!"

Luci's patient expression faltered. "You will?"

"My dad and Sheriff Weston are supervising at the hotel, so the teachers can go out to The Restaurant."

"But it's not Thursday."

"I think Angie wanted you to come tonight. There's something new on the menu." Sylvie nibbled at the strings of her hoodie.

"Okay then! Wednesday at The Restaurant it is." Luci's gaze met Mateo's, her eyes widening at this unexpected gift. "Awesome, I'll see you tonight."

"'Bye, Mateo!" Sylvie skipped from the room and headed down the hall to the library.

Mateo remained in the doorframe, gazing at Luci. She looked particularly *Luci* today, in a white skirt, a spring green sweater with a collared pink shirt underneath. Not a wrinkle or smudge in sight. Perfect.

"What's up?" she asked.

"Oh. I have a thing to show you." Mateo straightened and took a few steps into her room, then gestured toward Sylvie. "That was impressive."

"Just a pep talk." She tried to contain a smile as she leaned against her desk. "For a student who is late to play rehearsal because she's nervous about getting up in front of her classmates."

A spark lit her eye and Mateo grinned at the irony of the situation.

"It doesn't make her feelings any less real," she acknowledged.

"That's the thing about feelings. They're real even when they don't make sense."

She widened her eyes in acknowledgement, then glanced at the spreadsheet open on his computer screen.

"What's that?"

Mateo walked farther into the room. Student-made posters lined the walls, along with history memes and inspiring quotes. The room was lively, like her classes. Like her.

"I've been working on a plan for our students at the hotel." He held out the open laptop. "We don't have to use this, but I thought it could be a jumping-off point."

Luci's eyebrows knit. Her hands trembled a little as she reached out to take the computer, like she wasn't sure what he'd come up with this time. Mateo has been up late the night before, trying to combine Luci's desire for clear rules with his need for flexibility.

"I came up with three formulas, then examples of application."

"Nice math metaphor."

"I needed something to get me started."

Luci studied the three color-coded sections: respect yourself, respect others, respect the environment. He pointed to an application column.

"'Respect yourself' covers areas like curfew, lights out and study hours."

She nodded, brow still furrowed as she read.

"'Respect others,'" she read aloud, then pointed to the screen. "Is this a schedule for helping with meals?"

"It is, and I included ideas for looking out for one another. But I think we need to add more there."

She nodded, then pointed to an application of "respect the environment." "This is the cleaning schedule?"

"Yeah." He leaned against the desk so they could study the screen together. Not so he could be closer to her or smell the lemony shampoo she used. "What more should we add? And how do you want to handle consequences? Sorry, backing up. Are you okay with what I've got here so far?"

Luci drew the screen closer, reading in silence. Mateo was a little worried, so he kept talking.

"By having broad guidelines, we can loop in other applications as needed," he explained. "But it also gives us flexibility. Say one of the students has a big presentation in their social studies class the next day—doing well on it falls under respect for self. So if they need to exchange their cleanup duty with someone else, that's okay. And it saves us from situations where students might lie about being sick, or sneak away early to get out of cleaning."

Luci lowered the computer and stared at him, her

blue eyes bright and serious. "This is a masterpiece. This is the Sistine Chapel of house rules."

Mateo grinned. "You like it?"

"I like it more than I like the Napoleonic Code, and that's my favorite." She gazed down at the screen again.

"You're a big fan of the Napoleonic Code?"

"You aren't?"

"I guess I never really thought about it."

"Well, you should, it's still used as the basis for law in Louisiana."

"I'll keep that in mind the next time I'm at Mardi Gras."

Her shoulder brushed his and the sense of anticipation kicked up again. How had he never noticed how warm and inviting her room felt?

Luci exhaled, then glanced into his eyes. "Why don't we—" She paused, and pulled in a breath as though to strengthen herself. "Why don't we present this to the students, and ask for their feedback and ideas, then ratify it."

"Like wishy-squishy group norms?"

She laughed. "Just like that."

He pressed his lips together, trying to contain a smile that threatened to take over this whole body.

"Thank you," she said.

He nodded to accept her gratitude, but felt compelled to remind her of the truth. "I should have sat down with you the day we agreed to this and come up with a plan."

"The day we agreed to this, the hotel was overrun

with community members, one of whom I was threatening with a Good Vibes sign," she reminded him.

"The next day, then."

She smiled in acknowledgement. "Look, I get it. You were raised in a world where rules were about appearance, rather than substance. I wouldn't like rules, either, if I were you."

Mateo soaked in her understanding. "What about you?"

"What about me, what?"

"I don't know as much about your background," he said.

She looked directly into his eyes. The spark that sometimes raced between them was now doing laps. For the first time he felt like she might open up. Then she flickered one eyebrow and said, "Yep."

He chuckled. "I just wish I understood where you were coming from."

"I don't mean to be mysterious. In fact, I'd love it if I were the least mysterious person you knew."

Making that comment was about the last way to shed her air of mystery. But she didn't have to tell him a thing about her background if she didn't want to. What she needed was to know he was ready to work with her, and if he had to change to do that, he would.

That meant it was finally time to bring up the issue he hadn't been prepared to tackle the night before.

Mateo stared hard at the carpet as he said, "Sometimes I hurt your feelings, and I don't know what I've done."

She swallowed and nodded. "I know."

"I don't want to hurt you. But I don't know how not to."

"It's not always your fault," she said. "I get tangled up and I say the wrong things."

"*I* say the wrong things," he reminded her.

"But you don't mean to. You have impeccable manners. You make everyone feel comfortable."

"We're not talking about everyone, we're talking about *you*."

She raised her chin and looked directly into his eyes. Telling her how pretty she was didn't seem like the best way to make it through this tough spot, but dang, it was hard not to.

Mateo retrained his eyes on a poster detailing the Algerian independence movement. "You remember that one time, at the U of O, when you made a comment about how the class needed to have open and engaged dialogue and I laughed because I thought you were joking, but you weren't?"

Her face clouded. She tucked a lock of hair behind her ear and looked away. Aaaaand he'd stuck his foot in it, again.

"Okay, good example, I'm saying the wrong thing right now."

She shook her head. "I was just embarrassed. You're right, it sounds ridiculous."

"It sounds like something Today's Moment would say in a school-board meeting. It's not ridiculous, it's just not very Luci Walker."

Luci stood abruptly, keeping her face turned away

from him. "I'm overly sensitive. I know that. It's not your fault, nor is it your problem to solve."

"Upsetting you *is* my fault. When I hurt your feelings, it's my fault and I don't want to do it."

She gestured to the computer. "This formula for behavior management is fantastic. Thank you so much."

"Don't change the subject."

"I'm taking us back to the original subject," she countered. "You're the subject changer around here."

Mateo kept focused. "Can you, maybe, promise me that when I say or do the wrong thing you'll tell me? That way I can at least apologize."

She was still, as though weighing her options. Finally, she rolled her eyes. "Sure. I can promise some good old-fashioned 'open and engaged dialogue.' Can we get back to this math-formula rule-system situation now? It's fabulous."

Mateo mulled over the incident in graduate school. The more he thought about it, the more it sounded almost word for word like something Today's Moment would say, or had actually said.

He studied Luci again. "Did you know about Open Hearts before we moved to Pronghorn?"

"Did I know about a random intentional community in the least populated region of Oregon?" she scoffed.

He was upsetting her again. "I made you mad just now. And you sidestepping the issue is frustrating me."

She blinked, then looked up at him.

"You're right. I'm closing in on myself and we agreed that's no good. Maybe you and I need some ground rules, too?"

"You suggested a strategy," he reminded her. "I think a good start would be to assume positive intent. I don't ever want to hurt you or make you angry."

She smiled at him. "That's nice."

"It's true."

"Okay, same. And I don't want you to feel like I disrespect you, because I don't. You're a really good person and the best teacher I've ever seen. You've got everyone around here loving math and feeling confident. I don't know how you do it. Or rather, I do know, but how you have the patience for it is beyond me."

Mateo stared at Luci. It hadn't occurred to him that she even noticed his work.

"That's good. Assume positive intent." She leaned against her desk next to him again. "I was also thinking, if we do start to get mad at each other, we could list the good things about our situations, like you do."

"Great idea."

She squared her shoulders with mock pride. "Thank you. It fits with our school motto—"

"It could be worse," Mateo finished with her.

Luci gazed at the carpet, a smile playing around her lips. "Do you want to know something about me?"

"Yes." He wanted to know everything about her.

"Okay. Um. Worst boarding-school moment?"

"Sure. That's a good place to start."

"Assuming, of course, you have positive intent and won't use the information for your own nefarious purposes."

"While I'm curious about the type of nefarious purposes one might use your information for, you can trust me. I don't know anything about your past. I can name specific people who were on Tate's third-grade basketball team and I don't even know if you have siblings."

She gave a small laugh. "I don't have any siblings that I know of."

He let her words sit, giving her a chance to explain further because that was *not* how most people would answer that question. But she didn't seem to realize there was anything odd about it and continued with her original track.

"I did my best to fly under the radar at Breasely-Wentmore, and I was good at it. Participate just enough in class, be nice without attracting friendships."

Mateo nodded. The scholarship kids at St. Xavier tended to be extraordinary athletes, recruited to keep their teams returning to state meets year after year. They were roped into cliques and left alone by the teachers.

"Anyway, I had really bad teeth. By that point in life I'd learned about braces, but the idea of a dentist, much less an orthodontist, was so far from my experience. It never occurred to me that I could have good teeth, any more than it would occur to me now that I could be gorgeous like Harlow."

Mateo started to contradict her. She was every bit as beautiful as Harlow. More appealing, in his eyes. But that wasn't the conversation they were here to have.

"There was this upperclassman, Meredith, who was always so nice to me. From day one, she was kind. She helped me figure things out, let me know which teachers were the best, gave me tips on how to plan for graduation. I admired her and was grateful for her kindness."

"What happened?" Mateo asked. "Was she setting you up for a prank? Did she want you to be her little henchman and take the fall for her when she pranked someone else?"

"No, nothing like that. Breasely-Wentmore really did *not* prank the way you all did at St. Xavier's. I'm still kind of stuck on the bagpipes."

"It was horrible," Mateo reminded her.

"I'll take your word for it." She ran her tongue over her now-perfect teeth. "One day, Meredith pulled me aside and, very kindly, pointed out my bad teeth. She explained that people would never take me seriously with crooked teeth. I was shocked, and ashamed. I didn't know what I was supposed to do about it. She was all 'get braces,' and I foolishly asked if I could get them at the school nurse's office." She looked him in the eye. "I didn't know how a person got braces—that's how naive I was."

Mateo had a lot of questions about the first fifteen years of her life before she had this conversation. But he needed to listen and let her share what she was comfortable sharing.

"Two weeks later, the president of Breasely-Wentmore called me into her office. It was this big, gorgeous room with books and beautiful furniture, and windows overlooking the whole campus. The president was sitting with Meredith and her parents. Everyone was so nice. I couldn't figure out why we were there. I shook hands like I'd been taught to, but I didn't want to speak at all because I was afraid I'd say the wrong thing. Plus, Meredith had mentioned how bad my teeth were so I didn't want to open my mouth and show them my horrible smile."

Mateo tried to picture what she would have looked like. The same ski-jump nose, the same dimple. Maybe less confidence, which would break his heart to see.

"Then the president informed me that Meredith's family was going to pay for me to get braces. They'd already found an orthodontist nearby, and my first appointment was on Friday. I was confused. Like why did they care, and why was the president in on it? I was searching for all the clues I could find in their body language and conversation to explain why these random people were fixing my teeth, and why we were all taking up the president's valuable time as they told me about it. Everyone seemed to be holding their breath, waiting for me to say the right thing. At a loss, I thanked them."

She paused, staring ahead as though she was still

sitting in that office. Mateo nodded to show her he was interested, fascinated.

"I could tell immediately that's what they were waiting for. The president smiled at me so I laid it on a little more thickly. I said I never thought I'd get braces and was really happy. I explained that Meredith had suggested it, but I didn't know how to make it happen. Then Meredith's dad looked at his daughter with pride and patted her hand. That's when it hit me. They were buying me orthodontia, not because they cared about my teeth, or me, but so they could feel good about themselves. I was Meredith's service project. I don't know if you've ever felt that, like someone is helping you to alleviate their own guilt at their privilege. It's a weird position to be in. I needed braces. I was excited to have beautiful teeth like Meredith and the other girls. But the price was to grovel in gratitude before these people."

"I can't imagine you groveling," he admitted.

"I'm not very good at it. In fact, I needed help. Over the years, the president herself made sure I was writing thank-you notes, and she sent Meredith's parents pictures of my emerging smile. She did it because if they felt good, they would keep donating money to the school. The president groveled for a living and didn't see anything wrong with it."

Mateo shook his head.

"At Breasely-Wentmore, there was this hierarchy based on wealth and family connection. I was raised with the idea that no one is born any better than anyone else, everyone should have a place at any table. When you don't believe in hierarchy, and you find yourself in one that sentences you to the bottom, it's a bizarre feeling. I was furious and grateful at the same time. I wanted to thank them, but I didn't want to thank them as part of the school's financial-development plan. I guess I could have said no, but—"

"You were fifteen," Mateo reminded her.

"I was fifteen and I still admired Meredith. She was incredibly friendly and helpful. And I'm not sure saying no would have been the right thing. Good teeth are so important to our overall health. In fact, modern dental care is largely responsible for the extended human lifespan."

Mateo could feel history trivia coming in to take over Luci's narrative. "Back to your experience at school—"

"I'm serious. Think about it. If your teeth fall out, or hurt, you're not going to be able to eat nutrient-dense foods, like vegetables and nuts. You're not going to eat as much at all, then overall health declines and you die. Bad teeth are a killer."

"Where is Meredith now?" he asked.

Luci sighed. "She's married. Very active in a number of charities. Coming out as a modern debutante is more about stepping into your role as an adult and service to community, and that's very *Meredith*. She's not a bad person. She's just…"

"Clueless," Mateo finished for her.

Luci nodded. "When she found out I was teaching, she sent me a handwritten note, commending me for my sacrifice and giving back to my community." Luci gave a dry laugh.

"Did you tell her that Pronghorn isn't your community? Because I bet she'd be pretty disappointed to find out."

Luci glanced up at him, then shook her head. "No, I just wrote back and said thank you, resisting the urge to include a picture of my smile."

Mateo leaned against the desk. He had a hundred more questions for her. Where was her family now? What were they like? How had they sheltered her so heavily that she didn't know about orthodontia? Why was she unsure if she had other siblings?

But she'd shared more with him in the last few minutes than she had in the years he'd known her. There was only one thing to say.

"Thank you."

"It's kind of a disappointing boarding-school horror story, I know."

"Not at all. What would you say to the family now, if you had a chance?"

Luci crossed her arms and gazed up at the ceiling. "Good question."

"I pride myself on good questions."

She gave an appreciative nod. "I'd say 'Thank you. I am so grateful for the thousands of dollars you donated toward giving me a beautiful, healthy smile. Every time I catch a glimpse of my teeth, I think of you in gratitude. Now, let's take a little bit of your abundant free time and wealth, and get busy creating systems where every family has the opportunity to provide their own kids with great teeth and a world-class education.'"

Mateo laughed. Luci glanced into his eyes, her truly beautiful smile shining, accompanied by the little dimple. A spark of joy ignited in his chest.

"I hope I'm not interrupting you." Mrs. Moran appeared in the doorway.

Mateo stood quickly. Luci straightened. They were very much interrupted, but he wasn't going to say that to Mrs. Moran, of all people.

"It seems as though Amber Danes is at the hotel and your expertise is needed."

"Is Neveah okay?" Luci asked.

"Oh, yes. She's at rehearsal. I don't believe she knows her aunt is here."

Mateo and Luci exchanged glances. They might have had bad experiences with boarding school, but every indication suggested Neveah was thriving in their institution. Did her fiercely protective aunt see it that way, or was Amber there to pull Neveah out of school again?

LUCI PUSHED OPEN the front door of the school with Mateo on her heels. Amber Danes was not a bad person, but she'd been throwing up roadblocks for her niece since Pronghorn High had reopened in September. They'd learned, over time, that Amber's own experience with public school in Pronghorn hadn't been great. Way less than great. Young Amber had been stuck in a system without the resources to help her, one that demanded she show up to a school that was failing her in every way.

So, yes, she had ample motivation not to trust the system. But she had to see how her niece was thriving. Neveah had found her stride when participating in the holiday pageant, her incredible voice bringing the house down. Neveah was one of the reasons, if not the main one, that Luci had agreed to the boarding school. She was not going to take it well if Amber tried to pull her niece out.

"You want to come up with a strategy?" Mateo asked, stepping over Connie as she lounged in front of the school.

"For dealing with Amber? How about you do your thing with the perfect manners and make her feel comfortable, then I'll hide Neveah."

Mateo laughed.

"I'm not entirely joking," Luci said.

They trotted through the courtyard and into the elegant lobby.

"Do we know where she is?" Mateo asked.

Luci peeked into the dining room, then heard voices in the kitchen.

Mateo frowned. "Why is she in the kitchen?"

"And who is she talking to?"

Luci strode toward the kitchen, but Mateo reached out and placed a hand on her shoulder. "Hold up. Let's not go charging in."

"Good call."

Mateo pulled in a deep breath, inspiring Luci to

do the same. "Whatever she's upset about, we need to listen to her. She's Neveah's aunt."

Luci nodded. "You're right. But after we listen…?"

"You move in with those logical arguments you're so good at."

"And you make her feel like it's okay that I'm right."

"Got it."

Together they turned and walked into the kitchen.

Where they found the unlikely pair of Amber Danes and Harlow Jameson washing potatoes for the baked-potato bar they'd been planning for dinner.

"Oh, hey," Harlow said, like she was surprised to see Luci and Mateo in their own kitchen. "You guys have a sec to talk with Amber?"

Harlow sounded chill, but her posture suggested otherwise. Amber didn't turn around from the sink, where she was furiously scrubbing a potato.

"Of course," Mateo said. His gorgeous smile and gesture toward a stool at the island were lost on Amber as she continued her work at the sink.

Dang, she was going after that potato.

"Hey there, Amber. Do you have concerns about Neveah?" Luci asked.

Amber sighed and shook her hands out.

Harlow gave Luci and Mateo a meaningful look, one Luci couldn't intuit.

"Well, for starters I wanted to work this all out with Mr. V, but that's not an option," Amber said. She turned from the sink to face them.

"Amber has a cool job opportunity," Harlow prompted.

"I was talking to Melissa Hayes—her daughter Cece lives here, too? And we were talking before the kids moved in."

"That's great," Mateo said, all confidence and smiles, as though Amber would drive into town simply to discuss her conversation with Melissa.

"She's got this job where she works from home, dealing with medical billing. It pays great."

Mateo nodded encouragingly, but Luci could already see where this was going.

"They're looking for people to hire. I just need this, uh, certificate."

"What kind of certificate?" Mateo asked, oblivious.

The room silenced as they waited for Amber to explain why she was in the kitchen washing potatoes and telling them about a job opportunity. The intermittent dripping of the kitchen faucet picked up.

"You need a high-school diploma," Luci guessed.

Amber shrugged. "Yeah. I didn't exactly get that. The last time I was in school."

"There are a lot of Oregonians in the same boat," Luci said. She would have been one of them if she hadn't managed to leave Open Hearts when she did.

Amber glanced up at the ceiling. "When the school closed down, Neveah had to do all these packets. I did some of the reading ones with her." She paused for a second, then admitted, "I did them all with her. I got a lot better at reading. I think I can pass the language-arts test but…"

"But you need help with math?" Mateo asked.

Amber glanced at Luci. "And social studies."

"We are happy to help," Luci said. Not that they had a ton of spare time, what with full-time jobs and running a boarding house…

"I don't want to take it for free." Amber crossed her arms and stared at the floor.

"But it *is* free," Mateo said. "It's public education."

Luci placed a hand on his arm. This wasn't exactly like her braces, but it had potential. Amber didn't need them acting all magnanimous.

"I've looked into getting certified as a GED instructor," Luci said. "It would be a nice addition to my résumé. If I could help you study, I could see if I liked it."

Amber snorted, clearly not buying it.

"And then maybe you could write me a letter of recommendation if I do a good job."

Amber tilted her head to one side, considering this.

"Yeah," Mateo said. "Same."

"You know, I'm not the only one around here without a high-school diploma. Not by a long shot."

"I do know. There are a number of young adults at Open Hearts who, while educated by their community, don't have—" Luci scrambled to remember Amber's words "—that certificate."

"That's what I'm sayin'—you guys could run a whole class for adults."

Luci glanced at Mateo.

When, exactly, could they find time to run an adult class? Literally, when?

Amber turned back to the sink. "What do you want with these potatoes?"

"Let's put them over here." Harlow gestured to a baking tray. She gave Luci a conspiratorial grin, then turned back to Amber. "Hey, we're kicking the teachers out tonight so they can have a break and eat at The Restaurant. Do you want to stay and help out?"

"Sure." Amber moved potatoes from the sink to the baking sheet without looking up. "Seems like you two could probably use some help."

That was the deal then—Amber would lend a hand at the hotel in exchange for lessons.

"Yes. Thank you," Mateo said, picking up on it, too.

"Absolutely," Luci confirmed. "Let me do a little research over the next few days about resources, then we can come up with a plan."

Amber nodded. "We can talk when I pick Neveah up on Friday."

"You mean, the day after tomorrow?"

Amber stared at her, and Luci could feel how anxious she was to get moving on the GED. But she just rolled her eyes and said, "Yep. Friday's the day after Thursday."

Harlow made eye contact with Luci and gave her a smile of thanks. Then said, "You all need to get out of here. Angie's not gonna be happy if you're late."

CHAPTER ELEVEN

"Took you kids long enough," Angie chastised the teachers as they walked into The Restaurant. She drew herself up and attempted to look down her nose. "I was beginning to think you didn't support local business."

Luci did not look at Mateo, because bursting into laughter wasn't the way into Angie's heart.

"We missed *one* week," Willa said.

Angie pointed squarely in the middle of Willa's chest. "You missed two weeks, because of spring break."

"I meant we—" Willa gestured to the group as a whole "—only missed one normal school week."

"Well, how was I supposed to know it was only going to be one week?" Angie asked, waving her hand at the table she had waiting for them.

The teachers headed over to their usual spot. They'd come a long way since their first meal at The Restaurant, where they'd nearly gotten themselves kicked out before they'd even placed their orders. Over time, Angie had learned to tolerate them, then love them as fiercely as she cared for the rest of her community. They'd come to appreciate what they'd originally identified as mediocre food, but now understood as mediocre food with its own special charm.

Luci glanced at the sandwich board, where Angie had scrawled the offerings for the day.

Pizza with meat, coleslaw and chocolate pie with whipped cream.

Pizza without meat, green salad and strawberry pie with ice cream.

"Pizza?" This was entirely new. Angie's fare was generally fried chicken, burgers, steak and various combinations of the three. Everything was served with gravy.

"What? You've never had pizza before?" Angie snapped.

Mateo held out a chair for Luci. "Pizza sounds great, Angie. I'll take a pizza with meat and a Coke please."

"I'd like a pizza without meat," Luci said.

"What's wrong with meat?" Angie barked.

Luci started to snap back that random, unidentified meat had a lot wrong with it. Mateo sat next to her, offering a subtle wink. Luci changed her tack. "Nothing, but I was thinking about all that is right with strawberry pie."

Angie harrumphed, but accepted the answer.

The teachers settled around the table, silently communicating their trepidation over tonight's menu options.

"Anybody want to make a guess about what the pizza will be like?" Tate whispered.

"Nope," Vander said.

"I'm with Vander." Luci lifted her water glass.

"Let's just see what happens and be grateful for ice cream."

"And that we're all here together," Mateo said, raising his glass.

"Yes!" Tate chimed in, sloshing water over the edge as he held up his glass. "To our Pronghorn traditions, long may they live."

The teachers clinked their plastic cups in a toast. A wave of security flushed through Luci. She was with the best friends she'd ever had, in a place where the only unknown would be atop Tate's pizza.

It had been a big afternoon. Had she agreed to help a woman earn her GED after being swept off her feet by a gorgeous man with a well-crafted set of dormitory rules?

Maybe.

But strawberry pie was on the way.

Luci snuck a look at Mateo. He smiled back.

Assume positive intent.

She wouldn't have been able to identify it before now, but there was always a little piece of her that had suspected Mateo was judging her, mocking her lack of easy social graces. Ironically, she responded to her fear by judging and mocking his messy room, his breakfast choices, his wrinkled sweatshirts. She was so afraid of not fitting in she looked for ways to call out others.

But to be honest, if a person wanted to fit in around Pronghorn, a wrinkled sweatshirt wasn't a bad way to go.

"I'm just gonna say it," Tate announced. "You two are nailing it with the student dormitory."

"It could be worse," Luci quipped.

"You're doing great," Vander said. "Attendance is better than ever. Kids are feeling less stress due to decreased travel time."

"Stop—" Luci tried to place a hand over his mouth "—pretending like we've got this."

Vander raised both hands in innocence. "I'm just going over the data."

"We had three more kids join Ultimate Frisbee, because now they can attend practice without getting home so late," Tate said.

Luci glanced at Mateo for help, then remembered the value he placed on Frisbee throwing.

"Well, if it's not the chinchillas coming home to roost."

Loretta appeared directly behind her chair. Luci reached over and squeezed Willa's hand before she could respond to the mixed-up metaphor.

"How are you this evening?" Mateo visibly fought his urge to stand and offer a chair. They'd managed to train him out of this habit of standing when Loretta approached the table. Manners were all well and good, but not when they resulted in their volunteer principal joining them for dinner.

"Took you long enough to ask!" Loretta said, batting her long, tangly eyelashes at him. "This afternoon, I sold the Public Trust bank building."

After a stunned silence, the teachers all swiveled their heads to look out the front window. Sure enough, the three-story brick building in between Mac's store and The City Hotel had a Sale-Pending sign out front.

A Sale-Pending sign written on a piece of notebook paper with a Sharpie, but a Sale-Pending sign nonetheless.

"Wow! Loretta, that's great!" Tate said, holding up his hands for a double high five.

Loretta waved back at him with both hands, fingers wiggling like she was playing air piano. "I sold it to two gals from Eugene. They're going to sell nack nacks."

"Nack nacks?" Luci asked.

Willa swallowed, as though summoning generosity. "Do you mean knickknacks?"

"Nack nacks," Loretta stated. "Like you use to go hiking."

"Backpacks?" Mateo asked.

"Knapsacks?" Tate suggested.

"All of it!" Loretta waved her hands around, inspiring Luci to envision three stories of packing options for water bottles and trail mix. It didn't sound like a great business plan. Then again, mortgage payments on a building in Pronghorn probably cost less than the average trip to REI.

And what was incredible was that two humans were moving to town, and opening up a business. *That* was newsworthy.

"Congratulations," Willa said.

"Well, the town really sells itself, what with our young-singles scene and innovative market district."

She readjusted her yellow blazer. "Now, I need to talk to Angie about extending her menu. I might have oversold The Restaurant a tad. I told those two women this was a fusion place."

"Fusion?" Mateo asked. "Fusion of what?"

"I didn't specify. We'll leave it up to Angie." She waved at Tate again with both hands, then sashayed up to the counter.

"Are we the singles scene?" Mateo asked Luci.

"And that would make Mac's store the business district?" Tate mused.

"Oh, one more thing!" Loretta reappeared at the table with a bright yellow folder. Lazarus Real Estate, Raising the Market One Home at a Time was scrawled across the front, again in Sharpie. She dropped the folder in front of Mateo.

"There's something wrong with the books," she said.

"Which books?" Mateo asked.

"The books. For the school. I can't figure it out so I'm giving it to the math teacher."

"I'm happy to look at it for you." He opened the folder, then turned the papers right side up.

"I'm sure you can make the numbers work out!" And she was off, doubtless to convince Angie to offer menu items she'd never heard of.

Mateo took another glance at the folder, then set it on the table. He gazed at Luci, a smile barely repressed as he gestured to Loretta's business name. Luci giggled. Mateo held her gaze, his bright smile growing, crinkling up the corners of his eyes. She'd fought this crush, assuming it was unreturned, and that his kindness to her was simply good manners.

But right now, it was hard not to read in some *very* positive intentions behind his smile.

MATEO STARED DOWN the mishmash of receipts, lists and hand-scribbled notes Loretta had referred to as "the books." He'd taken a quick look earlier, but this was not a situation where a glance would yield anything other than confusion.

He was alone in the solarium, with space to think.

Problem was, all he could think about was Luci.

He gave his head a sharp shake, then spread out the papers on the old service counter. The windows were open, and the voices of Luci and the students came wafting in on the evening breeze. It was fun to hear her laugh with the kids and the other teachers in the courtyard.

Could she go for a guy like him? The day they'd met, he'd wanted to ask her out and get to know her better. Mateo didn't believe in love at first sight. But attraction with possibility? That was certainly a thing. Then he'd stuck his foot in his mouth and offended her in their very first class. They'd see-sawed like this for years, with his heart getting two steps ahead of his good sense, then his big mouth landing him back where he'd started.

But today changed everything. They'd had an "open and engaged dialogue," as she might have once said. She admitted to being sensitive, and that was helpful. There was nothing wrong with being sensitive. To some extent it explained why she was so good with her students. She understood how they were feeling. As of today, she finally understood that he never intended to hurt her. Even if he messed up, which he surely would, she at least knew he wasn't being malicious.

A warm breeze lifted a coffee-stained receipt off the table. Mateo caught it and refocused on the mess of papers.

This was one place Luci's interest in order would absolutely come in handy.

Mateo pulled out a sheet of graph paper and created a column for money in and money out, then began filling in numbers. Running through these books should be a pretty quick task.

AN HOUR LATER Mateo stepped back from the file folder. He mastered his rising panic, as he'd learned to over the years at St. Xavier's. Then he launched out of the solarium and ran down the stairs.

Luci and the kids were still in the courtyard, enjoying the warm evening. The students were busy, with homework out, and some were working together on a group project for Willa's class. Vander played guitar. Overhead, the sparkle lights Luci had insisted they put up for the holidays still crisscrossed the courtyard.

Mateo slipped his hands in his pockets and entered the space as calmly as possible. He nodded at the kids. Sylvie and Colter were still there. Mav, or course, was hanging out. They didn't have rules in a traditional sense at Open Hearts, but it still seemed bizarre that Mav was allowed to stay out on his own on a school night, and no one seemed to have an issue with it.

Luci glanced at Mateo from where she was watching her hedgehogs forage for food. Her bright smile drew him closer, making him momentarily forget why he was there.

"You want to say hello to Earl Grey?"

"Good evening, Your Excellency," Mateo said.

"I think it's 'my lord', in the case of an earl."

"Why is that information even in your brain?" he asked.

"Have you not been reading the Barbara Cartland novels in the school library? Those things are a wealth of information about Regency-era salutations."

He laughed. A little color rose to her cheeks as she pushed a lock of hair behind her ear. Why had he come over to talk to her again?

"How are the books?" she asked.

Aaaaaand he remembered.

"Yeah. Um. I was wondering if I could talk to you about that real quick."

"Sure." She turned back to watch her roly-poly little critters find the mealworms she'd set out for them.

Mateo tried again. "I think I should show them to you."

Her brow furrowed. "Is it bad?"

Mateo scrambled to find the right words. Luci was sensitive. This school mattered to her. Plus, he didn't want to spill the bad news when they were surrounded by students.

"Come check it out." He offered a hand to help her up. Luci slipped her fingers into his and a jolt of pleasure ran through him.

She looked into his eyes, as though surprised by the same wave of feeling.

"Ms. Walker, do you want me to watch the hedgehogs for you?" Sylvie asked.

Luci dropped his hand. "Yes. Thank you. Just be on the lookout for Connie. She feels the small friends are enemies to Pronghorn."

Sylvie's brow furrowed. "Why?"

"I don't think we ask why when Connie is involved," Mateo said. He gestured to Luci to walk ahead of him, back into the hotel.

"Where are we going?" she asked as they started up the stairs.

"I'm set up in the solarium."

She flashed a smile at him. They'd met up to grade in there a few times, and it had quickly become their spot. It definitely had benefits.

"So we have to look at these books in secret?" she asked.

Mateo paused at the landing on the second floor.

Did Luci think he was planning something romantic?

Her ponytail swung as she walked down the hall toward the solarium. She looked back over her shoulder at him, another bright smile on her face.

By that point, he couldn't even remember why they were here. *Was* he planning something romantic?

"How was Loretta's math?"

Right. The books.

"Nonexistent." He trotted ahead to get the door for Luci. She was in such a good mood, he hated to bring her down like this. But honesty was essential, particularly in a situation like this.

Luci stepped into the solarium.

"Have a seat," he said, gesturing to one of the wrought-iron table.

"Sounds ominous."

Mateo drew in a deep breath and sat down next to her.

"Okay, that *felt* ominous." She wrinkled her nose. "What's up? You're never this serious."

Mateo slid the piece of graph paper in front of her. "I want your thoughts here. I ran the numbers three different times, but I keep coming up with the same conclusion." He gave her a minute to look over his math.

"I don't understand this column," she said, pointing to the income.

"Yeah."

"And why is this…?" She furrowed her brow, then turned to Mateo. "I think you're missing some numbers."

Mateo drew in a deep breath. "Can I give you some bad news?"

"Can I say no?"

He tilted his head, acknowledging her statement. Luci stared at the paper, her hands starting to shake.

"If I've read everything correctly, and I'm pretty

sure I have, Loretta isn't charging any of the students the full price for rooming here. We assumed Neveah would stay for free, but Loretta also gave generous discounts to Cece, Oliver and several other students. The stipends attached to the exchange students could cover the gap, but Loretta already spent that money in January when she bought new computers for the school."

"What about the state?" Luci asked. "I thought the state could pitch in for some of the expenses?"

"They could, but Loretta never filled out the paperwork."

Luci's breath increased rapidly in short, desperate gasps. Mateo set his hand on the table between them and she grabbed it, weaving her fingers through his, clinging as though he was the only thing keeping her tethered.

"If there's not enough money, we're going to have to close the dormitory," she said.

Neither of them seemed to remember they were banking on asbestos to put a stop to this endeavor several weeks ago. This meant too much to the kids. Mateo gave himself a moment to reflect on how well they'd done, and to relish the feel of her hand in his, the pleasure of being the person she reached for in this moment of crisis.

Then he told her the rest of the truth, because it wasn't right to hold anything back.

"It's not just the dormitory," he said. "Loretta is one month away from bankrupting the school."

CHAPTER TWELVE

"IBN BATTUTA WAS far and away the most significant postclassical traveler," Mav said. "Seventy-five thousand miles, all over the Muslim world. There's no question."

"Zheng He went way farther than seventy-five thousand miles—" Ilsa began, but Cece cut her off.

"In a boat! He was literally just sailing a boat."

"Being on a camel doesn't make the travel more significant."

"I'm just saying, Zheng He was funded by the government, and he used boats. Most of his travel time was in the ocean." Cece crossed her arms. "Can we really call that exploring?"

"Yes, we can. Why are you so anti boat all of a sudden?" Mason asked.

"And he didn't have *a* boat, the treasure fleet was composed of three hundred and seventeen ships and sailed throughout Southeast Asia, India and the east coast of Africa. This shouldn't even be a discussion. None of the other travelers even come close to Zheng He," Ilsa said.

Luci was trying to listen and grade student participation in the debate, she really was. But how was she supposed to assess anything when the school might not even exist by the time she turned her grades in?

"Wait, wait, wait." Oliver held his hands out to stop the conversation. "It's not about how you travel, or how far you travel, it's about impact. By that measure, Marco Polo is clearly the most important explorer."

The whole class groaned.

"Marco Polo was a liar," Mav snapped.

"And you're saying Ibn Battuta *never* embellished his stories?" Oliver retorted.

On most days, Luci would have been thrilled to hear her students championing the postclassical explorer of their choice. It really was lovely to hear them take a stand. But today wasn't going down on her list of best teaching days.

She glanced across the hall at Mateo. His smile in response lifted her heart a fraction of an inch off the floor of her stomach.

They'd decided to wait until this evening to talk to their coworkers. Mateo wanted to talk to Loretta, then run the numbers one more time, when he was fresh. But they both knew he could run the numbers six ways to Sunday and the results would be the same. Loretta had mismanaged the funds, and no one, not the school board, not the teachers, not the community, had thought to question her. Loretta was to blame for the bad decisions, but they were to blame for leaving her alone to make and enact those decisions.

"Isn't that right, Ms. Walker?"

Luci jerked up her head at the sound of Cece's voice.

"Frame the question one more time?" she asked.

"I said more people read Ibn Battuta's *The Rihla* than *The Travels of Marco Polo*."

"But that's because more people in the Islamic world could read during the postclassical era," Oliver said.

"Exactly! Battuta was way more influential," Mav said.

"Not when you look at it in terms of what Polo's shared knowledge of China did to spur Europe into the Renaissance, scientific revolution and ultimately the Enlightenment."

"But Marco Polo literally made things up," Ilsa said.

Luci crossed her arms and put on her best listening face. Unfortunately, her listening *ears* weren't working. The depressing truth of the situation weighed down on her. She'd come all the way out here and had she really helped anyone? The students had attached to her popular coworkers, and they grew through the opportunities they offered. Luci hadn't managed to help anyone, not really. Sure, she was on hand to defuse tension when anything came up with the kids at Open Hearts, but had she opened their eyes to other possibilities? Her own journey from growing up here to creating her own life was fraught. While she was happy with her choices in many ways, those choices had also resulted in the loss of her identity. The little girl running through the marsh grass felt wholly unconnected to the woman in penny loafers.

If the school folded, she'd never have the chance to help kids from Open Hearts negotiate the huge question facing them, whether to commit to their community or take their chances with the greater world. And honestly, it didn't just apply to kids from Open Hearts. Everyone had to ask themselves a similar question at some point.

"Wouldn't that be cool?" Mav said.

"What was that?" Luci shook herself out of her thoughts.

"Wouldn't it be cool to be a traveler like Ibn Battuta?" Mav asked. "To travel all over the world, see things you've only heard about. See things you've *never* heard about. If I lived in the postclassical era, I'd be an explorer."

Luci gazed at Mav. He longed to see the world but lived in a community that asked people to make a choice to stay at a young age. As Luci began to see Open Hearts from an adult perspective, she could understand why people chose to move there. They wanted to opt out of the modern world and cultivate flowers in this beautiful place. The issue was that the kids raised there didn't fully get a chance to understand the world they were choosing to opt out of.

School was the one place kids had to get a sense of the greater world. She was not going to let it go under.

MATEO HAD THE information he needed laid out in the dining room. After a frustrating conversation with Loretta, he knew there hadn't been any mistakes in his work, only in Loretta's judgment. The school was on the verge of bankruptcy and Loretta's solutions of buying a lottery ticket, and/or recruiting volunteer teachers if there wasn't enough money to pay the ones they already had, did not sit well.

He was almost ready to explain the situation to his coworkers. The only thing he was missing was Luci.

He hadn't even seen her leave after school. Tate was busy with athletic practices, Vander had rehearsal and Willa was at a parent meeting to discuss curriculum options for next year. If there *was* a next year.

But before everyone got back, he needed to talk to Luci, and she was nowhere in sight. He'd checked in at Mac's and The Restaurant. Aida was at soccer practice, and Harlow wasn't in town so Luci wasn't hanging out with her friends.

Unless…

No, wait. She *was* hanging out with her friends. The roly-poly, spiny ones, and he had a good guess as to where they were.

Mateo took off up the stairs and raced down the hall to the solarium.

He was wholly unprepared for the sight that greeted him there.

Luci was wearing sweatpants and had her hair in a messy bun. She'd woken up her hedgehogs early, something she normally refused to do because it was akin to waking a human up before dawn with the expectation that they'd play with you. He took a glance at her mug and read the tea tag.

"It's four thirty," he reminded her. "Isn't it a little early for Sleepytime?"

She turned to him, eyes red-rimmed from crying. This wasn't the time to joke. Why couldn't he keep it together around Luci and stop himself from hurting her feelings?

"I'm sorry," he said.

But rather than snap at him, Luci stood. She had a hedgehog cradled in one hand and held out her other arm.

Did she want a hug? Because he definitely wanted a hug.

Luci crossed to him and wound her free arm around his neck. He paused, surprised by her touch, then wrapped both arms around her. She nestled into his arms. Mateo breathed in her warm scent.

There were very few good things to find in this situation, but this was one of them.

"We can fix this," he promised. "And even if the school folds—"

"The school can't fold."

"But if it does we can easily get jobs elsewhere. It could even be close by like Lakeview or Adaline."

"Adaline only has one business, a store and restaurant combined."

Mateo rubbed her back and didn't challenge her logic.

She pulled back and wiped her eyes with her free

hand, giving him a weak smile. "I don't want to teach anywhere else. I'm supposed to teach here."

Mateo took her hand and asked the question he'd had since seeing her with Loretta at the job fair. "Why here?"

She blinked. Her blue eyes connected with his and she swallowed hard. The air between them felt electric. Then Luci drew in a deep breath and seemed to make a decision.

She wove her fingers through his and spoke deliberately.

"Because this is where I grew up."

Luci WATCHED HER words settle on Mateo. She'd never told anyone about her upbringing. The story was on file as part of her applications to Breasely-Wentmore and Dartmouth. Harlow had guessed, but even then, they didn't talk about it. Luci had never had this conversation, and she was scared.

"You grew up in Pronghorn," he clarified.

"Just outside of town."

He dropped her hand. That was fair. She'd kept a secret, the ultimate sin in his book.

"You gotta start from the beginning, Luci. I don't totally get this."

She worked to make her voice sound neutral, even as tears pricked the back of her eyes. "Okay."

At her tone, he turned to her immediately, solicitous as always. He pulled a chair out at the wrought-iron table and gestured for her to sit. "I would be grateful if you explained this to me. You're not under any obligation—"

"No, it's okay. I... I don't know how to say this. I want to tell you. I almost did tell you, so many times." She placed the hedgehog in her lap, then pulled off her glasses and set them on the table. "But then I didn't, and no one else knew, and I don't want to be judged, so...no one knows."

He sat next to her and took her hand again.

Good call. Hand-holding was a much better idea than talking. Maybe they could just sit here with her hedgehogs and enjoy the afternoon?

Mateo gazed down at her hand, brushing his thumb over her knuckles as he readjusted his grip. Then he looked into her eyes and nodded.

It was time. She could do this. And with Mateo, she would assume positive intent.

"I grew up at the Open Hearts Intentional Community. I left when I was fourteen, without anyone's permission. I've never been back."

He froze with shock, then tilted his head, as though she might be joking.

"You...?"

He didn't even know what to ask. She didn't blame him, since the whole thing seemed preposterous.

"You grew up at Open Hearts?"

She nodded. Admitting it out loud brought visceral memories racing back. The whisper of the wind through the grass, the muggy heat of the greenhouses.

"Does Today's Moment know? Or your—your parents?"

She shook her head. "I don't think my mom is there anymore. And no, Today's Moment hasn't shown any signs of recognition."

"*No one* recognized you?"

"People see what they want to see. I'm a prep-school girl who steams her sweaters and wears a watch. No need to look further."

"You are an incredible teacher with a penchant for order," he corrected. "That's what people see."

"Yeah. Well, it's not what anyone had in mind for my future."

Mateo studied her hand as he seemed to choose his words with care. "What happened?"

"My mom moved the two of us to Open Hearts when I was three. I don't know who my father is, and I don't know if she knew. It wasn't a bad place to be a little kid. I was allowed to run around all day—children are valued there, it was fine. But my mom was not fine. The patterns that had her seeking something new at Open Hearts continued. She went all in on the philosophy, intent on sheltering me from a world I was very curious about, even from a young age."

Memories were piling up inside her. The smell of the wetlands in the fall, the cozy group meals at the central hall, getting up early in the cold mornings to greet the sun.

"I was raised in complete ignorance. And I mean complete. We had something like school, where we learned to read and write. But without internet, every piece of information was filtered by the adults around me. In some ways it was okay. I grew up without the angst that a lot of children have today. But I was taught that Open Hearts was the best place to live, that outside of Open Hearts there were only ignorant people with misaligned values. I thought the outside world was Pronghorn. I didn't fully understand there *was* a world beyond Warner Valley."

She watched Mateo try to digest this information.

"There were no real rules beyond being vegetarian and wearing orange. But everyone I knew was vegetarian and wore orange, so it truly felt like there were no rules. I could do whatever I wanted. My mom was difficult, so I'd wander into other people's yurts. As I got older, I would leave the compound and go to town on my own. As an eleven-year-old it felt wildly dangerous, but I soon became a fixture around Pronghorn."

"Sounds like Mav," Mateo said.

"Exactly like Mav. I 'borrowed' dangerous books from the high-school library, like a copy of J. M. Robert's *The History of the World*. I enrolled myself in middle school because I was bored. And, in case you don't remember this from your own experience, middle school isn't when humans are at their best."

Mateo shook his head. "They're not."

"That's where I learned just how incomplete my worldview was. My behaviors and speech patterns and everything were so off. Everyone shared all these cultural references that meant nothing to me, like Disneyland and Netflix. Kids laughed at my orange clothing, they laughed at my hair. Teachers had all these unspoken rules I didn't understand. Every day felt like a battle, but unless I wanted to spend my life at Open Hearts, I needed an education."

"Were there any teachers who helped you?"

"They tried, I guess. But believe me when I tell you the prejudice against Open Hearts was *so* strong in those days. Mrs. Moran was nice, of course. She wasn't even my teacher since I was still in middle school. Still, she always—*always* said something kind when she saw me around town."

"How did the people at Open Hearts react? I thought this was the first year they let their emerging adults come to school."

"Yeah. I kinda ruined it for everybody else, for a long, long time. My mom was pretty unhappy about me going to school. But she didn't want to say no, because the whole Open Hearts philosophy is that kids should be free to make their own choices. That's the thing about not having clear rules, it puts the onus on the child to intuit what the adults want them to do, and figure it out." She shuddered, remembering the confusion and frustration. "Mom went to the leader to discuss the issue."

"Today's Moment?"

"No, it was a guy named Beat."

"Beat?"

"Yeah." Luci gestured with her free hand over her heart. "Like a heartbeat. I know Today's Moment seemed pretty rigid when we first got here, but she's honestly so chill in comparison. I mean, it's been incredible to watch her and the rest of the community embrace the school. I think she understands that kids need to know what they're choosing if they decide on a life at Open Hearts."

"I hadn't thought of it that way," Mateo said.

"I'm really impressed with her. Anyway, my mom met with Beat, and then we had this big community listening session about it. They decided the school in Pronghorn was a corrupting influence, but that every emerging adult should make an informed decision whether or not to go. The subtext was clear—they definitely didn't want us to go. So again, no rules, just the expectation that you figure out what others want you to do, and do it."

"Did you go back?"

"Not exactly. I mean, technically, yes, I stepped foot inside Pronghorn High. I went to Mrs. Moran's office, used her computer without asking, researched boarding schools and got myself a scholarship to Breasely-Wentmore."

"That's… That's incredible Luci. I can't even imagine what that took."

"I was… I mean, I don't want to boast, but I was pretty smart. And an essay about growing up at the Open Hearts Intentional Community is a compelling argument for admission."

"You're brilliant."

"I also got into Choate." She grinned at him. "But now I'm bragging."

"Of course, you did. But seriously, how? How did you just leave, and then thrive when you got there?"

"Well, I was mad. And you may have noticed, when I get mad, I'm spurred to action."

"Luci, you are amazing. I can't believe the guts it must have taken."

She shrugged, keeping her eyes on Rooibos as she waddled across the floor, sniffing for adventure.

"Then you came back. You could have taught anywhere, but you came back here."

"This wasn't the original plan," she admitted. "I knew I wanted to teach. I figured the school had closed down, the town had died. But do you remember the job fair?"

"Everyone remembers the job fair."

"Right. I saw Loretta, and I couldn't even believe it. Loretta Lazarus, right there in front of me. I started to walk away because I didn't want her to recognize me but she said, 'You there! The cute one in the sweater. Come talk to me.'"

Mateo laughed.

"I sat down and she had absolutely no recollection of me. It was a funny feeling, like I was relieved, but also sad. I'd spent so much time trying to hide who I'd been as a child. But coming back, it felt like that child had disappeared. As though I'd cut out part of me and lost the good moments along with the bad."

He wrapped his fingers more tightly around hers and gazed into her eyes. "I think I still see the brave, curious little Luci in there."

She laughed, then wiped at the tears rolling down

her cheeks. "My name's not actually Luci. It's Evening Light."

He pulled his head back, surprised. "That's beautiful." She let her eyelid twitch, calling him out. He adjusted their hands, lacing her fingers through his again. "Not as beautiful as Luci, but Evening Light, it's like your eyes."

She nodded, a fresh wash of tears running down her cheeks.

"What was the endgame?" Mateo finally asked. "Did you plan to teach here and just hope no one recognized you?"

"I didn't have an endgame, if you can believe it. When I applied to the ed program, I figured I'd teach at a place like Breasely-Wentmore. I'd be on the lookout for girls who didn't fit in and help them find their confidence, find a place. When I took this job, it was a *complete* impulse move. I figured I'd come here for a year or two. I imagined myself providing a place for any kids from Open Hearts who were interested in the wider world. I had no idea..."

She trailed off. She'd had *no* idea. Nothing that had transpired since coming to Pronghorn had been as she imagined it.

"In my life, I equate structure with freedom. Structure helps me understand the world I'm operating in, it alleviates stress. When I know what's expected of me, it frees up my mind and creativity to other tasks. That's why I love clear rules and expectations."

Mateo's warm brown eyes were sincere as he

nodded. A sense of relief flooded through her, as though she'd set down a heavy burden.

"I've just shared more with you than I have with anyone in the last nine years. I'm exhausted."

He gestured to her tea. "You're the one hitting the Sleepytime early."

"It's nine o'clock somewhere."

He laughed, his eyes crinkling at the corners, bright smile making her feel as though everything was going to be okay.

"What about you?" she asked. "How did Loretta rope you into an interview?"

He shook his head. "She didn't."

Chai was wandering toward a pile of old crates. Luci slipped her hand from Mateo's and went after her hedgehog.

"What, you saw a random woman in bright yellow representing a tiny school and thought you'd check in on opportunities for low pay in an underpopulated area?"

He gazed at her. "I saw the smartest, most interesting woman in our cohort talking at length with a representative from Pronghorn. After she walked away, I sat down to see what had Ms. Luci Walker so interested."

CHAPTER THIRTEEN

MATEO'S SCHEMES TO save the school were sounding more and more Loretta-like by the minute. He and Luci planned to tell the other teachers this evening, after the students went home for the weekend. But he wanted to have a few, surefire fundraising ideas in mind before they met.

If he couldn't give Luci absolute assurance that the school and hotel dormitory were going to stay open, and every kid from Open Hearts would feel valued and as though they had options in this world, he could at least throw out a few solid suggestions on how they could work together to make it more likely.

Mateo grabbed a pair of jeans, then checked his closet. He had a couple of button-down shirts. He pulled out a gray one, then put it back. Tate had a closet full of sharp clothes he'd brought with him from the posh Portland suburb he'd come from. None of it would feel right on Mateo. He'd look like he was dressing up on purpose, and that would tip off Luci. Not that holding her hand and staring at her as she told her story hadn't been a pretty clear indication of his feelings.

Last night, every confusing piece of the Luci puzzle had fallen into place. He'd always known she was brave, but what kind of guts had it taken for her to get herself into a boarding school on the other side of the country at the age of fourteen? If he'd thought she was extraordinary before, it was nothing compared to what he saw in her now.

He was not going to let this school fold, not after all she'd put into it.

But first he had to get dressed.

Mateo opened his dresser drawers, hoping something sharp but not too try-hard would appear. He dug through a pile of T-shirts.

At the bottom was a green T-shirt he'd been given at orientation, Puddles the Duck proudly repping the education school. Mateo grinned and pulled the shirt over his head. It might be a little wrinkled, but Luci *loved* that duck.

The hotel was quiet as he slipped out of his room. The kids didn't need to be up until seven, but Luci would be in the kitchen or courtyard, sipping a cup of English Breakfast. He'd check in with her, and let her know he was working on ideas to save the school.

He just wouldn't tell her that so far, the ideas were terrible.

Mateo jogged down the stairs, running a hand through his hair. He made a quick turn into the kitchen, his heart already beating in anticipation.

Empty.

He backed out and headed into the courtyard. Also empty.

That's when he started to worry. Luci was always the first up, first dressed. Sometimes he wondered if she even slept.

She was probably still upset. But what was he

going to do? Scour the hotel for signs of tea consumption? Knock on her door and wake her up?

Voices floated into the courtyard from the street. Mateo glanced out the arched entryway.

"I don't know what to do," Cece said. "My mom's gonna hit the roof."

"Is she?" Luci asked.

Luci and Cece were approaching the school. Steam rose from the cups of espresso they held. They must have slipped out to Mac's early.

"Wouldn't you be mad if your daughter wanted to move away?"

"Absolutely not," Luci said.

"That's because you're young and cool."

"As was your mother, at one point. And if you think it through, you might come to the conclusion that your mom is older and cool."

Cece laughed, then took a sip from her mug of espresso.

"But my mom and I are, like, a team. She's gonna be really sad if I move away."

"I think she would be far more disappointed if you didn't follow your dreams."

Mateo leaned up against the bricks of the entryway and watched their approach.

"But we're not talking about moving away yet. You're only a sophomore. Give your mom the chance to surprise you."

Cece nodded. "And then there's like, another problem."

"Okay." Their quiet voices managed to create an echo in the mostly empty street.

"Mason."

"Is he bothering you?"

"If by bothering you mean I can't sleep because I think about him all the time, then yes. Solid bother."

Mateo clamped down on an impulse to chuckle.

Luci nodded. "I get it. So why is this a problem? Mason is great."

"I just feel like, you know, like I don't even know how to…what? Date someone? I mean, I know Mason, and we hang out. Sometimes I think we might be on a date but then I don't know. It's like…"

"It's like there's no way to practice?" Luci suggested.

"Exactly. In a normal town there are dances, and kids have parties. There would be a way to figure out if he likes me, and here—"

"Here we have a boarding school in an old hotel and The Restaurant."

Cece laughed, then held up her cup. "Plus espresso and ice cream."

"Which mug did you get?" Luci asked.

"I got the cute puppies." She turned the cup so Luci could see the image. Luci's mug was shaped like an elephant, with a trunk for the handle.

"I wish we were a normal school, with dances and social activities and more than thirty-four kids," Cece said.

"Do you?" Luci asked. "I love our tiny school."

"I guess we are kinda quirky."

Luci held her thumb and forefinger about a quarter of an inch apart. "Little bit."

Mateo laughed, and Luci's head shot up, her gaze connecting with his. Her eyes ran to the image of Puddles the Duck on his shirt and she smiled. "Nice shirt."

"Thanks."

"Are you getting espresso?" Cece asked, suspicious.

"I'm just heading over there, yeah." It was tempting to assure Cece that he hadn't heard a thing, but that would be lying.

"Oooookay." Cece turned to Luci. "Thank you, Ms. Walker."

"Anytime. We can talk more later if you like."

Cece nodded, then disappeared into the building, leaving Mateo and Luci alone on the street.

Well, Mateo, Luci and Connie the cat.

"Thank God you're here. Drink this." Luci handed him the cup.

"You don't like Mac's espresso?"

She looked at him blandly. "Have you noticed that I can be a little high-strung? This does not help." She held out the mug. "I've already had my caffeine intake for the morning. Double dipping is really not an option for me."

Mateo laughed and accepted the espresso. "Thank you." He paused before taking a sip, gazing at her from over the rim of the mug. "You always buy espresso when you don't want or need it?"

"I found Cece moping in the lobby at six thirty. She didn't seem to think a cup of tea would fix anything, so I suggested we go grab espresso and have a chat."

"And the problem is she has a crush on a boy who also has a crush on her?" Mateo took a sip of espresso, then looked up, surprised. "Is this a cortado?"

"Is that what you call it? I asked Mac to give me whatever you order. It's good. I had a drink."

He took a longer sip, keeping his gaze connected with hers. Then he asked, "Did you plan on giving your coffee to me?"

A flush ran up her cheeks.

"Are you asking if I had a plan? Don't you know me well enough by now? I always have a plan."

An idea solidified in his mind. Mateo savored the coffee, then gave a firm nod.

"I figured it out."

"You figured what out?"

"I know how we're going to save the school."

"Just like that?"

"Just like that."

Luci grinned at him. "You sure it's not just good vibes?"

Mateo had excellent vibes at the moment. The best vibes.

"We're going to throw a gala."

"In Pronghorn?"

He gestured to the hotel. "This place used to be a travel destination. People would come from all over the US to see the antelope and the wetlands. Our hotel has a ballroom."

"Okay, we have a ballroom, but only about seventy-four residents. I feel like a gala has to have more than seventy-four people."

"We start by inviting everyone who went to Pronghorn High, then extend the invitation to the surrounding areas. If we can get three hundred people at a soccer game, we can sell that many tickets to a gala."

"We're just going to throw a gala? That's a lot of work. Have you ever been to a gala?" she asked, narrowing her eyes.

"I volunteered at two galas a year, every year of high school. It was expected at St. Xavier's."

A smile pushed at her cheeks, encouraging her dimple. "Me, too. Except we didn't work at the dances, we attended." She locked eyes with him. "This is going to be great for the kids. A real dance."

Mateo held her gaze. He wasn't thinking about the kids at all.

"Oh, wait." Luci's expression faltered. "They don't know how to dance. We both had it pounded into us at prep school but—"

"But their PE teacher knows how to ballroom dance, and would like nothing better than to pass that skill on."

Luci raised her eyebrows. "And we can help."

If teaching the kids to ballroom dance meant holding Luci in his arms as they demonstrated, he was all in.

A spark lit her eyes. "Ballroom dance is a seriously underrated life skill."

Mateo set his coffee mug on the front steps, then reached out and took her hand, his feet already stirring in the memorized movement of the jitterbug. Luci slipped her fingers into his and let him twirl her under his arm. He could almost hear the snare drum, the cheerful horns. Luci's penny loafers picked up the beat, as though she could hear it, too.

She followed his lead easily, a laugh escaping as he drew their arms out wide, then pulled her in close again.

It wasn't even 7:00 a.m., and he was dancing on the empty street in a tiny town in the middle of nowhere. Exactly where he wanted to be.

He spun her closer, wrapping an arm around her waist. She placed a hand on his chest, his heart responding to her touch with a warm and steady beat. Surprise and delight reflected in her gaze.

As though this was exactly where she wanted to be, too.

Then Luci stepped out of his grasp, but kept ahold of his hand and tugged it.

"Come on." She turned and headed into the hotel. "Let's go tell the others we're almost bankrupt and are therefore going to throw a huge party. I'm so excited!"

SUNSHINE STREAMED ACROSS their table by the front window at The Restaurant, illuminating every scratch in the old wood. But it also illuminated Mateo as he sat across from her.

Luci printed Invitations! on a blue sticky note and placed it on a list with Sofi, Taylor and Morgan's names across the top. "They did such a great job with promotion for the holiday pageant, they'll rock this."

"You're having a lot of fun for someone whose school is going under," he accused.

Luci glanced up from the spreadsheet, grinning. She placed a green Post-it note that read Coat Room! on the list in front of Mateo.

"I might be."

He laughed, somehow even more handsome today than he had been the day before. How did he manage that?

"It feels like I'm doing something positive in the face of certain ruin. I love that feeling." She took a sip of her ice-cold, somewhat watered-down Coke. "What about parking? Do we have everyone park at the field adjacent to the school?"

"That should work. How many students do you think we'll need for valet service?"

"How many of them can actually drive?" she asked.

"Good question. Maybe we can find out before we make the general announcement."

"How many times have I told you I love this plan?"

"Eight."

How sweet was it that he kept track?

"The best part is, rather than saving the school for the students, we're helping them take part in what will become an annual fundraiser for their own education. That feels fantastic."

It had been Mateo's suggestion that they assign the majority of the work to their students. He'd remembered her complicated feelings around charity and came up with a way students could provide real value for the money people donated.

A basket of fries landed squarely in the middle

of the table. "What have I told you kids about ordering Coke without French fries?"

"Sorry, Angie," Mateo replied.

"It's not good for you to have too much sugar on an empty stomach."

"Noted," Luci said, still grinning. She felt generous with everyone today. And if she had to eat a few French fries to make Angie happy, so be it.

This basket of fries looked extra fresh and crispy. Luci grabbed one and took a bite.

Ooh! Okay, no salt on this particular batch.

She could remedy that once Angie's back was turned.

But Angie wasn't turning her back. She grumbled a few insults about the glorious spring weather but didn't leave the table.

Luci's gaze connected with Mateo's. What were they missing here?

Finally, Angie gestured to the fries. "I suppose you'll be wanting some of my special sauce with those."

Right, sauce. That was it.

"We would love sauce, thank you, Angie," Mateo said.

She stalked off toward the kitchen and Mateo grabbed the saltshaker, liberally seasoning the fries.

"Thank you," Luci whispered, then asked in a reasonable voice, "Do we know if Vander has checked in with Harlow?"

"Yeah, I forgot to tell you." The muscles in Mateo's arm flexed as he reached for another French fry. Who would think a guy could look so good eating fried foods? "Harlow is stoked."

"No surprise there. This is right up her alley."

"She's gonna see if she can get a Nashville musician out here."

"Seriously?"

Mateo nodded. "Trey Tucker comes to her ranch for songwriting retreats."

"The guy Vander works with?"

"Yep. She's pretty sure she can convince him to play."

"That's so exciting! And we can play music from the last several decades, so everyone has songs they know and love, and that will encourage them to dance."

A small steel bowl landed on the table, a little of Angie's truly special sauce sloshing over the edge. Angie looked expectantly at Mateo, then Luci.

"Thank you, Angie," Luci said, hoping she had the tone right. You couldn't be too grateful, or Angie would get mad. It went along with her rule about overtipping.

Angie huffed.

"These fries are great," Mateo said.

"They're *French fries*," Angie commented.

Mateo and Luci exchanged a glance. They'd done something wrong, and not even Mateo, with his perfect manners, could figure it out.

He started to rise from his seat, and gestured to an empty chair. "Would you like to join us?"

Angie's face screwed up in derision and Mateo sat quickly. "Sorry."

The proprietress crossed her arms and looked over her shoulder at the mostly empty restaurant. Mac, Ed and Pete sat at one table, drinking coffee and talking about whatever seventy-year-old guys talked about on a Sunday afternoon.

"Are you two planning on making this a regular occurrence?"

"Um…" Luci widened her eyes at Mateo.

"If we're not taking up space from other customers," Mateo said. "This is a nice place for us to focus outside of school."

"And you need to focus because you're planning some kind of gala because Loretta mismanaged the funds?"

Mateo and Luci locked gazes. There had been no announcement yet. They planned to tell the kids on Monday. But that didn't stop news from spreading in Pronghorn. It was like Canada thistle—seed of the stories carried on the wind, while extensive root networks guaranteed survival of even the most flimsy tale.

"Well, you don't need to beat around the bush," she snapped.

It definitely felt like there was bush beating, but Luci was pretty sure neither she nor Mateo held the stick.

Angie looked over her shoulder again, then lowered her voice. "You're gonna ask me to cater, and that's fine. I can do barbecue sliders, and a vinaigrette coleslaw, but don't even think about requesting green salads. No one pays a hundred dollars a ticket for lettuce."

Tears pricked at the back of Luci's eyes. This was *so* Pronghorn. "That's a lot of work, Angie. Can we help—"

"My boys will help. And their friends. I have more help than I want."

Mateo smiled gratefully. "Thank you. We may need to pay you in installments, and can only give you a partial payment up front."

Angie scoffed. "You're not paying. What do you think I am, some kind of opportunist?"

"I guess you'll be needing the beef for those sliders donated," Pete grumbled from his table.

"Unless Angie wants to go with pork," Ed cut in.

Angie placed her hands on her hips and turned to the table of old guys who drive trucks. "It's a *gala*. Pretty sure these fancy people, or whoever these two think they can find to show up, are gonna expect a choice."

This inspired an argument between the three of them about how many choices fancy people expected, and whether beef barbecue or pork barbecue was more posh.

Mateo grinned across the table at Luci. "Barbecue sliders will be perfect. We can lean into the upscale, down-home vibe."

"Love it!" Luci pulled out another piece of paper and wrote Food! across the top.

"We have all those fancy dishes at the hotel,"

Mateo noted. "We can use bone china and crystal to serve sides."

"Who doesn't love a cut-glass bowl full of potato chips?" Lucy made a note in her planner.

Mateo grabbed a piece of paper and wrote Donations! across the top, including the exclamation point Luci had subconsciously employed.

"Is this killing you? All the sticky notes and lists?"

"Not at all," he said.

Behind them Pete, Ed and Angie were discussing drop-off plans for their donations and comparing freezer space. Mac glanced their way, then slipped out of his seat and approached their table.

"I couldn't help but overhear you're planning a gala to raise funds for the school." Mac spoke quietly while Ed, Pete and Angie continued to argue about meat. "I'd like to donate the beverages, if I may. I get a wholesale discount, so it makes sense that I could cover sparkling cider and champagne, if that's what you intend to serve."

Luci thought back to the champagne coupes nestled in the top kitchen cabinets.

"That's very generous of—"

Mac waved away the compliment before it could land. "My business has tripled since the school reopened. What with the ice cream and espresso, I can barely keep up. I need to do something with the extra money."

Because heaven forbid someone had extra money lying around in Pronghorn.

"Thank you," Mateo said. "That's huge. Thank you."

Mac glanced out the window. "Looks like I have a customer." He gestured to Mav entering the store. He pulled out his wallet and left two dollars on the table with Ed and Pete, then headed over to wait on his "customer." Luci couldn't imagine where Mav had gotten the money. Kids at Open Hearts didn't traditionally have access to cash.

"Can you believe all these donations?" Luci asked.

"I can't tell if it's funny or touching."

"Both," Luci confirmed. She glanced at her watch. "It's already two thirty. We have an hour and a half until the kids show up at the hotel. My guess is if these guys know, the kids already know and have wild expectations for the gala."

Mateo chuckled. "Good point. I'm glad we'll have a solid plan before they get here."

She raised her eyebrows at him. "You don't want to be flexible? Plan the gala in the moment?"

He grabbed a French fry and dipped it in the sauce. "This is a time for organization, and fortunately, I'm working with the empress of strategy."

Luci tucked her hair behind her ear.

"We are going to plan this gala down to the last detail," he said. "We're gonna plan so well and so hard, space-shuttle launches will look sloppy."

Luci laughed, a squeak of pleasure drawing attention from the other patrons.

Mateo raised his glass in a toast to her. "This is gonna be our magnum opus of planning."

"I'm on it," she said, raising her drink. "For Pronghorn Public Day School Boarding School."

Mateo held her gaze as he clinked his plastic cup against hers.

Totally for the school. Zero thoughts of planning a gala where her date might be a gorgeous man who knew how to waltz.

A tap on the window drew her attention. Suleiman and Antonio were standing outside waving at them.

Suleiman's voice was muffled as it came through the glass. "When are you guys coming back to the hotel?"

Mateo sighed. "I guess it's nice they want to be around us?"

"I guess."

Antonio held up a Frisbee and pointed at Mateo.

"Five minutes," he said, holding up five fingers and enunciating the words so they could understand him through the window.

The boys raised their arms in triumph and whooped as they headed down the block.

"Really? You're going to spend your last free hour before we're responsible for kids with kids?"

"If I keep them entertained, you can have some time to yourself. Steam a few sweaters."

Luci held back a smile as she gazed at him, mock serious. "You see me."

"I do." A flush ran up his neck. "I see you, Ms. Luci Walker."

CHAPTER FOURTEEN

LUCI AND MATEO exited The Restaurant into the sunny Pronghorn afternoon. He was quickly swept up by a pack of students running across the empty street as they tossed the disc back and forth. Luci glanced into Mac's store to see Mav still there, discussing something. Probably trying to talk his way into some ice cream. Luci fought the urge to run in and buy it for him. Mav would learn more by negotiating with the world around him than he would by her trying to save him from disappointment.

"Ms. Walker?"

Luci turned to see Taylor and Morgan Holms standing on the porch of a small, seemingly abandoned house next to the post office. She waved.

"Can we do the 'Thriller' dance at the gala?" Morgan asked.

Luci didn't stop to ask how they knew about the gala. She just shot back with a clear, straightforward answer. "No."

"But—"

"No." Luci was trying to loosen up, she really was. Mateo had helped her see that flexibility and grace had their place alongside clear rules. But the "Thriller" dance in May? Not a chance. "It's spring. You can't do the 'Thriller' dance in the spring."

"But—"

"Morgan?" The door to the little house opened and Raquel emerged. "I need help with a window, it's stuck." She nodded to Luci but didn't offer any explanation about why she needed help fixing a window in an abandoned house.

Morgan set her brow at Luci in a we'll-see-about-that furrow, then followed her mom back inside.

"Mom, I'll be back in a bit," Taylor called to Raquel, then crossed the street toward Luci. "Ms. Walker, can I talk to you about something?"

"Sure, is everything okay?"

Taylor glanced at the field where the Frisbee game raged. Suleiman leaped up to catch the disc then sent it spinning toward Cece. "Yeah. I need, um, advice."

"Okay. I was just going to—" Luci paused. Was it weird to talk to a student while steaming sweaters? There'd been a lot in her education program about setting appropriate boundaries. Where did wardrobe prep fall on that scale? "Make a cup of tea," she said, ad-libbing. "Join me?"

Taylor took one last look at the Frisbee game. Suleiman waved to her, trying to get her to join in. Taylor gestured to Luci like it was her fault she couldn't join the game.

"What's up?" Luci asked as they approached the hotel.

"Well, first off, there's some drama between my mom and Today's Moment."

Luci's scalp tingled. The community had come so, so far since her first weeks back in Pronghorn.

Were old grudges resurfacing? "I'm sorry to hear that. How can I help?"

"I don't know. It's about flowers for the gala. Like, everyone at Open Hearts thinks that any flower donations are their thing, and my mom feels like all decor is her turf. So now they're totally into this polite argument and my mom won't drop it."

Luci rubbed her brow. She was putting off steaming her sweaters for this?

They stepped into the lobby to find Willa lounging in a chair, reading a thin, worn book with an illustrated cover of a woman in regency dress.

"Which Barbara Cartland novel are you on?" Luci asked.

"*A Ghost in Monte Carlo*," Willa said, not looking up from the book. "Trying to figure out what exactly happens at a gala."

"According to Ms. Cartland, big secrets are revealed, then the hero and heroine have a swoony dance."

"Sounds great." Willa turned another page in the old book, a smile playing on her lips as she said, "I can't wait for our gala. What shocking secrets does Pronghorn have in store?"

"I think most of those are hidden in Angie's kitchen."

Taylor followed Luci into the hotel kitchen. The scene before them had Luci skidding to a stop.

"What—?" Luci couldn't get any further with her question. Just *what*?

Every single cabinet was wide open. Drawers,

too. The industrial kitchen was strewn with cut-glass bowls, serving platters, cake plates, champagne coupes, so many teacups. It looked like someone was preparing high tea for the entire western hemisphere.

At the center of it all stood Amber Danes and Melissa Holms.

"Oh, hey!" Melissa said. "We thought we'd get a jump on organizing service for the gala."

Neveah emerged from behind a pile of dinner plates. "There are so many pretty dishes!"

Taylor glanced at her friend, then at the other adults. Her expression morphed into one of practiced confidence. Whatever it was she needed to talk to Luci about, it wasn't going to happen here.

"That's great!" Luci said, sincerely hoping they were planning on putting it all back. "Thank you. Taylor, do you want to—"

"I'll help." She walked decisively toward the central island. "What are we doing? Taking inventory?"

Amber eyed Luci across the room, then explained the protocol to Taylor, who jumped right in as though this was the only thing she wanted to do with her afternoon.

It definitely wasn't part of Luci's plan. But she couldn't bail on this crew.

Or could she? They hadn't been interested in her help when they got started.

"We've got this," Amber said, picking up on her indecision. She stalked across the room and grabbed an old tote bag, rifling through it to pull out a file folder crammed with papers. "I have a thing for you."

A thing was the thick packet of homework Luci had given her two days ago to kick off their lessons. The work was supposed to take her a full week. She pushed it into Luci's hands.

"Go on," Amber said, looking meaningfully at the assignment. "You've got enough work to do."

Luci glanced at Taylor, attempting to reopen the avenue of conversation.

"What?" Taylor asked, already elbow-deep in a stack of salad plates.

This town, seriously.

"I'll check back later," Luci said.

She made her escape up the stairs, the jovial noise of the kitchen fading behind her. The world quieted as she walked down the carpeted hallway, past the bright windows and gilt-framed pictures of flowers. Once in her room she gratefully shut the door. The tidy, beautiful space felt like stepping into a hug. Next to the neatly made bed, her little family of hedgehogs slept in their basket, breathing together. From outside the window she could hear Mateo and a group of students playing Ultimate Frisbee.

Luci set up her steamer, the familiar smell of heating water calming her as she went through her clothes. Late April in Pronghorn meant cool mornings, with heat rising steadily throughout the day. Perfect for a sweater she could wear in the morning, drape over her shoulders midday and tuck away in her bag by late afternoon.

She pulled a pale yellow cardigan out of the closet. A comforting click signified that the steamer was ready.

Then a gentle tap sounded on her door. "Ms. Walker?"

Luci closed her eyes briefly. It was Taylor, again.

She pulled in a deep breath and opened the door.

"There's one more thing." Taylor walked confidently into Luci's room and sprawled on the settee near the window. "Can I hold a hedgehog?"

Luci left her door open, then brought the nap basket to Taylor. The girl ran her hand over the spiny, sleeping critters. Her expression morphed into confusion, then sadness.

Luci sat down in the chair across from Taylor. "What's really going on?"

Taylor sighed.

"What is it? Because I don't think you ditched your mom and sister to talk to me about flowers."

Through the open window they could hear the Frisbee game. A string of French suggested the game was not going the way their exchange student from Senegal wanted it to. Taylor listened carefully, her hand resting on the sleeping hedgehogs.

"Can I talk to you about Suleiman?" she finally asked.

"Of course."

"I really like him."

Luci managed *not* to say how obvious this was.

"And, at first it was like, just fun. I mean, he's the hot exchange student—"

"Maybe not use the word *hot*?" Luci suggested.

Taylor laughed. "Okay, the cute exchange student. But then he's like, funny. And really smart."

Luci was having trouble tracking what the problem was. She kept her expression neutral and listened.

"But he's going back to Senegal."

There it was.

"Taylor, we can't enter every relationship thinking it's going to last forever, particularly at your age."

"I know. But this is different."

"I understand, believe me. It's hard to let yourself feel for someone who you may never see again."

Tears sparked in Taylor's eyes. *Oof.* This was worse than Luci anticipated.

As an adult, Luci understood that Taylor's feelings for Suleiman would change over time. He'd go from the one true love of Taylor's life to someone she missed to a former boyfriend whom she remembered fondly. Eventually, they'd become Facebook friends and celebrate the milestones of one another's children.

Or who knows? Maybe they'd meet back up in their thirties and live happily ever after.

But right now, this confident, connected student was facing a new challenge, and needed help.

"Did you ever have a crush on someone like that?" Taylor asked. "Someone you knew there was like a firm expiration date on?"

Luci nodded. "Yeah. Absolutely. You know I went to a boarding school in South Carolina?"

"That must have been so fun."

Luci shrugged. "We had all these social events with boys' schools, and the whole point was to introduce kids from wealthy families to kids from other wealthy families." She paused. Then, for the first time, told a student a concrete piece of information about her past. "I wasn't from a wealthy family. I was on scholarship."

"But I'm sure lots of boys liked you. You're so pretty and smart."

Luci laughed. "Thank you. That's very sweet. But it was a different world. I knew I wasn't heading for the same life as the other girls at my school. I always felt like if I acted on any of my crushes, I'd get rejected eventually." Luci was surprised to hear the words coming out of her mouth. She'd never fully thought it through, but much of her loneliness at boarding school was self-imposed. "I didn't act. I missed out on friendships and fun and the opportunity to learn about relationships. I'd like something different for you."

"But if Suleiman and I get together, he's just going to go away."

"That's going to be hard no matter what. We're all going to miss the exchange students."

"I know. I just don't know what to do about—" she gestured toward the window "—anything."

"Have fun," Luci said, giving her the advice she wished all kids would follow in their teens. "Spend the next few months getting to know Suleiman. Learn about the give-and-take of a relationship. And expect to break up when he leaves. This would be my advice to most high-school students, expect to take a break when you graduate. See the world, follow your path. Learn French."

Taylor laughed.

"Know that the world may still have plans for you and Suleiman. Reuniting with a love from the past isn't uncommon. But over the next few years, you need to line things up for your law career. Suleiman has big dreams of professional soccer. Have fun now, then give yourself permission to focus on yourself in your late teens and early twenties as you put your life on the path you've chosen. You really don't know what the future will bring."

"Thank you, Ms. Walker."

Luci soaked up the gratitude. It felt good to help, and it was pretty good advice. Off the cuff, but good. Now she needed to figure out what she was going to do about *her* crush.

Taylor headed for the door, then turned back toward Luci. "Is there anyone from your school you'd like to reunite with?"

Mateo's voice came wafting in the window, celebrating someone's catch.

"Not from high school, no." She smiled and kept talking before Taylor had the chance to ask more questions. "Think about what you want. If you want more than a friendship with Suleiman, ask him out."

Taylor nodded thoughtfully as she gazed out the window, leaving Luci to consider the same question.

What did *she* want?

She wanted to dance with Mateo. To feel unguarded, to share her secrets with him.

She wanted to be a person he celebrated with. She wanted to look into his warm eyes and not feel like she had to look away.

She wanted to let this happen, no planning, no rules, just get in there and see where it took them.

But she also had a real specific end goal of *where* she wanted it to take them.

And she wanted it more than an organized wardrobe and freshly steamed sweaters. She felt like sidestepping her plan and living in the moment.

She grinned at Taylor. "Shall we see if we can get in on the Frisbee game?"

COMPETITION IN THE Sunday afternoon Ultimate game had become fierce. Mateo raced to make a catch while tracking his teammates. If he caught the disc, Mav was in a perfect position to make it to the end zone to receive.

Then he stopped cold, the Frisbee sailing straight past him as he stared at the entrance to the hotel.

Luci emerged from the building under the arc of roses. Her blond hair swirled around her face, and she brushed it back as she grinned at him. She was wearing sneakers, jeans and a UO T-shirt.

The group stampeded past him, but Mateo was frozen on the spot.

"Is there space for two more players?" Luci called out.

Mateo finally noticed Taylor walking next to her. He might have been speechless, but Suleiman quickly claimed Taylor for his team.

And that was the moment Mateo's feelings finally made it through his thick skull. He wanted Luci on his team.

When they'd met, he'd seen a woman who was beautiful, smart and funny, the whole list of attributes he thought he wanted in a partner.

But now, she was more than that. She was Luci.

At her expectant look, he snapped out of it. "Yes! Absolutely. You're on my team. With me. We're on the same team."

Her dimple appeared. "So what you're saying is that you and I are on the same team?"

"In so many words. Or too many words." He grinned at her. "Do you know how to play?"

"Not at all." She scanned the field. "What's the point?"

He stepped closer. "Fun. Exercise. Community building."

One of her eyelids twitched in what he was beginning to understand was amusement, not annoyance.

"I meant of the game."

"Oh."

"It's like the silk-road simulation," Mav called to her. "You trade off the goods until someone can send it across the finish line to a teammate."

This seemed to land. Luci pointed to one end

of the field. "So is that imperial Rome, or Han dynasty China?"

"China."

"Got it. Let's go! Make that money!"

The kids whooped to see Luci in the decidedly un-Luci situation.

At least, it began as an un-Luci situation. She quickly picked up on the flow of the game and her competitive side kicked in. What she lacked in skill with the disc, she made up for in strategy and teamwork.

Those skills were part of what had made Luci a star in their education program. She was the brave one, always willing to clarify an assignment with a difficult professor, head up a group presentation, or volunteer to supervise in the student section during a pep rally.

What happened in those days? He'd had a crush on Luci the moment she walked into his life. He could have asked her out at any time. Why had he settled for arguing, rather than partnering with her?

He watched Luci as she ran next to Tate, trying and failing to catch the Frisbee.

He hadn't wanted to face the possibility that they wouldn't work out. If he tried and they didn't work out, that would be it. He couldn't bear the thought of being banished from her circle.

A little bit of Luci was infinitely better than no Luci at all.

But since then he'd learned a few things about the way they worked together.

They did well in a crisis.

Their strengths balanced each other.

They could spontaneously parent eleven teenagers and have fun doing it.

There was every indication that they could succeed in any kind of a relationship together. But at this point there was only one kind of relationship he was interested in.

"Mateo!" Cece called. The Frisbee spun toward him and Mateo made the easy catch. He scanned the field to see Luci near the end zone.

Large, athletic kids jostled around her, but Luci held steady. Rather than aiming high, Mateo gave a low toss toward the end zone. Luci sped ahead and snapped up the Frisbee just as it sailed across the end line.

"Success!" she yelled, raising her arms. "We scored!"

Mateo ran toward her, no thought but how beautiful and happy she was in this moment. Then she started running toward him, arms wide in triumph.

He scooped her up and spun her around, every piece of him feeling the only right thing in the world was Luci in his arms.

Slowly, he lowered her to the ground. Her smile was so bright.

"That's what strategy gets you!" she said, triumphant and happy.

That was what he needed, then. A strategy.

CHAPTER FIFTEEN

"AM I LATE?" Colter asked as he ducked into Mateo's classroom.

"You're right on time. Have a seat." Mateo gestured to an empty chair in between Tate and Vander at the front of his classroom.

It was Friday afternoon. The building had cleared quickly as the kids who lived in the dorm would be heading home with their parents or host families for the weekend.

"What's up?" Vander asked. "Is everything okay?"

"I hope so." Mateo erased the board, preparing for the wealth of ideas he expected from his friends.

"Is it about the gala?" Tate asked.

"No. This a gala-free zone for the next hour."

"Good," Tate said. "Because while I do not want to shirk my responsibilities, I have put in my time teaching thirty-four high school students how to swing dance."

"No, man. You're doing awesome."

"I'm doing my best." Tate ran his hands through his shock of dark hair. "I never realized how insufficient my best was before now, but the foxtrot made it clear."

"Don't say that." Colter tapped Tate's shoulder with the back of his hand. "The kids are doing great—"

"At complaining."

"Hmm." Mateo tilted his head to one side. "They might be complaining, but that's not stopping anyone from practicing back at the hotel."

Tate laughed. "Good to know."

"I didn't ask you here to talk about the gala. Luci's planned that thing to within an inch of its life—it's perfect." Mateo wrote "The Plan" in block letters across the top of the chalkboard. "I've asked you all here to help me come up with a strategy."

He faced his friends and finally admitted the truth. "I need a foolproof, surefire plan to inspire Luci Walker to fall in love with me. Where do we start?"

The room erupted with a hurricane of hooting, hollering and every possible version of "I knew it!"

As expected.

"Quiet!" Mateo glanced out the door. "She'll hear you."

"She's gonna have to know eventually," Colter noted.

"Why do you need a strategy?" Tate asked.

"It's Luci," Mateo reminded them, turning back to the board to draw a heart next to the word *Plan*.

"Does she find strategy…romantic?" Vander asked.

"You know Luci. Probably."

Colter sat forward, elbows on his knees. "Tell her," he began.

Mateo wrote "Tell her" on the board, then waited for Colter to finish his sentence. When he didn't, Mateo swiveled back around.

"Tell her what?"

"Just tell her you like her."

Mateo lowered his hand and scowled at Colter. "That's your plan?"

"Yeah, I think that'll cover it." He glanced at the others from confirmation. "Won't it?"

"You should plan a great night out," Tate said. "Come up with a string of fun activities and show her you put some thought into it."

Mateo wrote this on the board, despite the fact that they lived in a town with one restaurant and one store.

"Maybe you two should go for a hike, under the stars," Vander suggested. "Mars is visible right now."

"Okay." Mateo kept writing.

"And buy her some earrings. Women love Raquel's jewelry."

"Yeah, I thought about that but—"

"But it's Luci," Tate reminded everyone. "Raquel makes artistic turquoise pieces set in silver and Luci—"

"There's nothing wrong with Luci's style," Mateo said, cutting him off.

"No one would suggest that," Colter said, as Vander mumbled, "Pearls are nice."

Mateo studied the list.

Tell her
Plan a big date
Look at Mars
Buy earrings

This wasn't the wealth of information he was hoping to mine from his engaged friends. He sighed, then addressed the group.

"Here's the deal with Luci. She's amazing. Beautiful, smart, funny, caring. But she can be a little like a hedgehog—"

"I *wouldn't* compare her to a hedgehog," Colter interrupted.

"No, I only mean—"

"Seriously, dude." Tate held a hand out. "Do *not* compare women to rodents. Ever."

Vander shook his head. "Hedgehogs aren't rodents. They're considered spiny mammals, like porcupines, part of the Erinaceinae subfamily."

"Whatever," Tate said. "My point is—"

"Oh, I agree with your point." Vander glanced at Mateo. "Maybe the strategy is you stop comparing her to her pets? It could be pretty simple."

Mateo let out a breath in frustration. "One, you guys clearly don't appreciate hedgehogs. Two, I only meant that I have to take it slow with Luci because she will fold in on herself if she feels defensive."

"I'd feel defensive, too." Tate crossed his arms and leaned back in his chair. "You're the one comparing her to spiny mammals, or whatever Vander called it."

"You are not helping!" Mateo pointed at the board. "This is a terrible list. How are any of you engaged?"

His friends mumbled apologies, and reflected that they, too, were a little surprised they'd managed to win the hearts of such an incredible group of women.

The sound of sneakers running in the hallway

hit his ear. Mateo whipped around and erased the board.

"Mr. V!" Neveah appeared at the door, breathless and excited. "Harlow's here!"

Vander shot up, his leg getting tangled in the chair. "She didn't tell me she was coming this weekend."

Neveah's eyes shone. "She said it's a last-minute surprise. Come on, you have to see what she brought!"

Vander shot out the door. Mateo stared after him. He'd had Vander's back all year long. He'd supported his friend through every crisis, and now he was just ditching Mateo and his strategic planning?

A beat later, his friend looped back into the room. "Sorry. Can we, uh…" He pointed in the direction of the hotel, where the love of his life had arrived with some sort of surprise.

"Yeah," Mateo said, absolutely getting it. "We can finish up with a strategy at the hotel."

Colter slapped Mateo on the shoulder. "Keep it simple. Tell her how you feel."

Tate joined them. "She likes you, too, man. It's gonna be fine."

Mateo nodded, but his friends really didn't know what they were getting into. This was Luci they were talking about.

"THINGS HAVE BEEN…DRAMATIC," Luci said, answering Mrs. Moran's question. "Way more dramatic than I ever expected."

Mrs. Moran gave her a gentle smile. Luci took another sip of tea and readjusted herself on the bucket. She was here to tell Mrs. Moran about her past. It was time to accept where she'd come from, and find a way to share the truth with her community. She was ready.

Or almost ready. Telling Mrs. Moran would be like a soft launch.

Luci needed to honor the little girl with the big question, and admit that her path, while unconventional and rocky, had brought her to a place where she was happy.

And maybe once she had reconnected with her youth, the Jenga tower of emotion wouldn't sway so perilously. She could let herself feel without fear of being overwhelmed. She could let herself love.

The question was *how*? The town was going to freak out when they learned the truth. She would wait until summer break, for sure. Then the news could filter throughout the town and lose its impact before school started.

Right?

"How so?" Mrs. Moran asked.

Luci jerked up her head, tea sloshing over the side of her cup.

"In what way are things dramatic?" Mrs. Moran prompted.

Luci managed a smile. "I guess I didn't entirely understand what I was signing up for when I took this job."

"No one told you teaching included living with eleven students in an old hotel, working with a

Mad Hatter principal and hosting a gala to save your job?" Mrs. Moran asked. "Funny. They really should have offered a class on that."

Luci laughed.

"How is the gala? Is everything coming along?"

"It's coming alright. Like a freight train."

As though to underscore her words, a trampling of feet sped past the broom-closet office, along with the voices of her male coworkers. Luci leaned back to peek out the door. Tate, Vander, Colter, Neveah and Mateo were joking and jostling each other as they headed out. As they got to the door, Mateo looked back and saw Luci. His brilliant smile broke out as he waved. Like maybe he'd been thinking of her, too. Then he slipped out the door.

Luci gave her head a sharp shake.

"What do you suppose that's about?" Mrs. Moran asked.

Luci stared after them. When Mateo left the building, a piece of her heart went with him, pulling her to follow. "Who even knows anymore?"

"It didn't sound like a someone-is-in-danger stampede," Mrs. Moran noted.

"No, it was more 'there's something cool and unusual happening at the hotel.'"

Luci turned from where she'd been staring at Mateo's exit to find Mrs. Moran smiling at her.

"Shall we go find out?"

Mrs. Moran held her gaze. Luci hadn't shared the secret she intended to, but she had the feeling she'd totally given away another. Luci grinned back at her.

"Let's."

They set their teacups on Mrs. Moran's desk, then headed out past Loretta's aggressively inspirational signage and into the street.

"I hear some little towns are sleepy, peaceful places to live," Mrs. Moran said idly.

Luci laughed.

"But in Pronghorn it seems to be one thing after another."

"So true," Luci said.

Like literally. What's next around here?

As they entered the hotel courtyard, a familiar hubbub of voices came tumbling out of the lobby.

"Harlow must be here," Luci said.

"What makes you think that?"

"There's a specific pitch to the excitement Harlow brings. And if you listen—" Luci paused, waiting for the timbre of another voice. "You hear that?"

"Vander?"

"Right. Normally he's pretty quiet in a social setting, but something about Harlow makes him want to talk. And play guitar, and write love songs."

They entered the hotel lobby to find an explosion of color and noise: silk and sequins and students. So many students. Way more than actually lived here. And since it was Friday, no one was supposed to be here at all.

"Hey!" Harlow called to Luci, waving from across the room. "I brought dresses!"

Flashy, silky dresses of all kinds were strewn over

every available chair, settee and even the check-in desk where Mateo used to keep his grading.

"So I surmised," Luci said.

"For the kids," Harlow clarified as she rummaged in a bag. When she straightened she was holding an off-the-shoulder, lavender silk dress. "Where's Cece?"

Luci planted her feet and awaited further information.

"OMG!" Sylvie yelled. "It's vintage Versace." She pulled a dress to her chest. "Harlow, where did you find this?"

"I told you, I messaged a few friends and asked if anyone could donate a cocktail dress or two for the cause."

Luci's heart sped up as a familiar scent pulled her attention from the activity. Mateo had made his way across the room to stand very close to her. She widened her eyes and gestured to the clothing. He shook his head in amazement.

"How many friends do you have?" Mateo asked Harlow, then muttered to Luci, "And what are their lives like?"

Luci giggled, then called out to Harlow, "This is *amazing*."

Harlow wove her way through the throng of students, stopping to greet Mrs. Moran as though she was an A-list celebrity. Which the elderly Spanish teacher absolutely was, in Harlow's estimation.

Luci picked up a sparkly black dress by its thin

straps. She glanced at Mateo. "The kids are going to look like they're club hopping in Nashville."

He laughed, setting her heart racing even harder. "Which one will you wear?"

"I'm not sure there's a Ms. Walker dress in this mix."

Harlow appeared next to them. "I didn't think there was a good place nearby for prom wear, so I asked a few friends to check their closets and see if they had anything to donate."

Luci reached out to hug her. "You are an absolute wonder, Harlow Jameson."

Harlow accepted the hug, pulling Luci tight to her as she whispered, "I thought about you and me at this age. We would have appreciated a room full of dresses."

Luci tightened her embrace. "I *still* appreciate a room full of dresses."

"For Antithesis!" Sofi said, holding up an orange-and-red dress that looked like a column of fire.

"Yes," Sylvie agreed.

"Let me see!" Antithesis called from the other side of the room, jumping up to look over the crowd.

"I guess we need to start thinking about the guys," Tate said.

Colter looked over his shoulder at Mateo and said meaningfully, "Yeah. Maybe Mateo can come up with a *strategy* for that one?"

Mateo come up with a strategy? For nice clothing? Luci glanced at him for an explanation, but nothing seemed to be forthcoming.

"Ms. Walker, do you have a dress?" Sylvie asked.

"Uh, I think so? Maybe." Luci had two, knee-length wool shift dresses. They were technically interview dresses, but one of them should be fine.

"Oh, I brought something for Ms. Walker," Harlow said, winking at Luci.

"What did you do?" Luci asked.

"Nothing." Harlow ducked behind the reception desk and emerged with a pink shopping bag with fancy black lettering across the front.

"*Not* nothing. What did you buy?"

"You need something for my bachelorette party," Harlow said, defending herself. She returned to Luci and held out the bag. "It's a present."

Mateo glanced into the bag. Luci kept her gaze on Harlow's face.

"You didn't need to buy me a dress."

"True statement, but I wanted to. As you know, it's hard to stop me when I want to do something."

Luci opened the bag to find an elegant slip dress, the color of a Pronghorn sky the moment before sunset. It was cut on the bias, so it would outline her figure, but not cling too tightly.

It was stunning. Like, this dress could attend the gala on its own and turn heads.

Luci gazed at the dress, not even knowing what to say.

"Wow." Mateo's eyes tracked from the dress to Luci and back again. A flush ran up her neck as she imagined him imagining her in the dress. "That's, uh...wow." Mateo slipped his hands in his pockets and spun away from Luci. "Hey, Tate? Colter? Can we get back to that planning session? *Now.*"

A conspiratorial grin lit up Harlow's face. "Are the guys fleeing?"

"They don't want to rifle through dresses anymore?" Luci wrinkled her nose. "Weird."

Harlow blew a kiss to Vander as he left the room. "I think they were in the middle of something earlier."

Luci held up the dress. The little girl, Evening Light, seemed to reemerge inside of her, a part of the path that led her to a beautiful place with good friends and engaging work. She'd nearly come full circle, reconnecting her past with her purpose as an adult.

Taking steps toward a relationship with an incredible man.

Luci blinked, then leaned against Harlow as they watched the girls go through the dresses. "Thank you, friend. This dress is magical."

"You're a little magical, too, you know." Then she addressed the girls. "Okay, who wants to help pick out a dress for Mrs. Moran? I have several options."

CHAPTER SIXTEEN

WAS THERE ANY other place in the world where a gangly young man from an alternative community would be dancing the Lindy Hop with an opinionated Dutch midfielder? Ilsa's movement was precise and powerful, like when she played soccer. Mav was all flailing arms and legs, but they were having the time of their lives.

Only in Pronghorn.

The ballroom shone as it must have in its glory days. Over the last few weeks, students and community members had cleaned the space, down to the final piece of dust caught in the decorative molding. Every detail of the gala had come together—if not perfectly, then like a patchwork quilt where mistakes made the whole that much more appealing.

Saturday was the big day, and they still needed to finalize the playlist.

Luci clapped her hands to get students' attention.

No one stopped dancing or talking.

Mateo ambled over to cut the music playing on his phone. Kids who a few weeks ago complained about having to learn these dances as part of their PE curriculum now grumbled about being made to stop.

Luci jumped up on the dais. "May I have your attention! The gala is three days away and you have done a wonderful job preparing for the big night. Mateo and I would like to remind you of your role as hosts."

Mateo joined her on the dais. "We've sold over three hundred tickets, and have received several large donations. Now, we need to make sure your donors have fun and are excited to keep donating in the future."

"We want our guests to feel cared for and to have a blast," Luci said. "We're not groveling for donations, we're meeting a real need in this area by throwing a fabulous party. Our job is to get the party rolling by greeting people, chatting with folks, telling them about your experience in school and listening as they tell you stories of their good old days."

"Let's be clear," Mateo added. "You need to walk up to adults you don't know, and ask them what brought them here."

The students nodded, like this was a reasonable ask.

"Then you need to listen to the entire answer," Luci added.

That directive was greeted with a little more skepticism.

"As much as we can, we want our guests to take part in the festivities. To connect with old friends, enjoy the food and, most importantly, to dance."

"That means creating a playlist aimed at our guests," she said.

The kids immediately began to grumble. The current playlist was a mash-up of big-band music and Beyoncé. Which, Luci had to admit, wasn't a terrible mix, they were just missing six decades of music in between.

"You all had an assignment to ask community members what songs they'd like to hear."

"We did," Antonio said, defending the crew. "We're gonna play that one song from the sixties."

"That one song from the sixties?" Luci asked. "I feel like there was more than one song in the nineteen sixties."

"We need to include popular music from the last seventy years," Mateo reminded them. "The music should spark good memories for everyone who comes."

"Then why can't we do the 'Thriller' dance?" Morgan asked, *again.*

No sooner had she said it than the whirling bass line and lyrics of the Michael Jackson megahit got stuck in Luci's head. Again.

"Wrong time of year," Luci reminded her.

"Who cares? It's a fun dance."

"Do you really want to see Gen X moms storm the floor for a Halloween-themed dance?" Luci snapped.

"Yes!" the students responded.

Luci glanced at Mateo and muttered, "This is going to be *so* different from the galas at Breasely-Wentmore."

He grinned back at her. "I feel like that was already implied."

That's when a serious omission hit her. "We don't have a waltz."

Groans and imitation retching filled the room.

"Seriously. Waltzing is fun!" Even as the words left her mouth, Luci knew she sounded like a twenty-five-year-old grandma. Mateo tried to back her up, but no one was listening.

"It doesn't matter, anyway, because Coach Tate didn't teach us a waltz," Morgan said.

Luci and Mateo exchanged a baffled look.

"How did he not teach you a waltz?" Mateo asked.

"Because waltzing is boring?" Taylor suggested.

"Okay, that's not going to stand. Waltzing, with the right person, is about the least boring thing." Luci's eyes flicked directly to Mateo.

Could you be any more obvious?

She cleared her throat. "I have history on my side here. The waltz was scandalous when it first came out, shocking. Like, it was banned by mission priests in California."

"Why? Because it's so dull?"

Mateo disengaged from the argument, heading over to his phone.

"Because it was so intimate," Luci explained.

"Women also didn't used to show their ankles," Sylvie noted. "Times have changed."

"This discussion isn't about whether or not the waltz is still scandalous, it's about how fun it is. I can't believe Coach Tate omitted this dance." Luci glanced over to Mateo as he fussed with something on his phone. "Could I get some backup over here?"

Mateo looked over his shoulder at her as music filled the room, the first strands of the old classic "Can't Help Falling in Love with You." She furrowed her brow, listening. Then she heard it. The song was in three-four time, perfect for a waltz.

Were they really going to do this?

He advanced on her, his hand outstretched.

Oh, yes.

Luci met him at the center of the dance floor and let her palm rest against his. Mateo grasped her hand lightly, then slipped an arm around her waist.

They both knew how this was done. They might not have enjoyed their time at prep school, but both reaped the benefits. Their hands knew the correct positions, and instinctively, they would execute the steps and hold the exact right amount of space between their bodies.

Their hearts, on the other hand, weren't following the rules at all.

Mateo initiated the dance and Luci responded, letting the song flow through her. She caught his scent, and his stubbled cheek brushed hers.

Luci lost herself in the waltz. Mateo was strong and confident as he led, spinning her in his arms. The room blurred out of focus, all she could see was Mateo, smiling as the song expressed every simple truth about their beautiful, complicated, enduring friendship.

More than friendship.

Mateo had always been more than a friend. The moment she met him her heart responded with a sure and steady beat meant only for him. No amount of bickering could change that. This was the man she wanted.

The song ended, their feet stilled. Luci remained in Mateo's arms, in the warmth of his gaze. They had a strict rule about no fighting in front of the kids, but what about kissing?

A noise intruded on their bubble. It took Luci a moment to recognize it as applause. She scanned the room and saw that students were already imitating their movements.

Luci tried to catch her breath. Mateo gave her hand a subtle squeeze, grinning at her.

Then to the group, he called out, "Who's ready to learn?"

IF MATEO HAD taught a room full of kids to waltz, sent home the students who weren't living in the hotel and gotten everyone else upstairs and in their rooms for the night, he couldn't remember. All he could see was Luci.

Except for right now, because she was tucked up in her room.

Mateo stood in the hallway, outside his own door. It was eleven o'clock. They both had to be at work by seven thirty tomorrow morning. He really should get to sleep.

He gazed at her door. The white molding, classic paneling and crystal doorknob of the entry to her room seemed even prettier than the rest of the doors. As though the hotel itself wanted to straighten up and look good for her.

Or it was possible that she regularly cleaned her door and polished the crystal handle. This was Luci, after all.

He stared at the portal, willing her to step out into the hallway, to give him five more minutes. The pretty door stayed resolutely shut. Was that her voice, chatting with the four hedgehogs?

He closed his eyes and leaned against his unremarkable door. He had it *bad*. He'd had it bad for a long, long time. But the last few weeks made it clear—he and Luci could work together, they could thrive together.

It was the perfect imperfections that he loved in her. But how should he move forward? They worked together, lived together, had lives so intertwined that he couldn't make any mistakes as he pursued a relationship with Luci. He had to get it right on the first go. It required thought and planning, but the moment he looked at her any hope of a functioning frontal lobe flew right out the window.

"Hi."

Mateo's eyes snapped open. Luci stood in her open doorway, her pink flannel pajamas a little too long in the wrists. Her hair was down, her glasses slightly askew on her perfect ski-jump nose.

"Hi."

She smiled at his greeting, then blushed as she tucked her hair behind one ear. The tiny scar at the apex of her ear where she'd once had the piercing that identified her as an emerging adult at the Open Hearts Intentional Community was barely visible.

"Can't sleep?" she asked.

"Nope." He gazed into her eyes, letting her know exactly who was keeping him awake. "You?"

She shook her head, the mischievous smile curving her lips.

Mateo gazed at her. "Do you remember the day we met?"

"You were talking to Puddles the duck. I was so nervous, but then I saw you, and Puddles, and you smiled at me. You were wearing a rumpled green sweatshirt, and had mud on your boots. Your smile, and your kindness with the Pixar character... I never told you this, but they were exactly what I needed."

"I wasn't talking to you just to be nice," he admitted, taking a step toward her.

"You were wondering where I got my sweater?"

"I was wondering how I was going to focus on my studies with such a cutie in my cohort."

She flushed a deeper red, and glanced down at her bare feet. He took a step toward her.

"Do you remember when I suggested we get pizza after our first class?"

"Track Town pizza." She grinned at him. "That was a fun night."

He nodded. "I was trying to ask you out. On a date. But I accidentally wound up inviting the whole cohort."

Her gaze connected with his. She took a step toward him, her hands peeking out of the cuffs of her pajamas.

"Do you remember the study groups we used to have at the Knight Library?"

"Very well."

"It took me forever to realize you stood and offered chairs to everyone when they entered." The dimple in her cheek was present as she said, "At first I thought it was just me."

He glanced at the carpet, then back at Luci as he admitted, "I used to get to class and study sessions early and leave all my stuff on a chair so I could offer you the seat next to me when you arrived."

Her flush deepened. His heart beat hard and steady in his chest as he took a step toward her.

"Do you remember when you got your placement at Churchill High School?" she asked. "I was supposed to be at a different school, but I pestered that really cool woman into taking me as her student teacher. I was so nervous, I felt like I needed someone from our cohort down the hall. And you were the person I most wanted teaching three doors down."

He hadn't known. He only remembered the relief of realizing they were going to be at the same placement.

"Do you remember when I suggested it would be bad for the environment if we didn't carpool?"

She laughed. "Thank you for all those rides. I didn't have a driver's license. Still don't."

The unfolding pieces of her background continued to surprise him, and he imagined they would for years to come.

"Do you want me to teach you how to drive?"

She held his gaze, nodding slowly as she took another step toward him. "I would love that."

She was less than a foot away from him now. Mateo couldn't wait for driving lessons, for history lessons, for their inevitable arguments about the superiority of coffee over tea.

Her eyes were a perfect twilight blue as she gazed at him and said, "Do you remember that one time, when you put on a romantic song, and we taught a group of kids to dance?"

Mateo laughed out loud, taking the final step toward her. They stood in the middle of the hall together. Tentatively, he placed his hand on her cheek. She gazed into his eyes.

"It was really fun," he admitted.

"I thought so."

Mateo could barely breathe. He could barely think at this point. He was only aware of the beautiful, complex woman who was so close but not nearly as close as he wanted her to be. Her scent caught him and he felt dizzy. Then Luci slipped her arms around his waist and drew him into a kiss. His eyes closed, cherishing the moment. Her soft lips against his, her baggie pajamas, the wholeness of Luci in his arms.

He wrapped his arms more tightly around her, deepening the kiss, trying to express all he felt for her.

This was the only strategy he needed.

LUCI WAS STANDING in the hallway, kissing Mateo Lander.

She'd dreamed of this kiss. The stubble on his cheek, his clean, warm scent, the way he couldn't stop smiling as he kissed her.

It all felt like a gloriously good idea.

His hands cradled her cheeks. He kissed her dimple, the tip of her nose. "I really like you."

She laughed.

"I like everything about you," he went on.

Somehow, that made her laugh even harder, which turned into a laugh-squeak.

"That, right there," Mateo said. "The sound you make when you laugh, the way you get mad when a student is in danger of not appropriately learning a concept, the way you light up when explaining a random history fact. All of you."

Luci felt weightless, as though Mateo had lifted the cloak of worry and fear obscuring her heart. She floated, free and easy. Mateo liked all of *her*.

"Even with my weird past, and the fact that I kept it from you?"

"We all have things in our pasts we don't like to talk about," he said.

She gazed at him frankly.

"Yours is, admittedly, a little more complex than most people's. But I think you're amazing *because* of where you've come from and what you've accomplished, not in spite of it."

Luci let the warmth envelop her. She needed to say something similar. Let him know how much he meant to her. Mateo was always good with words, good at knowing what to say, and when and how.

She opened her mouth to speak. The emotions piled up. She was way past liking and admiring by this point. She'd always known she would fall hard and irrevocably for this man if she let herself. And here she was, gleefully plummeting into love with her friend. She couldn't help falling in love.

"I think you're—" Luci placed both hands on his chest as she looked into his eyes to find the right words. "I think you're my favorite."

He held her cheek in his palm, his sparking, dark eyes connected with hers. A smile lit his face, as though her words were exactly what he wanted to hear. Then he drew her lips to his again, and they were kissing.

This was exactly where she was meant to be.

CHAPTER SEVENTEEN

MATEO JOGGED DOWN the front steps of the school. Friday's lesson plan was "get ready for the gala." The students were working on food, decorations and preparing the town for the influx of visitors. That suited Mateo fine. There was no way he would have been able to focus on teaching math with Luci existing across the hall from him. With Luci existing anywhere within a hundred-mile radius.

They'd stayed up late the previous evening, long past curfew. Laughing, talking, kissing, confessing, more kissing. When they finally returned to their rooms, Mateo drifted off to sleep on a cloud of joy, anticipation and relief. He could finally admit how crazy he was about Luci. This morning he woke up in the same haze of happiness.

Presently, his orders were to check in to see how the food was coming along and determine whether or not Angie needed extra help. Then he would transport the champagne and sparkling cider to the hotel and somehow make room for it in the refrigerator. Luci and her crew were cleaning the hotel's ancient crystal and china, getting it all polished up and ready for the big night. So as soon as he did his rounds, he'd wind up back in the same building with her, and with any luck the same room.

Cleaning teacups had never sounded so appealing.

"What are you smiling about?"

Mateo looked up sharply. The combination of sunshine, euphoria and the lingering scent of Luci made his head spin as he tried to redirect his focus.

Willa waved a hand in front of his face. "Good morning?"

"Oh. Hi. Good morning!" He hugged Willa, because who didn't deserve a hug on this glorious day? "What are you up to?"

"Colter and I are mapping out parking." She gestured to the field beyond the school, where Colter was supervising a team of kids earnestly chalking parking spaces and quibbling over signage. "You're in an awfully good mood for someone who got to bed so late."

"I'm just happy."

Willa raised her brow. "Sylvie told me you and Luci gave the class a dance demonstration last night. Said you both made the waltz look good."

Mateo grinned. The whole world could know as far as he was concerned.

"It's a great dance," he said.

"So I've heard." Willa winked at him.

"How—" Mateo paused, unsure of how to phrase his question. From the moment they all stepped off the bus in Pronghorn, Willa had been the mom of the group. He valued her opinion. "How obvious—?" He pointed at the hotel, which contained Luci, then at himself.

"Very." She placed an arm around his shoulder in a sympathetic half hug. "And completely charming."

He laughed.

"Now, go check on Angie. Not because she needs help but because she's going to be mad if a teacher doesn't try to get in her way."

Mateo trotted down the steps, heading to The Restaurant. People were already arriving for the gala, staying with friends or relatives in the area. It was fun to see former Pronghorn residents exclaiming over changes to the town.

Tate stood in front of the old Public Trust bank building, talking to two women in their early thirties. "Mateo!" he called. "Meet Meghan and Lara. They're the ones who bought the building."

"Nice to meet you." Mateo shook the women's hands. "I hear you're selling nack nacks."

They laughed, clearly already acquainted with Loretta's style of communication.

"We *make* custom backpacks," Meghan said.

"And chalk bags for climbers, portable hammocks and other special-order outdoor gear," Lara added.

"Okay, *that* makes more sense." Mateo gave a firm nod. "Loretta made it sound like you were opening a backpack emporium."

Lara laughed. "Not quite. We wanted to live in a small town with affordable prices and access to outdoor activities. Plus Pronghorn is part of the Dark Sky Sanctuary and Meghan is an astronomer."

"Amateur astronomer," she clarified. "This place is awesome."

"It *is* awesome. You're gonna love it here," Mateo asserted.

"They're gonna run a small storefront," Tate said, gesturing to the front windows of the building. "And they *both* have coaching experience! Volleyball and dance team."

Mateo laughed. "How long did you wait before asking them?"

Tate glanced at the women, running a hand through his hair. "I said hello first, right?"

The soft hiss of the infamous Lyfcycles ridden by the Open Hearts members caught Mateo's attention. He turned to see Today's Moment and several others riding into town on their Segway/bicycle things, orange robes flapping in the wind. They were towing small trailers, each loaded with flowers for the gala. The group maneuvered expertly around Connie where she lay stretched out in the middle of her street.

Meghan furrowed her brow. "Is that the 'religious diversity' the real-estate agent told us about?"

"Yes," Mateo said. "The folks from Open Hearts are good people. A little quirky, but so is everyone else around here."

"Oh, for sure. But is all this activity normal? Is there something happening around here today?" Lara asked.

Tate gestured to the hotel. "There's a big gala to raise funds for the school. I hope you both can join us."

Across the street, the door to the tiny, abandoned house next to the sheriff's office clapped open and Raquel came charging out.

"If she thinks she's going to sneak in there and arrange those flowers without me—"

"Mom, chill." Taylor followed Raquel out of the little house, which, on a second look, wasn't as abandoned as it used to be. Had someone cleaned those windows?

"I'm *not* going to chill. Today's Moment and I had an agreement."

"Then I'm sure she's going to follow through," Taylor said. "You still have work to do on the shop."

Tate and Mateo exchanged a glance. *Shop?*

Mateo studied the tiny house more closely. Likely built in the 1920s, it was so small and weathered he hadn't even noticed it the first few months they were in town. But it looked like the front porch had been spruced up, and an understated sign hung over the front door.

Holms Custom Jewelry

"Raquel!" Tate ran into the street. "You have a jewelry store!"

Raquel attempted to wave away the attention, but Tate continued to bellow. He slipped one arm around Raquel's shoulder and raised his other hand. "Attention citizens of Pronghorn! Our most distinguished artist is opening her own shop!"

"Shush!" she scolded. "It's mostly just a workshop. I don't want to bother Mac by keeping a display in his store."

"This is the best jewelry!" Tate shouted across the street to Meghan and Lara.

"If you have any hopes of me finishing that special order for Aida's birthday, you need to lower your voice right now," Raquel snapped.

"Congratulations," Mateo said, at a more reasonable volume.

"Thank you." She gave an understated nod. "And I know Luci is hard to buy for, so I made a pair of little drop earrings with turquoise and pearls."

Mateo blinked. Okay, Willa was right—he was that obvious.

"Of course, when I was her age I was much more adventurous with my jewelry. Heaven forbid that girl go out on a limb and try something asymmetrical."

"Mom!" Taylor admonished.

At that point, Aida exited her office and threatened to cite her fiancé for disturbing the peace. Tate introduced her to Pronghorn's newest residents, while Mateo ducked into Raquel's nearly finished shop. As always, he was amazed by Raquel's artistry, her ability to create the perfect setting for each stone. He found the earrings she'd designed for Luci right away. They were simple, ethereal. A pearl stud gave way to a thin silver chain holding another pearl, and finally a sky-blue turquoise stone. Mateo was tempted to wax on about how perfect they were, how thoughtful Raquel was to create something Luci would enjoy. But that would only make her uncomfortable. He simply purchased the perfect earrings, and knew Raquel would feel the compliment every time she saw Luci wearing them.

The day continued at a similar level of excitement and activity. The Restaurant was packed with students as they helped Angie with the slow-cooked barbecue beef and pork, and prepared mass quantities of coleslaw, mac and cheese, and baked beans. They had it all under control.

By the time Mateo made it to the store, Mac and Mav were already hitching a trailer full of beverages to an ATV. It was funny how Mav had allied himself with Mac. When the teachers had first arrived in Pronghorn, the awkward teen drifted aimlessly around town, getting in everyone's way and challenging people to arguments over generally agreed upon social constructs, like which side of the street cars should drive on. But over the course of the school year, Mav became more intentional about where he spent his time. For the last three months, he was seen more and more often at Mac's shop. And Mac never complained.

"This is enough champagne for the Met Gala," Mateo commented.

"If there's extra, keep it. I hear you have a few friends getting married over the summer." Pronghorn's unassuming store owner walked past him before Mateo could acknowledge the generous donation. "Mav, you have it all loaded up?"

"Yep. Can I drive the ATV?" Mav asked.

"Do you know how?" Mateo countered.

Mav shrugged, which meant no. Then he turned

to Mateo and said, "You're a teacher, you could teach me. I don't even need a license to drive an ATV."

Mateo stared down at the finicky, camo-painted vehicle, imagining what a rolled ATV and twenty cases of fizzy beverage crashing on Main Street would look like. He drew in a deep breath, mentally waving away the thought.

"And there's no time like the present. Let's do this."

A quick tutorial on the handlebar controls, a few lurching starts and stops and the two of them were finally puttering toward the hotel.

"Go slow," Mateo instructed. "There are a lot of new folks in town today."

Mav was all focus as he drove roughly two miles an hour down Main Street. He parked the ATV and trailer by the side entrance to the hotel, next to the kitchen. He turned off the engine and remained in his seat.

Mateo hopped off the ATV. His first driving lesson had gone well. The next one would be in a car, with a supercute social studies teacher.

Then Mav sighed.

Mateo got really nervous. He was always willing to help out a kid, but Luci had been covering most of the relationship drama. Mateo had the feeling he was about to be on the receiving end of a string of questions about Ilsa.

But instead, Mav said, "I have a job."

"You do? That's great."

Or is it? At Open Hearts, kids were given their first job when they committed to staying with the community. It was a big deal, accompanied by a celebration and new clothes. But Mav seemed to want more than a life at Open Hearts.

And since the kid hung out at the store, in the dormitories and everywhere else in town, it wasn't an unreasonable suspicion.

Mav leaned back, out of his slouch, and looked at Mateo. "At Mac's. I'm a barista and I restock the floor."

Oh. Whoa.

"Mav, that's…*not* a job at Open Hearts."

"It's not," he said, eyes forward.

"Congratulations." He tried to infuse the word with hope and enthusiasm. "That's a big decision."

"Everybody at home is all wanting to engage in open dialogue about it," Mav said. "It's been kinda hard, because like, *everyone* wants to discuss it with me. It's good to talk about your feelings, but nobody understands my feelings and they keep trying to convince me this is just a phase."

"I hear you." Mateo said, but he didn't come close to really understanding. He did, however, know someone who would.

Mav stood and walked around to the trailer. He grabbed a case of sparkling cider and lifted it. Mateo followed suit. He didn't speak, letting silence invite Mav to offer more of his thoughts.

"Ms. Walker inspired me to do it."

Mateo followed Mav into the kitchen. "Did she talk to you about it?" That would be incredible, if Luci had opened up about her past to Mav.

"No, but she's brave. You know?"

Mateo smiled. "I do know."

"She doesn't let anything get in her way. Even when you can tell she's nervous, she still gets things done. It's cool." Mav set the case of cider on the counter.

Mateo set his case next to Mav's and waited. Noise from the adjoining dining room filtered in. Luci and a group of students would be setting up a buffet, setting out the china and freshly washed and pressed table linens.

"Ms. Walker gets us."

"She has a real understanding of her students," Mateo concurred.

"No, I mean *us*." Mav turned and walked back to the door. "Me, and Antithesis, and Spring Rain and the other kids from Open Hearts." They stepped into the sunshine and grabbed second cases of cider. "Ms. Walker sees the good and the bad of the community but she never judges us. She, like, I don't know how to say it. She *gets* us. She knows how to frame a discussion, and why it's good to go into the sun when our emotions are running high. I can't explain it." Mav turned so he could push the door open with his shoulder.

They set the cases of sparkling cider onto the counter. Mav stared at the beverages as though they might contain the answer.

"I can't explain it," he said again, then he looked at Mateo. "Can *you*?"

Mateo locked eyes with Mav. The kid didn't want

to ask outright, but he clearly had a sense of Luci's background.

This wasn't Mateo's secret to share. But it would be so good for Mav to have someone to talk to, and it would be so good for Luci. A burst of laughter came from the next room.

"Ms. Walker's life experience is unique," Mateo said, trying to answer the question without lying, but without saying too much.

"Is it?" Mav asked.

Well, no, not by Mav's standards.

"Maybe you should talk to Ms. Walker about all this."

"I tried. At the solstice, I was describing lime cakes, which are so good. It was like she knew what I was talking about. And that's when I noticed her scar." Mav touched the piercing at the top of his own ear.

Mateo froze. Mav was observant, and once he was on the lookout for signs that Luci was raised at Open Hearts, he would have picked up on everything.

"I just need to know. Is Ms. Walker the girl they talk about, Evening Light?"

The question seemed to expand through the room. The longer Mateo took to answer it, the more obvious the answer was.

So much good could come of Mav knowing about her background. Not the least of which would be Luci finally unburdening herself of this secret.

And Mav was asking a direct question. Mateo

wasn't going to lie. He knew all too well the harm that came from lying, the webs of deception created when adults withheld information.

"You need to speak to Ms. Walker directly," Mateo said.

"I tried but sometimes she can be intimidating."

"I understand, but you should—"

"Can you just tell me?" Mav asked. "Did she grow up at Open Hearts and then leave?"

Luci's laugh rang out from the adjoining room.

Mateo made his decision. He would answer Mav honestly, then go get her. She wouldn't be happy with him, but she *would* want to help Mav. That was why she was here, wasn't it? That was why she was so desperate to save the school, so she could be here for Mav and the others as they faced this difficult decision.

Luci had told him she would do anything for Mav.

"Yes," Mateo said.

"Oh, wait, what?" Mateo looked up to see Cece standing by the door. "Ms. Walker grew up at Open Hearts?"

Mateo opened his mouth to speak but Cece's exclamation had attracted Oliver.

"No way!" Oliver glanced back into the dining room, where Luci was chatting with the students.

Mav spoke quietly as he approached his friends. "You guys, we're not supposed to know. I asked because—"

"Ms. Walker?" Oliver clarified. "Ms. Walker grew up at Open Hearts?"

"I can't believe it!" Cece clapped her hands over her mouth, eyes wide. "I *don't* believe it. Ms. Walker?"

"WHAT'S THE DRAMA?" Luci appeared at the door. Always on the alert for trouble, she'd sensed something was up. The students stared at her, eyes searching for clues.

She glanced across the room at Mateo. The familiar spark lit, then quickly faded as she asked, "What's going on?"

The lack of response chilled her. Sweat pricked the back of her neck. Most of the time, when kids had done something wrong, they would start talking immediately, trying to cover their tracks. No one said a word.

Cece and Oliver glanced at each other. Mateo stared at the countertop. Only Mav made eye contact.

Everything shifted into place.

Luci kept her voice steady. "What happened in here?"

"Kids, I need to talk to Ms. Walker alone. Can you wait here while we duck outside—?"

"I want to talk to Ms. Walker," Mav said, not taking his eyes off her.

Mav *knew*. Emotion rose in her chest as she glanced at Mateo. The man she was falling in love with held eye contact briefly, then dropped the connection.

Mav knew, because Mateo had told him.

Luci widened her stance and folded her arms over her chest. "What. Happened?"

"Ms. Walker, is it true?" Cece asked.

Her stomach churned, as emotions began to pile higher.

Mav gestured toward the door, a combination of hurt and curiosity on his face. "Ms. Walker, I think we should go out into the sun."

The events unfolded like an anxiety dream. Luci half expected the kitchen to morph into the dining hall at Breasely-Wentmore, a little girl in orange half the size of the other students getting crushed by a society she didn't fit into.

Mateo advanced on her, his expression serious, remorseful. Was this really happening? She opened her mouth, ready to demand clarification again, but stopped. As long as no one said anything, she could stall the truth.

Mateo had told these kids her secret.

He'd taken her trust and shredded it.

He'd destroyed their friendship for what? A moment of honesty?

She would have no one to lean on as she dealt with the aftermath of his casual cruelty. He had simultaneously broken her trust and sent her into a storm of repercussions. She'd have to explain her actions and admit she'd been lying. She'd have to deal with the anger and hurt from people from Open Hearts. Her students would never trust her again.

And all the while, she would be deprived of the one person she would have gone to for help in this nightmare situation.

The sound of students' hushed and fascinated chatter encroached on her thoughts.

Luci forced herself to lift her head and meet Mateo's gaze.

"I'm sorry," he said softly.

Luci shook her head.

Stop. Don't destroy us by letting this be true.

"Mav asked me a direct question."

He reached for her hand.

"Mav asked me a question and I didn't want to lie."

She stepped back.

Mateo winced at her reaction. "Luci, I'm sorry. I know you're angry."

"Your need for honesty does not trump my desire for privacy."

He looked surprised, as though it hadn't occurred to him that other people had important core values as well. Then he moved closer and whispered, "Luci."

She backed into the refrigerator, emotions building, swaying. The Jenga tower of feelings stretched up, unstable.

"You did this on purpose."

"I can assure you I didn't. Mav asked me."

She was aware of Mav saying something, of other students talking. "You did it on purpose because you don't respect my desire to keep my past private."

"Luci, no." Mateo's eyes were pleading, as though it really all had been a mistake. "Please, I know I misstep and make you angry sometimes."

"Misstep? You shared a deeply personal secret. I trusted you. You are the only person I told. The only person I trusted—"

Mav was suddenly right next to her, claiming his space in the argument. "You shouldn't have secrets. It's not good for you or the community."

Fury ignited inside her. She did not want to hurt Mav. She'd worked too hard for too long to be in a place where she could help him. But if she looked at Mav right now, her response was not going to be pretty.

Mateo kept talking, kept trying. "You know I would never intentionally upset you. Mav asked."

"It was unintentional?" She pressed her fingers against her twitching eyelid. "You unintentionally told the entire student body a key fact about my background I have chosen to keep private?"

"I told Mav, because he needs your guidance."

"Then Mav can ask me." Luci pinned Mateo with a glare. "Mav can take care of his own curiosity."

Mav's head drooped next to hers. "You're not always the most approachable person."

Her grasp on her control finally started to slip. Mateo said something to Mav about stepping back for the moment. The room buzzed with student voices.

Luci was exposed, humiliated. And, apparently, unapproachable. Tears threatened. She tried to speak, but not much more than a whisper came out over the lump in her throat.

"You had no right to share my past with anyone."

"Luci, I'm sorry." Mateo sounded desperate. "I just meant to tell Mav—"

"Because you're always the cool teacher, the one who *cares* about his students. Unlike Ms. Walker, with the strict rules and need for privacy."

"No!" He let out a frustrated breath. "Let's back up here. Assume positive intent."

Luci's throat constricted. It hurt to speak. "How dare you ask that of me?"

He stretched his arms wide, indicating the students. "From day one, you have done everything you can to support the students from Open Hearts—"

"I've done everything to support *all* my students."

"We all talk about it," Mateo said. "Everyone sees how you seek out and care for Mav, Antithesis and Spring Rain. It wasn't a huge leap for me to assume you'd want to help Mav now."

"Helping someone and exposing my past are two very different things."

"Think back to your former self. Wouldn't you want to help that girl who struggled?"

"That girl is gone. I have no past. I have nothing except for this work." Luci swiped at the tears streaming down her cheeks. "And you have taken it upon yourself to irrevocably complicate my work and break my heart in the process."

Her words landed in the silent room, the meaning instantly absorbed by the students.

Once again, she was overreacting. Her emotions had gotten the better of her and she was publicly humiliating herself. She and Mateo had broken the one rule they'd agreed upon, to never fight in front of their students.

Tears of embarrassment and frustration coursed down her cheeks.

Luci shouldered past Mateo, past the blur of horrified students and into the alleyway behind the hotel. She could hear him giving instructions to the kids, and no doubt, he appeared normal and sane. Just tell your students someone's deepest secret, then come off looking like the noble one, the champion of honesty.

Luci sobbed. She felt so out of control. She was furious with Mateo and furious with herself, but when she scratched the surface beneath the anger, sadness rushed in. She began to tremble against the nightmare Mateo's revelation had no doubt unleashed. She'd have to face the people at Open Hearts, their anger and accusations. Her friends would be hurt that she'd never told them, they'd see her for the fake that she was. Willa and Aida might not even want her to be in their weddings anymore. Harlow would stand by her, but Luci would be faced with a choice. Was she really going to bring her drama to Harlow and Vander's happy day?

Her friendships would fall away. She wouldn't be respected in her work.

Her relationship with Mateo was over.

"Luci."

His voice wrapped around her. She was so exhausted and hurt, her instinct was to turn into his arms, bury her face in his neck as he held her.

She glanced at him. His frustration took her by surprise.

"I'm *sorry*," he said, with deliberate enunciation. "I made a mistake."

"You think?"

"It just happened. Mav had already put it together and was asking for confirmation. I was trying to do the right thing." He looked into her eyes. "Please forgive me."

Her chest ached with hurt and longing. This was Mateo. The man she was in love with. Someone who could carelessly speak, then charm his way out of it. She'd be left to clear up the mess, while he'd smile and sleep well, waking up refreshed and ready to hurt her again tomorrow.

"I can probably forgive you, because forgiveness is important to me. I work hard at it and try to understand people within their context." She readjusted her glasses and swallowed the last of her sobs. "But I will *never* trust you again."

Luci walked past Mateo, through the silent kitchen full of students. She held her head high, tears streaming down her cheeks as she passed parent volunteers in the lobby. She didn't start running until she hit the landing at the top of the formal staircase. She sprinted to her room, desperate to keep the sobbing at bay until people couldn't hear her. Breathless and exhausted, she closed the door of her bedroom, and finally, mercifully, dropped onto her bed and wept.

CHAPTER EIGHTEEN

"YOU GET HOW bad this is?" Tate asked.

Mateo's closest friends stared at him from around the wrought-iron table. Morning sunshine washed through the courtyard, and birds chittered in the shrubs. Luci had taken such care of the roses and boxwoods so her hedgehogs could play in something like a hedge. Luci had taken care of the entire hotel, cleaning the shared spaces as though this home were a precious gift to be cherished.

He wouldn't be surprised if she was packing her bags right now.

"Yep." Mateo was so miserable he could barely speak. It hurt his chest to force air through his lungs, but he managed to say, "Clear on that point."

She refused to speak with him. He'd knocked on her door, tried her phone, sent notes in when others were finally allowed in her room. He'd spent hours in the hallway outside her door until Vander and Tate had forced him to go to bed.

Luci didn't want to have anything to do with him, and who could blame her?

"You had no right to share her background with anyone, much less the students," Willa reminded him.

There was an undertone of sympathy in her voice,

but the reaction had largely been mass confusion at how he could have been such an unfeeling idiot.

"In my defense—" Mateo began.

Vander shook his head. "You can't defend this, man. I know you, you're a good guy and would never willingly hurt Luci, or anyone. I'm sure you had your reasons. But the upshot is, she's distressed, and now she has to deal with everyone knowing about her past."

Tate gave his head a sharp shake. "I still can't believe it. Luci grew up at Open Hearts?"

Willa put a hand on Tate's arm to quiet him, but Mateo could read the confusion in her expression. She couldn't believe it, either, and was as hurt as anyone that Luci had kept this secret from her. But Luci hadn't just kept the secret from her friends, she'd kept it from everyone save a few admissions counselors.

She had completely disassociated from her past in order to have the future she wanted. Then she'd been brave enough to come back here to help kids who found themselves in the same situation.

Within the hour, the hotel would be inundated with students and community members setting up for the gala. Mateo didn't know how he was going to make it through the next fifteen minutes, let alone the next twenty-four hours.

Or the rest of his life.

"Where is she?"

"Harlow is with her," Willa said. "I think they're in the solarium. Harlow made her some tea, and as far as we've heard, she's had her nose in a biography of Cyrus the Great all morning."

Mateo's heart broke all over again. Luci loved Cyrus the Great. To the point that Mateo had been a little jealous of the ancient Persian champion of civil rights.

He pressed his palms against his eyes. This was such a nightmare. He'd been excited, walking on air, so full of love for Luci. Then Mav came at him with the questions and that kid could be so determined. In the moment, Mateo honestly felt like he was doing the right thing, doing what Luci would want.

It was like being at St. Xavier's. He thought he was doing the right thing, then out of left field he got in trouble for something he didn't realize was against the rules.

"If you guys want to rehash what a jerk I am, I'm in. I spent all of last night going over it, so I've got plenty to add on the subject." Mateo drew in a breath. "But I *was* trying to help. It's important to me that you know that."

"You're not a jerk. You are among the kindest people I've ever met," Willa said.

Mateo straightened at her words. He didn't deserve any kind of compliment, least of all such a broad statement from Willa.

"Your actions were jerklike," Vander amended. "But you're a good guy."

Tate leaned forward in his chair. "We all know how this went down. We've been watching you and

Luci for eight months now. She's supersensitive. And given her background, I get it. She cares so much about you, and your opinion. When you told Mav, you issued judgment on her decision to keep her past a secret."

Tate was right. Mateo wasn't being held up to arbitrary rules, rather he was the one making them. Honesty was important. Secrets could be harmful. But no one had appointed him the judge of when and how Luci shared this information with the community.

"Well, you sure stepped in it yesterday," a voice announced from the entryway.

Mateo didn't need to turn around to see who had invaded the courtyard to give him another verbal lashing.

"Good morning, Angie."

"I hope you're intending to get this fixed by the gala because I've got dinner for five hundred ready to go in my kitchen."

"She's not speaking to me."

She may never speak to me again.

Angie crossed the courtyard and set a grocery bag on the table.

"She can be real stubborn."

Mateo glanced up. Was she suggesting Luci had a part in all this?

"I mean, you messed up, but you did it because you love her," Angie said. "And you care about the kids."

Mateo sat up, suspicious. "How do you know I'm in love with Luci?"

Angie rolled her eyes. Fair point.

"You've seen what she's done in the community. Probably because you can't take your eyes off her. That girl has turned this town upside down, and for the better."

They all stared at Angie. Of all the teachers, Luci had seemingly caused the least stir. Until now, anyway, and that was Mateo's fault.

Angie continued, "It takes a lot to look past the orange clothing and see a real person, right off the bat. I would know. I was as bad as anyone else around here. Luci saw the kids from Open Hearts as people first, treated them as people. Like using orange for the soccer uniforms and merch, so no one stuck out as different. She gave Vander the idea of asking the Open Hearts kids about their solstice songs for the holiday pageant. She suggested I put a vegetarian offering on the menu. I figured it was just foolishness, but the first day I listed a no-meat option, I had five people from Open Hearts stop by. And once you sit down and eat with someone, they're family. I don't want to suggest the school wasn't key in smoothing out the issues between the townsfolk and Open Hearts, but without Luci, we'd never have gotten this far."

And Luci had done it all quietly and without expecting any recognition.

Angie gestured to him. "You were a real clod in getting her to fess up, but it was time."

"Thank you?"

She nodded. "It was past time. A secret like that had to be eating her up. And the longer she held it, the harder it would have been to say anything. While I'm sure she's furious, she's gonna get through this and be better for it."

Mateo glanced at his coworkers to judge their responses. The general vibe was that Angie might be right, but Mateo was still way in the back of the doghouse.

"Now, where is she?" Angie asked. "I made her some French fries, Mac sent over an espresso and Today's Moment brought her one of those lime cakes."

"French fries, espresso and a lime cake?" Tate asked.

Angie glared at him. "What's wrong with that?"

"Nothing. Great combo. Breakfast of champions."

Angie scowled at him for good measure, but Tate would always be her favorite.

"There's a nice letter in here from Today's Moment, too. Language is a little flowery for my taste, but she lets Luci know they're grateful for all she's done at the school, and can understand why she left Open Hearts when she did."

"You read the letter?" Mateo asked. "That's an invasion of privacy."

Angie leveled him with a look. "You're not one to talk right now."

Good point.

"Can I… Can I look at the lime cake?" Willa

asked. "After all the descriptions of them at the holiday pageant I'm really curious."

They all gathered around the small, dense cake. It smelled incredible. Mateo thought again of how brave Luci had to have been to leave her community and head out into the world at such a young age.

She'd been an outsider for years, unwilling to share the most basic information about herself with others. Then she'd finally come to this place. The teachers had created a home together in the hotel. He didn't know what it would take, but he had to find a way to show Luci that this was still where she belonged.

LUCI STARED AT the lime cake.

The fries had been a kind gesture, but they were cold on receipt and a little nibble suggested that Angie was skimping on the salt again.

She'd drunk the espresso gratefully when it arrived. After a night of no sleep, double caffeine was acceptable, exactly what she needed. Then she'd cradled a hedgehog and read Today's Moment's letter. It wasn't as bad as she'd thought it would be. It wasn't bad at all.

Typical of everyone at Open Hearts, it was verbose, a little overdramatic and three times as long as it needed to be. But kind and welcoming. Sweet, even.

No, it was a very nice letter, thanking her for all she'd done for her students, welcoming her back to Pronghorn and finishing with an invitation to come out to Open Heart's for some "open and engaged dialogue."

It was the lime cake Luci didn't know what to do with.

The buttery cornmeal base would be rich and sweet, soaked through with lime syrup. It would taste like the best days of her childhood. The decadent lime cakes were only served on special holidays: solstice, summer equinox, the spring renewal festival. Luci had loved those days. There had been many nights she couldn't sleep on the eve of a holiday, she was so excited to wake up the next day and eat her favorite treat.

The holidays were also associated with feeling like there was something to do. Children often had a place in the festivities, and those days held more meaning than a normal day of meandering around the property. Holidays also meant that her mom would be on her best behavior. Those were the days in her childhood she could connect with. Maybe that was a start to this bumpy, split existence she'd found herself in. She could focus on the good days. The lime-cake days.

"Ms. Walker?" A tap on the door followed. "Can I ask you a series of questions?"

Luci slumped in her chair, fighting the urge to yell *Oh, for fire's sake!* But Mav didn't need further reminders of where she'd come from.

Luci dabbed at her eyes and set Earl Grey in the basket next to her chair. "Come on in."

"Is the door locked?"

"Try the handle and find out."

Mav opened the door and entered. "I thought the door might be locked because you're upset," he explained.

"A reasonable assumption."

Mav dropped his lanky frame into a chair next to Luci and set a laptop on the table.

"Are you going to eat that lime cake?"

"Yes!" Luci launched protectively toward the cake.

"I was asking because they taste really good," Mav said.

Mav, for all the trouble he'd been a part of stirring up in the last twenty-four hours, was still a teenage boy. And she didn't blame him for eyeing her cake.

"Let's share it."

"Really?"

Luci nodded as she broke the little cake into two pieces, then offered half to Mav. She took a bite, then closed her eyes. So good. Tears pushed at her lids as the sweet lime hit her tongue, positive childhood memories washing out some of the stress and shame of her past.

"This is my favorite food," Mav said.

"Mine, too," Luci admitted.

"I have found I have a taste for ice cream, though."

Luci chuckled. "I still remember the first time I had ice cream. It's amazing."

"It is," Mav confirmed. "And potato chips."

"Also delicious."

He stared at the table for a moment. "Can we open up a dialogue? I know we have to get ready for the gala tonight, but I feel urgency for discussion with you. I had trouble sleeping last night because I want your opinion."

It didn't occur to Mav that maybe *Luci* had trouble sleeping because her deep dark secret had been unceremoniously spilled. Further proof that kids were kids, and teenagers could be oblivious no matter where they grew up.

"Sure. What's up?"

Mav straightened and opened the computer. "I found this job I wanted to ask you about."

"Okay."

"I was researching what lawyers do, because Harlow said I would be a good lawyer. And I found this." Mav pulled up an article entitled "Human Rights Lawyers and Religious Freedom." "This woman helps small religious communities. Do you know about Amish people?"

"I do know about Amish people."

"So she helps them live the way they want to, but—" Mav scrolled to another page in the article "—she also helps make sure people aren't harming others in the name of religious freedom, like she did with a different group in Washington who wouldn't let any of the girls learn how to read."

"That sounds like really valuable work."

"It is." Mav looked at her. "I think I'd be good at it. Harlow says I'm good at asking questions, and

I like to argue. Sheriff Aida says I have a lot of tenacity."

"And you enjoy research," Luci added.

Mav nodded, his eyes still on the article. "Maybe *this* is what I'm supposed to do."

The gangly, argumentative kid had grown so much in the last eight months. At the beginning of the year, she'd recognized his restlessness, and through his experiences at school, he'd found a direction.

"Would you like to do something like this?"

"It compels me. And if I had a career, outside of Open Hearts, I could visit Ilsa in Amsterdam."

"You could. You could save up and travel—"

"The whole world. I could see all the places we talked about in class. I could go anywhere, Tokyo, Buenos Aires, Budapest. I could go to *Maple Heights, Ohio.*"

Luci shook her head. "Maple Heights, Ohio?"

"The birthplace of Mary Oliver?" he said, as though the details regarding his favorite poet were common and widely discussed knowledge.

"Of course. Yes, Mav. That's the great thing about being in the world. You get to experience it."

His expression fell. "But I would miss Open Hearts."

Luci told him what she hoped was true. "I think they're opening up a little. I think you could still come back for visits."

"But the precedent has always been that if you leave, you can't come back at all."

"Maybe it's time for change? We could ask if the community would have a listening session about it?"

"Would you come?"

"I'll help lead it," she promised.

"Thank you." Mav closed the computer. "I'm glad you're here."

"Me, too."

"The gala is tonight," Mav said, abruptly changing the topic. "You should probably brush your hair."

"I intend to." Luci picked up a crumb of lime cake off the parchment paper with her finger. Her heart raced at the thought of the gala, or even leaving this room. Messy hair may have been dead last on her list of worries.

Mav stood and walked to the door, then paused in the open doorway. "I would have dropped out the first week if you hadn't been here."

Luci started to contradict him, but he shook his head. "You get one 'wild and precious life.' I'd like to express my gratitude at what you've chosen to do with yours."

CHAPTER NINETEEN

IT WAS AFTER five when Luci managed to cross the solarium and get her hand on the doorknob.

The next eight hours were going to be some of the worst in her life. Hosting a gala for a community that had probably been talking about her outburst nonstop. A bunch of people—hopefully donors—pulling into town, only to learn a teacher had been lying about who she was for the entire school year.

Facing Mateo.

Luci had to show up at the gala, that was nonnegotiable. And to do so she had to leave the solarium. She pulled in a deep breath, cracked open the door and peeked into the hall.

It was empty.

What had she been expecting? The whole town of Pronghorn assembled on the off-limits floor of the hotel to stare at her as she exited the room?

Okay, she *had* been half expecting that. Or at least her coworkers, waiting with questions.

But the coast was clear. Voices echoed down the wide, varnished stairwell. For the briefest moment, Luci considered risking the elevator so she wouldn't be confronted by whoever was descending. But no. She would have to see people sooner or later, and the elevator was just creepy. Luci closed her eyes briefly, then placed her penny loafers on the stairs, one step after the other.

The trampling of feet and the pitch of voices sounded like students. Luci turned the corner onto the third-floor landing and braced herself.

"Ms. Walker!" Suleiman cried, raising both his arms. "Do you like my suit?"

He was wearing pressed trousers and a rich brown jacket with Western detailing, circa 1975.

"Very sharp," she said. Taylor and Antonio joined them on the landing. Luci paused briefly, so they could all start asking her if *it* was true. But Suleiman just shot his wrists out of his cuffs and posed, setting his friends laughing.

"Where'd you find it?" Luci asked.

"Pete Sorel loaned us vintage jackets," Antonio said, strutting across the stairwell like a character from *Zoolander*, showing off a black jacket and bolero tie.

"You guys look fabulous. And Taylor, your dress!"

Taylor spun, the fringe on her sequined dress flaring. She wore dramatic eye makeup and an elaborate updo. Suleiman grinned at his girlfriend, then took her hand.

"We're the valet parking," Taylor said, kicking up her heel to show off a red high-top sneaker. "So we had to get ready early. But you're gonna be late if you don't get dressed. Harlow has everything set up in the girls' dorm room."

Of course, she did.

"Coach Tate is waiting for us," Antonio said. "Let's go."

"Have fun," Luci called as the trio stampeded down the stairs without asking her a single question about her mystery past.

Huh.

Luci continued up to the fourth floor, her stomach contracting at the thought of Mateo.

They'd tried and failed so many times, coming together and falling apart like a dance. At which point would one or both of them bow out gracefully?

Luci stepped onto the fourth floor. Excited voices emanated from both the girls' and the boys' dormitories.

She glanced at Mateo's room. Where was he right now? Helping downstairs? Getting ready? Playing Frisbee because he forgot there was a gala tonight?

Luci peeked out the window at the field behind the school. Guests were already arriving, but no one was currently engaged in a game of Ultimate.

The door to the girl's dormitory flew open.

"Ms. Walker!" Cece cried. "You need to get ready. Hi."

Luci gave a short laugh. "Hi. You look incredible."

Cece spun, showing off her shimmery lavender dress. "High three, am I right?"

Luci held up three fingers for Cece's version of a high five, then let the girl pull her into the room. She was supposed to have helped the girls get ready, instead of moping in the solarium with her hedgehogs.

Cece gazed at her, then said quietly, "I'm really

sorry I started yelling in the kitchen yesterday. I was just surprised."

Luci froze briefly. Then she said, "I was surprised, too."

"I didn't mean to tell everyone." Cece's expression of remorse shifted something in Luci's chest. No one meant to hurt her in all this. The news was shocking, and students responded as anyone would.

"Of course, you didn't."

"Hey, gorgeous," Harlow said, holding eye contact with Luci. She stood at the center of the melee wearing a floor-length, emerald-green dress, holding a curling iron in one hand, hairspray in the other as she turned Ilsa's bobbed hair into finger waves. "How you feeling?"

"Good," Luci said. "Hungry, actually."

"Same!" Cece said. "The food smells so good."

A young woman came skipping over to Luci. "Ms. Walker, I didn't know you grew up at Open Hearts!"

It took Luci a moment to recognize Antithesis. She wore a one-shoulder, deep orange dress, her long hair woven into an intricate braid.

"I didn't tell you, so there's no way you could have known." Luci acknowledged her part in all this.

"But *I* could have known," Antithesis said. "You remember the first day, when my emotions were running high and I wanted to leave, but you convinced me we should open up a dialogue?"

Luci nodded, remembering that nerve-wracking first day of school, and an argumentative young woman who refused to take part in testing because she didn't want to be judged.

"I would have left and never come back if you hadn't been there."

Luci blinked, unsure of what to say. She decided to go with the truth. "I was pretty nervous myself. It was nice for me to see you, and Mav and Spring Rain. You guys made me feel better, too."

"Antithesis, can you help braid my hair?" Sylvie asked.

"Sure! Just a second." Antithesis gave Luci a hug. "You have a special spirit."

Antithesis scooted off to help her friend. Luci scanned the room. It wasn't just the girls who lived at the hotel dormitory in here. The entire eighteen-and-under female population of Pronghorn and the surrounding area had gathered to get ready for the big night. The girls were kind, and careful with her. But no one was freaking out.

Luci and her drama just weren't that big of a deal. *Awesome.*

The door opened and Willa stuck her head in. "Hey, you doing okay?"

Luci nodded. "Is everything on track downstairs?"

"It's all going according to the brilliant plan you made. Everyone showed up, did their job and we now have a hundred people milling about in the street because if you're not twenty minutes early in Pronghorn, you may as well have missed the event."

Luci let out a chuckle.

"Fortunately, Aida's on parking duty with Tate,

so she doesn't have time to hand out tickets." Willa lowered her voice. "You don't have to come if you don't want to."

Luci let herself consider this option. Everyone was so caught up in the event, maybe they wouldn't miss her at all? Maybe she could put off the awkward conversations for another few days.

"Why wouldn't she come?" Morgan appeared next to them, then gave Luci's outfit a once-over. "You need to get dressed. Harlow, where's Ms. Walker's dress?"

"I'm good," Luci said to Willa. She *was* good. Maybe she shouldn't have kept this secret, but she did, and now she could deal with it. And getting ready and looking fantastic was the first step in dealing with anything. "I'll be there. I just need to steam my dress."

"Already steamed it!" Sylvie called.

"And we borrowed your steamer to do everyone else's dresses, too," Harlow admitted. "I hope that's okay."

"I'm only upset that I missed it. Steaming clothing is so satisfying."

"Right?" Sylvie confirmed.

The girls brought Luci the pale blue slip dress Harlow had gifted her. Since everyone else was mostly finished getting ready, they descended on her like a storm of personal stylists. Morgan took charge of her makeup, Cece helped with her hair, Sylvie and Sofi exchanged opinions on her shoes and finally presented her with a pair of kitten heels. The kids had her suited up in no time.

"It's like the scene with the woodland creatures in *Cinderella*," Harlow noted.

Luci started to nod like she knew the reference, then corrected herself. "I've never seen *Cinderella*."

"How have you not seen—" Harlow started to ask the obvious question, but stopped abruptly.

"I grew up without television or internet," Luci said out loud for the first time in her life.

"I haven't seen it, either," Antithesis said.

"Me, neither," Ilsa said. "Can we watch it tomorrow afternoon?"

"Sounds perfect. Hopefully we'll have an internet connection." Luci had a suspicion about the school's seemingly random pattern of internet connection. She intended to ask a certain Spanish teacher about it later tonight.

A loud knock sounded on the door and Oliver called, "Let's go!"

It wasn't the most dapper invitation to a dance, but no one seemed to mind. Antithesis was out the door first. Oliver's double take was so comical Luci nearly laughed out loud. The girls streamed into the hallway, beautiful and confident. Harlow had done an amazing job of finding dresses that celebrated each girl's unique beauty. The boys quickly lost their self-consciousness and joined them. They descended the wide staircase en masse, a kaleidoscope of butterflies, ready for the world.

"Yay," Luci said as she watched them go. "Just, yay!"

"Yay," Harlow echoed.

"Thank you for…" Where did she even start here? "Thank you for jumping in, getting everyone ready, bringing the dresses in the first place…dealing with my drama."

Harlow wrapped her in a hug. "It's not drama. It's life."

Luci sighed, allowing her friend to soak up her angst.

"How is Mateo?"

"Wretched."

Luci leaned her head against Harlow's shoulder as she let the statement settle.

"How horrible am I if it kind of makes me happy that he's wretched?"

"I'd think you were weird if you didn't."

Luci gave a weak laugh. "You're not supposed to use the word *weird* when talking about someone from Open Hearts."

"Then it's a good thing you're on track with taking a little pleasure in his misery then." Harlow rubbed her back. "Mateo feels horrible. He's desperate to make this up to you."

Luci shook her head. "It wasn't just him. I over-reacted."

"Your reaction was completely valid."

"I broke our one rule, though. I yelled at him in front of our students."

"He feels like he had it coming."

"But I know him. He didn't do it to hurt me. He

wanted to help Mav. And we all know Mav and how persistent he can be. We never would have gotten in this situation if I'd been honest with everyone to begin with."

"You are not allowed to pin this on yourself. Mateo made a mistake," Harlow said. "It's okay to be mad. It's also okay to let it go."

"But what if…" Luci trailed off.

"But what if he makes more mistakes? What if you make mistakes? What if you have another disagreement and it feels awful? Because it's gonna happen."

"Are you telling me there is no happily-ever-after?"

"No, there's definitely happily-ever-after. But it's more like, happily-ever-after with periods of adjustment, recalibration, the occasional stress argument and an underlying understanding that you are so incredibly lucky to have the privilege of fighting with and for each other."

"You and Vander fight?" Luci asked.

"Of course, we argue. Have you met me?"

Luci laughed.

"We argue because there is so much at stake. We are all in. I don't ever want to face this world without Vander next to me. But 'all in' is going to include some disagreements from time to time."

Luci considered this. She did kind of enjoy some of those debates with Mateo. Particularly the way he always made her laugh somewhere in an argument.

Harlow opened her tiny beaded bag and pulled out a small package wrapped in craft paper. "Yesterday afternoon Mateo bought this present for you. He asked me to give it to you, not as an apology, but because he wants you to have it."

Luci glanced behind herself to the boy's dorm room, then she squared her shoulders like she'd seen Harlow do and opened the package.

A gorgeous pair of pearl-and-turquoise drop earrings were nestled in a layer of tissue paper, along with a simple note.

I miss you.

Harlow continued, "Mateo has been working on a strategy to inspire you to fall in love with him, you know. While that's clearly had a few hiccups, he did buy earrings to go with your dress. It doesn't make up for his mistake, but it's evidence of a pattern of behavior."

Luci gazed at the earrings.

What's good in this situation?

The kids get to have a fun evening.

The rest of Pronghorn does, too.

Harlow is my friend.

These earrings are seriously gorgeous, and I don't have to pretend to feel comfortable wearing the cool, chunky pieces Raquel usually sells.

Mateo and I can work this out; he's desperate to work this out.

She let the good thoughts, or vibes, if you will, shimmer in the air around her. A sense of lightness, relief, wafted through as she realized…

I don't have to pretend anymore.

"Are you ready for this?" Harlow asked.

Luci slipped in her earrings and headed for the stairs.

"Let's do it."

MATEO STEPPED OUT of the cloud of Axe body spray and Old Spice from the boys' dormitory, just as Luci and Harlow headed down the stairs. He leaned against the wall and watched them walk away.

A lump rose in his throat, followed by a fresh wave of remorse.

He took a few steps after them, and then he started to run. If he was going to lose her, then it was what it was, but he couldn't let her go without telling her how much she meant to him.

He grabbed the stair railing to steady himself as he followed the voices of Luci and Harlow.

Then his phone buzzed in his pocket.

How did they actually have cell service today?

He glanced at the screen as he trotted down the stairs, then stopped. It was Mrs. Moran.

"Hello?"

"Hello." Her kind voice made him feel a fraction better. "Are you busy at the moment?"

Mateo stared at his phone. Was he busy?

Not at all, just, you know, hosting a gala and trying to win back the love of my life.

"I could use your help," Mrs. Moran said. "I'm over at the school."

"Of course." Worry shot through him. The octogenarian had never asked for help. "I'll be right there."

"I'm upstairs," she said, then disconnected the call.

Mateo stared at his phone for a second, then trotted down the stairs. The lobby was overflowing with guests, holding vintage champagne coupes and chatting amicably. He scanned the room for Luci but she'd already disappeared into the crowd.

He was going to have to wait to find her. If something was wrong with Mrs. Moran, Luci would want him to put her first.

Mateo exited through the courtyard, where more people were enjoying the warm evening. He waved but didn't stop to chat.

Once inside the school, his footsteps echoed through the empty hall. There was only one way upstairs that he knew of, an old door with peeling paint and a Do Not Enter sign. He opened the door and slipped into the stairwell. Dim light shone through windows that hadn't been cleaned in decades. Mateo's heart beat with concern as he stepped into the upstairs hallway. He passed posters advertising a prom that took place in the 1980s, and a football game against a team from a town that no longer existed.

A large set of double doors opened without ceremony.

"Come on in," Mrs. Moran said.

Mateo paused, trying to make sense of what he saw. Mrs. Moran was wearing an elegant, flowing dress with a vibrant pattern of flowers on a bright blue background, standing at the entrance to what looked like an apartment. He stepped closer to investigate. Mrs. Moran ushered him through the doors. High windows facing the back of the school allowed light to fill the space but ensured privacy. At one end of the large apartment was a cozy living room, decorated with pottery from the southwest, woven fabrics from South America and a batik hanging he thought might have come from Indonesia. A tidy kitchen with a large farmhouse table took up the center of the space, and to the other side, carved wooden screens created a bedroom.

"This is the old home-ec room," she said, as though that made complete sense of the situation. Then she smiled and gestured to the sofa. "Please sit. I need to tell you a few things."

"You live here?" he asked, taking a seat on the cozy sofa.

"I do." She sat opposite him. "I moved in here after my husband passed away. Our house was too quiet."

"Is that…legal?"

"I can't imagine it's legal. It really is impressive what a woman can get away with once she's over the age of seventy-five. Plus, my best friend is the sheriff's grandma." Mrs. Moran waved a hand, dismissing all legal concerns. Then she pointed at the west wall. "From that window there, I used to watch Luci, or Evening Light as she was known in those days, wander up to the school and try the doors. She'd always wanted to be here."

Mateo shook his head, trying to get all, or any, of this new information to settle. Then he asked the most burning of his questions. "How did no one recognize her?"

Mrs. Moran shook her head. "I recognized her immediately. I would have known that smile any-where."

Mateo started to speak, to tell Mrs. Moran about the braces, that Luci's smile had changed. But then her smile was so much more than her perfect teeth, wasn't it? "Did she always have a mischievous glint in her eye?"

"Like a little imp," Mrs. Moran said.

"Or a Shakespearean fairy—" Mateo could feel his face reddening "—with dimples."

"Just so." She gazed at him. "I recognized her. A little over a month in, Today's Moment realized who she was, and she told Pete Sorel. We were all so relieved that she was okay, that she was thriv-ing, we decided to let her tell us in her own time."

Mateo cradled his face in his hands. "I sure messed that up."

"You sure did," Mrs. Moran said cheerfully. "But we all mess up from time to time. Now, I'd like to make three deals with you before you take me to the gala."

Mateo furrowed his brow. Shouldn't they be dwelling on his mistakes a little longer?

"Deal number one." She leaned forward and lifted a check off the coffee table. "This is for the school, from the Open Hearts Intentional Community."

Mateo glanced at the check. Then he nearly dropped it.

"Whoa." He looked up sharply. "How can they afford—?"

"They have a number of very secure investments," she noted. "And their flowers are highly sought after. They have realized the importance of an outside education for their 'emerging adults,' so the teens can make an informed decision about whether or not to commit to living at Open Hearts as adults."

"That's incredible."

"That's Luci's doing. Today's Moment asked me to give you this generous donation on the condition that you take over as the school's financial advisor."

"Deal," Mateo said. There was enough money to shore up for hard times, and as they moved into the next year, they could work with the state to make sure they received proper funding for the dormitory.

"My second requires a little explaining." She sighed, then admitted, "There's nothing wrong with the internet at this school. I turn it on and off at will."

Mateo stared at her. All year long they'd struggled to do their work without reliable internet and all that time…

All that time kids hadn't been able to hide behind their phones. They connected with each other, their studies and school activities. For that matter, the teachers hadn't been able to hide behind their screens, either.

She shrugged. "I just don't love everyone being on the internet all the time. It has its place, of course. But so does conversation. So the deal is, if I tell you and the others where the router is, will you take a few shifts of turning it on and off? I get the sense that it's nice to watch a film together at the dormitory on Sunday nights, and I know Amber Danes could use it for a few practice quizzes for her GED. I can't keep up with everything at the dormitory, as much as I'd like to."

Mateo nodded, unable to get the right words out for what a diabolical genius Mrs. Moran was. What else were eighty-year-olds up to these days?

"Third deal…" Mrs. Moran picked up a tiny red leather box from the table and handed it to Mateo. "Open it."

Three bright diamonds in an antique gold setting winked out at him. His eyes darted from the ring, to Mrs. Moran, and back again.

"I love that ring. I love my husband." She swallowed, then drew in a breath. "But it's not doing any good in a box. I'd like you to have it."

He studied the ring, a smile growing as he caught her intention. "What's the catch?"

"You know I would never tell you what to do with your life, but I think you should take that ring, and when you're ready, give it to the smartest, kindest, most resilient woman you can find."

Mateo held Mrs. Moran's gaze, allowing hope to move through him. "I may have someone in mind."

Her bright smile warmed him to the core. "It's all settled then." She stood. "Shall we?"

Mateo hopped up and offered her his arm. "Let's do it."

CHAPTER TWENTY

THE GALA WAS PERFECT, far beyond Luci's wildest dreams. The eclectic crowd was joyful and energetic. Everyone danced, inspired by the old-school beauty of the hotel. No one could get enough of Angie's food, filling the hotel's delicate china plates with barbecue sliders, coleslaw and potato chips. In addition to the Pronghorn residents, people had come from all over. Some had grown up here, others had friends or family in the area. There were even some groups of young professionals from Portland and Boise who had heard about a formal gala in the middle of nowhere and bought tickets on a lark.

A number of Harlow's Nashville friends were in attendance as well. Wilson Range, a former country star turned producer, stood at the bar in the dining room, chatting with Raquel. Pronghorn's most opinionated mom laughed at something he said. He was wearing a distinctive turquoise ring, the sort of thing only Raquel could design.

Hmm.

A few steps away, a group from Open Hearts were filling their plates with vegetarian fare. Today's Moment caught Luci's gaze, then touched her thumb and forefinger to her chest, over her heart, and nodded. Reflexively, Luci returned the greeting, then grinned. Today's Moment smiled back and wiped a tear from her eye.

Luci wasn't ready to talk to the community just yet, but she would. And when she did, it would be fine, possibly even great, definitely open and engaged.

But presently, she was still running on half a lime cake and a lot of caffeine, and the food looked incredible. Luci grabbed a teacup full of mac and cheese, then scanned the buffet for something more. That's when she noticed the barbecue beef.

Would it be weird to make Mateo's signature heartbreak meal out of the stylish gala buffet?

Was she ready for Mateo's signature heartbreak meal?

Who was she kidding? She was *always* ready for this meal, no matter what state her heart was in. And what was the worst that could happen? Someone might talk about her behind her back because she did something unusual?

Already happening.

Luci headed to the barbecue station and scooped the slow-cooked goodness on top of her mac and cheese, then savored a bite.

"Ladies and gentlemen!" Harlow's voice rang out from the ballroom. "May I introduce Pronghorn's famous songwriting duo, Trey Tucker and Vander Tourn!"

Over the cheer of the crowd Luci heard someone next to her ask, "You coming?"

Luci turned to see Aida. The sheriff was stunning in an olive-green mini dress and strappy sandals. Luci grinned at her friend. "Is that what you're wearing for Harlow's bachelorette party?"

"How'd you guess?"

"Are we really going to Las Vegas?" Luci asked.

Willa joined them on their way to the ballroom, and said, "She's already booked the tickets."

Luci looped one hand through Aida's arm and the other through Willa's. "We're lucky."

Both women snuggled her close as they headed to the ballroom. "I think so," Willa said.

"The luckiest," Aida confirmed.

They entered the ballroom just as Vander and Trey finished their first song. Kids and adults alike crowded the stage, cheering.

Trey Tucker waved, his smile and Western-inspired ensemble gleaming in the makeshift spotlight. Vander kept his eyes on his guitar, but inspired the same excited fanfare.

"For our next song, we'd like to invite a special guest up on stage." Trey gestured to an elegant young woman in a floaty pink dress, her hair in a casual updo with tendrils framing her face.

It was Neveah.

The girl who had begun the school year with inconsistent attendance, hiding behind her lank hair, no connections at school and failing grades, now waved with confidence as the whole town cheered her on, no one more loudly than her teachers.

Except maybe for her aunt Amber, who put two fingers in her mouth and let out a whistle. Luci was going to need to learn how to do that, so she could celebrate the same way when Amber earned her GED.

Neveah dipped her head to acknowledge the cheers. Luci wondered what soulful ballad the girl had prepared this time. The kids had been listening to Beyoncé's new album nonstop, so maybe something from that collection was the choice?

"Thank you for inviting me to join you." She nodded to Trey and Vander like she was Taylor Swift dropping in on an Ed Sheeran concert.

"I told my friends a few weeks ago about the song I've prepared for tonight. It's an old song, from the nineties."

Wilson Range gave a whoop of approval.

"After I told everyone what I had in mind, my friend Cece asked if she could dedicate the song to a special person. To Mason."

Every head in the room turned to look at Mason. The kid looked shocked for half a second, then a huge grin broke out on his face.

Neveah continued, "And, like, five minutes later, Mason asked me if I would dedicate the song to Cece."

A collective "Awwwww!" was heard. Cece flushed purple, coordinating with her dress.

"And over the next two days, Taylor asked me to dedicate it to Suleiman, Oliver asked to dedicate it to Antithesis, and vice versa. Mav asked me to dedicate a poem to Ilsa, and I told him that's not how this works, but you know Mav." The crowd laughed. Neveah held up her hands. "So here you all go. This is my rendition of the Patty Loveless song 'I Try to Think About Elvis.'"

Tray and Vander picked up the beat and Neveah launched into the fun, up-tempo song about a person so in love they couldn't think about anything else.

It really did explain her classes over the last few weeks.

Harlow came over to join them, and they all cheered on the band. Luci found herself surrounded by friends, dancing and laughing while eating mac and cheese with barbecue beef.

The gala was going so much better than expected.

The song finished to mass applause, but Neveah didn't leave the stage. She glanced at Luci, then looked toward the back of the room. Luci followed her gaze to see Mateo, looking sharp in a black suit and white shirt open at the collar, Mrs. Moran on his arm.

He looked good. Like *good.*

Luci passed off her teacup to Aida as she let her nervousness simmer. This conversation with Mateo would be hard.

Or would it?

She always braced for life to be difficult. Was ready for the worst possible scenario. Maybe they could just apologize and move on? His one major flaw was that he was so confident in his ability to see the best in everyone, that he unintentionally hurt people.

As far as major flaws went, it wasn't *that* bad.

To quote the school motto, it could be worse.

Neveah continued, "This next song is for my teachers, Mateo and Ms. Walker, from all of your students. We think you need to waltz it out."

The music shifted. Vander's guitar picked up the familiar chords first, then Trey joined in, strands of a familiar song floating through the ballroom: "Can't Help Falling in Love with You."

Next to the dais, a clump of students—Taylor, Suleiman, Cece and Morgan—looked a little guilty.

Then Taylor straightened and pointed to the dance floor.

Space cleared and there stood Mateo, his hand outstretched to her. Luci took a tentative step toward him, then another as Neveah began to sing.

Before she could slip her hand into his, Mateo said, "Luci, I'm so sorry."

Somehow, she didn't need the words, or the confession anymore. "I know."

"I never should have—"

"I *know*."

He was so handsome, so *Mateo*. And while most days she loved arguing with him, she really didn't want to hear it right now.

"Please believe me when I say—"

"Mateo." She stepped closer and slipped her palm against his. "This song is only so long, and it may be the only waltz we get tonight." She grinned at him. "Less apology, more dancing."

Shock registered on his face, then he grinned, grasping her hand firmly in his.

"You want a waltz, Ms. Walker?"

"I do."

He pulled her close and kissed her dimple as she laughed. Neveah's voice filled the room, leading the haunting notes of Vander and Trey on guitar. Mateo straightened, positioning one hand on the small of Luci's back, holding perfect form. And then they were waltzing. Spinning and laughing. As the song stretched out, their friends, then their students, then other community members joined in the gorgeous, once scandalous, waltz.

As much as it pained Luci to admit it, they were all Dancing Like No One Was Watching.

Finally, the beautiful song came to a close. Luci's heart beat hard in her chest as she gazed at Mateo. He lifted a finger to the turquoise-and-pearl earrings.

"I missed you, too," she whispered.

He pulled her closer, his familiar scent wrapping her in warmth and safety. "I missed you so much. It's been a horrifying twenty-eight hours."

She laughed, but he wrapped her even tighter in his arms. "I mean it. I've had the privilege of seeing you nearly every day for the last two and a half years. Classes, study sessions, our student teaching experience, then this whole, wild experiment. No matter how bad things got, you were always there." He held her face in his hands, and his voice trembled as he said, "I thought I'd lost you."

"I'm still here."

He kissed her forehead.

"I like being here," she reminded him.

He gazed into her eyes, cradling her cheek in his hand. "You sure?"

"Very sure."

"You can forgive me?"

"Already forgave you." She paused, then said, "And myself. I forgive myself for not knowing how to handle everything perfectly all the time."

He pressed his forehead against hers, threading his fingers through her hair as he whispered, "Thank you."

Luci basked in his rush of emotion, then whispered, "In some cultures, it's appropriate to apologize with a kiss."

Mateo couldn't stop grinning as he drew her into the sweetest kiss. If there was any reaction from the students, the residents of Pronghorn and all their invited guests, she didn't care. Mateo wrapped his arms tighter around her, drawing her deeper into their private world.

Until the sound of a creaking door and heavy footsteps intruded on their moment. Somewhere, a wolf howled. Luci looked at Mateo in confusion. How were they suddenly in a haunted house?

A synthesized drumbeat filled the room.

Oh, no.

"Out of my way!" Loretta yelled.

The undeniable first bars of "Thriller" had every Gen X mom handing off her champagne coupe and racing for the floor.

Luci and Mateo tried to get out of the fray, but Morgan blocked their progress. "I know you know it." She pointed at Luci. "You're always telling us to go out on a limb. I expect no less of you."

Luci shook her head, trying not to smile. But her feet were already tapping to the beat, and if there was going to be a Halloween-themed dance at a spring gala, that was pure Pronghorn.

Luci rolled her eyes at Morgan, then lifted her arms in front of her chest, like a zombie pterodactyl, and joined in with her community.

Because sometimes, a girl just needs to live in the moment. Mateo jumped in next to her, the perfect reminder that every day was, after all, one of their Good Old Days.

EPILOGUE

"Mateo, we're going to be late!" Luci called from the courtyard of the hotel. "Graduation starts in twenty minutes."

"Coming!" his voice echoed out of the lobby.

Luci widened her eyes at her friends. Everyone looked sharp in suits and summer dresses, but her boyfriend was taking a little longer than the others to get dressed. Luci didn't love waiting, but it was totally worth it to see Mateo in a suit again.

"I love that we have an in-person graduation day this year," Aida said, kneeling down to scratch Greg's ears.

Tate gave a dry laugh. "I love that we made it to graduation."

"Right?" Luci asked.

"How did this school year fly by, when the school days felt so long?" Willa asked.

"The *minutes* felt long," Vander said. "But here we are. What a year."

What a year, indeed.

Twelve months ago, Luci had sat down across from Loretta at a job fair, and set in motion a chain of events she never could have imagined. In Pronghorn, the teachers' skills and patience had been stretched to the limits, but somehow they'd made it through to graduation.

No, not somehow. With each other.

And now, it was graduation day. The afternoon would be filled with celebration, and tears, as they said goodbye to the exchange students. Or goodbye for now, given that the kids had been extracting promises from everyone from Angie to Pete Sorel to come visit. Luci's only concern was that folks from Amsterdam, Dakar and Rio were going to have a really warped sense of Americans after this crew showed up. *Oh, well.*

Any of the graduates or exchange students would have a place to stay if the returned for a visit. Luci and Mateo had committed to running the dormitory for the foreseeable future. They'd have help, as Amber found she enjoyed working with the kids, and the school could now afford to hire her as a part-time assistant for the dorms. Mav had negotiated with the Open Hearts community and would stay in the dormitory his senior year. Mac was already helping his first and only employee research the prelaw program at the University of Oregon.

Luci looked forward to running the dormitory with Mateo, and saving up the extra money for summer travel. They had plans to see the world together.

But right now they weren't seeing anything together as he was taking so long to get ready.

"Mateo, seriously!" Luci called. "We're leading the procession of graduates."

Willa patted her arm. "It's fine. There are only three graduates. There'll be twice as many adults on stage as students."

"Four," Mateo corrected her, jogging into the courtyard. "Amber passed the GED test last week so she's walking as well." He grinned at Luci, then pulled his head back. "What?"

Luci attempted to pick her jaw up off the bricks. Mateo looked incredible. He was always handsome, but in a new tailored suit with a bright smile just for her? And an actual tie? How was she supposed to pay attention to graduation, or even know when she was supposed to pretend to pay attention?

She faked a casual shrug. "I like your suit."

"Even more than my Puddles the Duck shirt?"

She held up her thumb and forefinger, indicating a little bit.

"I figured since I'm spending the next three months in other people's weddings, I needed to step it up."

Luci gazed at him, thinking about another wedding she sometimes imagined him being in. He wove his fingers through hers, eyes shining as he said, "It's going to be a fun summer."

The funnest.

Loretta's voice echoed through her bullhorn, wafting across the expanse of prairie grass and sagebrush, into the hotel courtyard. She directed community members to the chairs set up on the soccer field, mixing metaphors and throwing in tips about staging houses.

"We should get out there," Harlow said. "I want to save a seat for Mrs. Moran."

"Hold up." Tate held out his hand and gestured for

the others to circle around. They piled their hands together. "Pronghorns, on three."

"One, two, *three*," Luci counted down, and together they all shouted, "Pronghorns!"

Laughing, they broke out of the huddle and headed out of the courtyard.

"Luci?"

She paused before the exit. Mateo stood in the middle of the courtyard, gazing at her.

"You look so pretty."

She twirled in her pale green, silk shantung dress. He caught her hand and spun her under his arm as their feet picked up a dance. She placed a hand on his chest.

Where she felt a lump.

"What's in your pocket?" she asked, pressing her palm against the small cube.

"Um…"

She pressed a little harder and looked into his eyes. There were worse things than being in love with a man who was incapable of lying when asked a direct question.

"It's… I—" His breath caught as he gazed into her eyes. She was surprised to see the spark of a tear. "I'm in love with you, Luci."

She gazed back at him. While she was super happy to hear it, they had been over this before, and it didn't really have anything to do with what was in his pocket.

Unless?

Mateo dropped to one knee. Luci's heart vaulted in her chest. She pressed her fingers to her lips.

"Luci, I love you. I love all of you. I love the ways we are different, and am grateful for all the values we share. Plus, you are the cutest, funniest, most Luci person alive. I can't help falling for you. There's nothing I want more than to spend our lives together. To spend our school years wrangling students and our summers exploring the world." He opened the box, where an antique gold band with three bright diamonds shone. "Luci Evening Light Walker, will you marry me?"

Luci was transfixed by his eyes, bright and soulful, so sincere. She would have the privilege of gazing into these eyes for the rest of her life, on the well-known streets of Pronghorn, or in a warren of cobblestones on the other side of the world. Tears sparked in her own eyes.

He motioned with the box, reminding her it was her turn to speak.

"Yes!" Like there was any way she'd say no? "Mateo, yes, always. What would I do without you?"

Mateo slipped the ring onto her finger, the cool, gold band warming her from her heart out. She glanced at the diamonds.

Wait, did she know this ring?

Mateo wove his fingers through hers, turning her hand so they could look at the ring together. "Mrs. Moran offered it to me on the condition that I give it to the smartest, kindest, most resilient woman I knew."

"How much does it thrill me that Mrs. Moran thinks we're a good idea?"

He nodded, eyes crinkling at the corners. "That's a solid endorsement."

Luci wrapped her arms around his neck and kissed him, so happy to be in this beautiful place, with this incredible man, her future on track with her dreams unfolding before them.

"Are you two coming or not?" The words startled them, reverberating through the courtyard as Loretta spoke through her bullhorn.

Luci grinned at Mateo. "We're on our way!"

He pulled her close. "We are. We are on our way, and there is no one I'd rather be traveling with."

Laughing, she tugged his hand and they ran out of the courtyard, setting rose petals scattering. Across the street, the community had gathered to celebrate. *Their* community: the one of her childhood and the one she'd chosen as an adult, if not seamlessly merged together, happily coexisting. Luci felt ready for every possibility with Mateo by her side.

"Watch out for the cat!" Mateo laughed. Luci leaped over the feline, and they were absorbed by their mass of students, ready to celebrate.

CONNIE WATCHED THE last pair of humans make their way to the gathering. Then she stalked back into the middle of the street, and stretched herself out on the blacktop. A breeze brought the scent of the antelope watching the proceedings from a distance. A tumbleweed rolled past. Connie eyed the couple as they merged with the crowd, then her lids lowered. She stretched her paws an inch farther, belly warmed by the pavement. Safe in the knowledge that all was right in Pronghorn, she closed her eyes and purred.

* * * * *

If you loved this book,
check out the previous books
in Anna Grace's
The Teacher Project miniseries:

Lessons from the Rancher
Winning the Sheriff's Heart
Mistletoe at Jameson Ranch

Available now at Harlequin.com!